LAST CHANCE ROAD

A JAKE CALDWELL THRILLER

JAMES WEAVER

WOLFPACK
PUBLISHING
— EST 2013 —

To my good friend and fellow author Robert E. Dunn.
Your books and characters always thrilled me,
and your talent turned me green with envy
more times than I can count.
You will be missed.
RIP

ACKNOWLEDGMENTS

It's hard to fathom that this is Book #7 of the Jake Caldwell series. Book 7! When I started *Poor Boy Road*, I had an idea this cast of fantastic characters could be extended to multiple books. But I don't know if I would have believed we'd have seven books over the course of six years. Looking back, my posse of helpers has grown and the product you hold in your hands is so much better because of them. I can't thank these folks enough. If I left anyone out, my humblest of apologies.

My wife, Becky, for not only putting up with me for more than a quarter of a century, but for never complaining when I disappear to my office to write into the wee small hours. I hope you know how much I appreciate and love you.

Fellow author Jodi Gallegos who is officially my favorite person in the world that I've never met face to face. Someday! She's an uber-talented writer who provides insightful feedback that is invaluable. I treasure our meme battles on social media. Please go check out her page-turning *High Crown Chronicles* trilogy. Seriously, go buy them now.

Fellow author and biggest Jake Caldwell fan Laurie Bell for continuing to be a beta reader. I love reading her reactions as she progresses through the manuscript along with her awesome ideas and suggestions. She hit the nail on the head so many times with *Last Chance*

Road on where I missed the mark. You have no idea how many times I pop out and read your reviews of my previous books that help stoke the writing fire. Thank you. Don't forget to check out her work—*White Fire*, *The Butterfly Stone* and *The Tiger's Eye*.

Editor and author Rebecca Carpenter for her fantastic copyediting of all my books. I still can't quite get those damn commas right, but I'm getting better! If you need a copy editor, you'd be a fool not to look her up. And don't forget to check out her excellent *Metamorphosis* series starting with *Butterfly Bones*.

My forever beta reader and good friend Jim McKernan who always turns around the beta read in the blink of an eye and manages to catch things nobody else notices. Thank you for your continued support and one of my biggest writing regrets is shooting your character in the throat in *Ares Road*.

Fellow writer Barry Brakeville who hacks and slashes what I think is pretty damned polished and makes the work better. We may not always agree on what needs to stay or go, but I take your advice more often than not. I look forward to our next round of cervezas and to see that awesome memoir of yours in print.

Jake Caldwell would not exist without fellow author and friend Kate Foster who saw a diamond in the rough and took a chance on me. I appreciate having her in my corner as she manages to crank out her own books. Check out *Paws* and *The Bravest Word*.

My dad who is always the first to read what I write to let me know if I'm on the right track and to hold my feet to the fire with my Warsaw references. Thanks, Pop!

Brandy and David Fajen for their valuable insight

into the foster care system. These two have done some amazing things, taken in so many children and made a true difference in the world. Thank you for what you do and for sitting down with me. I don't know if my resolution ended up being technically correct, but I do know you both helped shape Daisy, one of my favorite characters I've written thus far.

The excellent folks at Wolfpack Publishing for their support, promotion, and getting the Jake Caldwell series out there for public consumption. Appreciate everything you do.

And last, but certainly not least, to the fans of this series. Jake, Bear, and the rest of these characters would not continue to entertain and thrill without you. The fact that we're now on Book 7 is a testament to your continued support and I thank you from the bottom of my heart. And to put any fears to rest based on this latest title, this is not the last you'll see of Jake and Bear.

LAST CHANCE ROAD

CHAPTER ONE

MERLE WADE WHITE-KNUCKLED THE TIRE IRON AS HE approached the woman kneeling at the flat tire of her broken down Chevy Blazer, his work boots scuffling along the cracked asphalt on the shoulder of Highway 7. He wavered between the desire to bury the cold, forged steel into the back of her skull or apply it to the tire. His shadow slithered over the woman as he stepped in front of the headlights of his truck. Her ponytail whipped over her narrow shoulder as she turned in his direction.

Her hooded eyes scanned him up and down, locking in on the tire iron swinging at his side. She jumped up, drawing her arms in tight, hugging herself as she stepped back toward her open driver's side door.

"Evenin'," she said, her voice drawling out the words. Her eyes locked on Merle's face for a moment before scanning her surroundings, widening as if realizing her isolation between the walls of black woods on either side of the road in the middle of nowhere. Crickets chirped in the Ozark night as a sliver of moon peeked between bruised rain clouds, the musty scent of showers filling the air.

Merle stopped at the back end of the Blazer. Even though he would likely appear to her as a dark silhouette against the truck's headlights, he forced a tight-lipped smile. Revealing his jagged teeth tended to scare women away. "Howdy. You got yourself a flat?"

She nodded. "And no jack."

"Spare?"

"In...in the back."

Merle glanced over his shoulder, past his idling truck to the road beyond. No headlights. But there could be some at any moment, so it would be risky to try to take her here. He could be in the middle of dragging her body back to the truck when someone rolled down the highway, and it would be all over for him. Still, his muscles trembled with the urge to take her back to the ranch to make sure she was a match.

The woman was thin, just like the others. The way *she* was. The hair color was wrong, but he could fix that. She was a few years past optimal, but close enough. He couldn't stop staring at her eyes. Her wide, fearful eyes were the same as hers, and the eyes were the most important part.

"You want some help changing it?" He rocked back and forth on his heels. "I could do it lickety-split."

"I...I called a friend," she said, jerking a thumb over her shoulder toward the blackness beyond Merle's headlights. "He and his buddies oughta be here any second now."

Merle was good at telling when people lied to him, especially women. He'd followed her at a distance from the meeting and watched her pull to the shoulder, climbing out seconds later. She hadn't called a soul.

He shrugged his broad shoulders. "Well, if you wanna wait by the side of the road by yourself in the middle of the night, you can. Or you can let me help you, and you can be on your way. At least until your friends show up, that is."

The woman chewed on her bottom lip as her eyes flicked between Merle and her flat tire. She rested her hand on the open driver's side door, and for a moment he thought she would get in and lock the doors. Half of him hoped she would. The other half, the bad half, tingled with anticipation and hoped she didn't.

"It's Rebekka, right?" Merle offered.

She drew back. "H-h-how'd you know that?"

"I was at the meeting tonight," he said, stepping out of the direct glare of the headlight so she saw his face. "Sat in the back. Heard you speak and, now don't tell no one I said this, but I caught a tear in my eye."

Her shoulders relaxed. "I did see you there. So you're—"

"Same demons as you. Just tryin' to make amends, and you could help me out by letting me help you, Rebekka."

She threw on a half-smile. "I guess that'd be okay. Thank you."

Merle slipped behind the back of the Blazer, opening the latch for the hatch with his T-shirt. The hatch groaned open, revealing a back filled with white trash bags stuffed with clothes and open-topped boxes with knickknacks and electronics. The spare tire would rest underneath it all.

He studied the mess and leaned around the back

end. "Your spare tire's under all this stuff. What do ya want me to do with it?"

The woman's fists opened and closed at her sides as her bottom teeth raked against her upper lip. Despite recognizing him, he could tell she knew he was wrong. Given the disappearances in this region over the last year, she should listen to her gut. They may be fighting the same demons, but she knew what he was, and he felt the maniacal urge to tell her to run. He didn't want to hurt her, but if she came to the back of the Blazer, he wasn't going to have a choice. His limbs trembled as he waited.

The woman took a step toward the back, and Merle's heart skipped a beat. She paused and peered up and down the blackened highway.

Merle side-stepped from behind the Blazer and smiled again. "Listen, I get you're a bit nervous, and you should be with what's happened around here. If you just wanna wait for your friend, I'll get back in my truck and mosey back home. No harm, no foul."

The woman's gaze darted from his face to the dark road behind him, as if hoping her fictional friends were about to come roaring down the road.

"In fact," he continued, backing up and raising his hands. "I'll even sit in my truck and wait until they get here, just to make sure you're safe. You can't be too careful these days."

The corner of the woman's mouth twerked up. "How long would it take to change the tire? I do got somewhere to be."

"You help me clear enough stuff out so I can get to the tire, and you'll be on your way in ten minutes."

He offered his best, most disarming smile and took another step back.

The woman shuffled toward the back of the Blazer. Merle waited until she got there, sucking in deep breaths through his wide nostrils. God, she even walked like *her*.

The woman grabbed a trash bag and set it on the shoulder. "Sorry I was nervous. Like you said. You can't be too careful."

Merle glanced up and down the dark highway. Help or hurt?

"No, you certainly can't." The decision made itself. He stepped forward, raising the tire iron as the woman picked up another bag.

He brought the tire iron down, her skull cracking beneath its weight. The woman dropped like a stone and sprawled on the ground. Merle moaned as orgasmic relief flooded through his body, cooling his ragged nerve endings. He crouched and jammed his fingers into her neck, her pulse weak against his fingertips. Scooping her up, he carried her limp body back to his truck, laying her gently on the tarp spread in the truck bed amid the wood he'd gathered earlier. He pulled the tarp over the top of the bed and secured it with hooks.

Slipping on a pair of gloves, he ran back to the Blazer, threw the clothes bag in, slammed down the hatch, and moved to the front, leaning in the open driver's side door. Snagging the keys, he hit the emergency flashers and shut the door. Jogging back to his truck, he hit the button on the key fob and locked it. That should buy him some time to get her situated before coming back for the car.

He climbed behind the wheel of his truck, glancing to his wife, Charlene—her frown dragging her already dour facial features toward the floorboards. She hooked her thick thumbs into the straps of her denim overalls, the crusted red flannel shirt bunching up underneath.

"You sure this time?" she asked, her tone sharp and disbelieving, accusatory.

Merle strangled the steering wheel as he slipped the truck into drive. "I'm sure. Wait 'til you meet her, honey."

Charlene's lip curled as she leaned in close, her breath rotten, like a grave. "That's what you said last time, and look where it got us, Merle. Look where it got us."

Merle ground his teeth and pressed on the accelerator. Despite Charlene's pessimism, he fought to suppress the smile he had no business wearing. This girl was perfect. She could very well be the one they'd been searching for.

CHAPTER TWO

JAKE CALDWELL SCROLLED THROUGH FACEBOOK ON HIS phone, his elbows resting on the advertisement-covered table in the Rusty Skillet, a diner located on Main Street in his hometown of Warsaw, Missouri. The diner was full of patrons, clinks of dishware, and the delicious greasy aromas of breakfast fare. License plates, hand-painted saws, and tiny, hanging cast iron skillets decorated the wood-paneled walls. Jake and his best friend, Bear, sat in a booth in the back near the restrooms under a curtain decorated with flying eagles. A sign hung on the men's room asking the question, "How can a man who can hit a deer at 250 yards keep missing the toilet?" Jake had been in the restroom. It was a valid question.

Bear pointed at Jake's plate. "You gonna eat that?"

Jake zeroed in on the lone strip of crispy bacon on his otherwise empty plate. A grin broke across his stubbled face as he took in the hopeful mug of his best friend sitting across the booth from him. Benton County Sheriff Bear Parley never met a piece of pork he didn't like, and his cholesterol proved the point. Bear looked like a stray dog hopeful for a treat.

"I'm still thinking about it," Jake said.

Bear scowled, lines crossing his tanned forehead. "What's to think about? It's bacon."

Bear reached across the table to take the meat candy.

Jake smacked his hand away. "You had two orders already. If I decide not to eat it, I'll let you know."

Bear sank back in the booth. "Asshole. You seem cranky. Can't handle all the new business?"

"Amazing how a little notoriety increases people's perceptions of desirability and competency," Jake said.

"Well, we did save the damned country. We're at least somewhat competent."

A couple months ago, Jake and Bear thwarted the plans of a maniac with the bright idea to bring anarchy across the nation by blowing up the radicals of each political party. His goal was to let the polarized sides go to war with each other and tear the nation apart. Jake ended the plan with a bullet between the man's eyes.

Jake rubbed his tired eyes with his free hand. "After that craziness, I'll take the bevy of surveillance cases thrown my way. Most PI work is boring as hell."

"Anybody I'd know?"

Jake resumed scrolling through the phone. "One. But your wife swore me to secrecy."

Bear tossed some bills on the table and stood. "Like I have the time or the energy to step out on Audrey. You guys still coming over tonight?"

Jake nodded as he spotted a young wisp of a girl slipping in the front door of the Rusty Skillet, her eyes scanning the patrons. "Yup. Maggie's bringing her peanut butter lasagna."

Bear took advantage of Jake's diverted attention and grabbed the last bacon piece. He folded it in his mouth with a grin. "I don't know what that is, but it sounds goddamn amazing. Then again, you could dip a turd in peanut butter, and I'd probably give it a shot. I gotta get back to work. See you tonight."

As he headed out the door, Bear slapped the backs and pressed the palms of a handful of patrons. The girl side-stepped and threw Bear a withering stare as he passed. She was cute in a rough kind of way, with a head full of tight auburn curls. Maybe four feet tall, rail thin with a 2018 Jubilee Days T-shirt hanging over ragged jeans. Her eyes burned a hole in Bear's back before returning to the Rusty Skillet patrons. To Jake's surprise, she locked eyes and strode toward his booth.

She appeared around ten years old, sunken fawn eyes and a pallid complexion like the sun hadn't kissed her skin in weeks. Sliding into the booth, she rested her scratched and scrawny arms on the tabletop, searching Jake's face for something. Jake scanned his mental Rolodex and didn't think he'd seen the girl before, a little uneasy she'd picked him out of the crowd.

"Hi," Jake said.

"You Jake Caldwell, the private investigator?" Her high-pitched voice dripped with a backwoods twang. A fierce steel resonated in her voice like no little girl should have. Between her appearance and fire in her eyes, Jake could tell she'd seen things.

"Yes, ma'am. Who are you?"

"Daisy Dawn Everleigh."

"Pretty name."

Irritation crossed her face. "I hate it."

"What's wrong with it?"

She curled her lip in disgust. "Daisy Dawn? It makes me sound like a dumb hick. What's *not* wrong with it?"

"Then why say your whole name?"

"My momma told me that's how you introduce yourself to people."

"I've never heard of that before."

"It's what she told me. What do I know? I'm only ten."

Jake chewed the inside of his cheek. "What should I call you?"

"Daisy, I guess."

"Well, Daisy, shouldn't you be in school right now?"

She squinted at Jake like he was a moron. "Ain't like I'd be missin' much, not that anyone's going to check on me."

Jake shifted his weight, wondering what this girl wanted. "How'd you find me?"

"I've been looking all over town for you the last week or so. Heard you eat here sometimes."

"Well, now you've found me, what can I do for you?"

Daisy dug into a pocket of her jeans and fished out a crumpled ten-dollar bill. She carefully unfolded it and ran it back and forth along the edge of the table to smooth out the wrinkles. When she was satisfied, she slapped it in front of Jake's empty plate.

"You buying me breakfast?" Jake asked.

"You're an investigator, right? I wanna hire you."

Jake blinked back his surprise. What would a kid need a PI for, much less a kid who looked like she couldn't afford to give away anything? "Hire me for what?"

"To find my momma."

Jake's eyebrows drew together as he leaned forward. "Who's your momma?"

The first crack in Daisy's steely demeanor showed. Her bottom lip trembled before the fire returned to her features. "Sharla Babin."

Jake slumped back in the booth and blew out a breath. *Shit.* Sharla Babin disappeared months ago into thin air. The prevalent theory was she was dead.

But her daughter obviously didn't think so.

CHAPTER THREE

"THIS SOUNDS LIKE A MATTER FOR THE SHERIFF," JAKE said. "You can probably still catch him."

Daisy rolled her eyes. "They ain't doin' shit. It's been four goddamn months. They gave up."

Jake blinked at the profanity rolling off the young girl's tongue, smooth as silk, like it had been part of her vernacular since she emerged from the womb. He started to tell her he knew for a fact Bear hadn't given up on Sharla Babin's case, but he didn't want to start off in opposite corners of the ring.

"I know you're all friendly with Bear," she continued, her mahogany eyes narrowing. "Would that be a... a...shit, what do you call it?"

"Conflict of interest."

She pointed her index finger. "That's it. I know ten bucks ain't much, but it's all I got. I can get you more later."

There was something about the girl, a grit only a hard-scrabbled life could bring. He didn't recall many details of Sharla's case—it wasn't one Bear liked to discuss. The one thing Jake knew was Sharla lived on the wrong side of town and, guessing from Daisy's appearance and demeanor, it hadn't been an easy life. He wanted to push the bill back across the table and tell her no thanks, but he was drawn to her, knowing that behind the rough-and-tumble hard shell was a scared girl Jake could relate to.

"What's your dad say about you wanting to hire a private investigator?"

"He could be eatin' in here and I wouldn't know. Momma said he split town the day I was born. Kissed me on the head at the hospital, left to get a beer, and never came back. My momma wasn't perfect, but she was trying. She was all I had. She..."

Daisy bit her trembling lower lip and dipped her eyes to the table. The waitress came by and asked if she wanted anything. Jake offered to buy her breakfast. Lord knows she looked like she could use it, but the girl just ordered a Coke.

From what Jake could remember from Bear and the news, Sharla Babin lived somewhere off Route MM in a ramshackle house. She had a criminal record of some sort and worked part-time at the Walmart in town. Bear said he heard rumors she sold a little weed now and again, but nothing in an amount that would put her on his radar. Marijuana was the least of Bear's drug worries these days. Oxy and fentanyl were the rage. Heroin was also making a comeback as the Oxy became harder to obtain. On the night she disappeared, Sharla was last seen by a neighbor in her front yard around sunset.

The waitress set the Coke on the table, and Daisy drank half of the glass in one turn before settling back in the curved, wooden booth and crossing her skinny arms. "You ain't gonna help me are you? I can see it in your eyes."

Jake held her gaze for a moment before speaking. "See what?"

"The fuckin' pity," she spat with enough volume to cause the elderly couple in the booth behind them to half-turn and shake their heads.

Jake winced. "Listen, Daisy. Can we turn down the volume on the foul language?"

Her lip jutted out. "Sorry, that's just the way I talk."

Jake folded his hands on the sticky table. "It doesn't have to be. Save the f-bombs until you're an adult. And I didn't say I wouldn't help you."

She perked up and pushed the ten-spot toward him. "Then you will?"

Jake pushed the bill back. "I didn't say I would either. Frankly, I'm not sure if there's anything I can do. Despite your apparent hatred of Bear and local law enforcement, I know they've been working on your mom's case."

"Not hard enough. Your buddy Bear couldn't catch a cold."

Jake fought back a smile. She wore her cynicism like a mask, hardening her delicate features. The girl had an old soul, a bitter old soul, but one that reminded Jake of himself at that age. Though her old man hadn't been around to beat her in a drunken stupor like his, it didn't mean she hadn't been through the wringer.

Jake placed his elbows on the table. "You living with relatives?"

"Don't have any. I was livin' with my gramma, but she died a couple months ago."

"I'm sorry to hear that."

Daisy downed the rest of her Coke. Her voice softened. "Me too. She was a nice old lady."

"Where you living now?"

"Foster family a couple blocks away. The Wilkinsons, for now anyway."

"What's that like?"

She scratched a dirty fingernail on the table. "The mom is okay, but their son ignores me, and the dad is lookin' at me funny."

The hairs on Jake's neck bristled. He didn't know the family but didn't like the way she talked about the dad. "Funny how?"

She shrugged. "Can't tell if he hates me being there or if he wants to do something else to me. I'll scrape his eyeballs out if he tries anything."

Jake's gut hardened. "If he does, make sure you call your caseworker—"

Her narrow nostrils flared. "It'll be too late by then, if they'd even do anything. They didn't at my last place before my mom came back. I was fuc...seven years old and they left me there."

"I'm sorry, Daisy."

She glanced up and shoved the ten-spot back to him. "Don't be sorry. Help me, Jake Caldwell. Help me find my mom. She's all I got."

Jake didn't know if there was anything he could do to find Sharla Babin, but it couldn't hurt to talk to Bear and poke around.

He pushed the bill back across the table. "You keep it. Save it for a rainy day." Jake slid a business card from his wallet and passed it to her. "I'll do some checking around. If I find out anything, I'll come find you."

Her eyes probed his. "You promise?"

"Trust me."

She sighed and slid to the floor. "I'll try, but every time I trust someone new, they end up remindin' me I shouldn't trust anyone at all."

She spun, strode to the front door, and disappeared down the sidewalk.

CHAPTER FOUR

Rebekka Hammill coughed herself awake as she sucked in a mouthful of dirt from the floor. Each cough sent searing shockwaves of pain reverberating through her skull. She wanted off the floor, but her limbs were made of lead. A wave of nausea swirled over her as she managed to work herself to a seated position, blinking away the fog—her eyes probing her darkened surroundings. Her head heavy as a safe, the room spinning as she righted herself.

She sat on a hard stone floor of a ten-by-ten room, encased on three sides by gray cinder blocks held together with rough seams of concrete. The front of the room was open—a wooden door on the left side of the opening and ropes of dull steel horizontal wire set eight inches apart, stretching from the doorframe to the far wall. Beyond the wires was an opening into a dim hallway.

Her only light source was an overhead, single bulb in a cobwebbed protective plastic cage attached to a wood beam. The beam stretched the length of the cell and disappeared into the darkness of the hallway. A thin, gray-stained mattress on a two-foot high black metal frame sat along the wall to her left and a foul-smelling bucket slumped against the wall to her right. *Am I in jail?* She winced with pain as she shook away the thought.

She tried to stand, but the world swam away, and she collapsed back to the floor, feeling the tug against her left ankle. Squinting against the dark, she reached with her hand to the rope of wire attached to a black ankle bracelet. Her fingers followed the wire to where it attached to the frame of the bed which was bolted to the floor. Her pulse skyrocketed, fear crushing her lungs like she was suffocating.

Where the hell am I?

How did I get here?

Her eyes widened, the back of her head thumping like a drum as she recalled the man from the meeting, the one with the tire iron. Reaching back, she gingerly probed the laceration on her scalp, crying out as her fingers scraped raw flesh. Nausea swept through her thin body as the wire ropes covering the door wavered, blending into a haze of silver. She turned her head and vomited into the bucket next to her, the shit smell causing her to wretch even harder and longer.

Wiping her mouth with the back of her hand and pushing away from the bucket, she worked her way to a sitting position on the mattress, the metal slats biting into her buttocks. She blinked away the haze.

She'd been moving bags from the back of her car for the man. *Why?*

She smelled the earthy, decaying leaves of the Ozark woods over the dank, moldy stench of her cell. She heard his footsteps behind her, crunching the sandy grit on the side of the highway. *Why was he there?*

The flat tire.

She had the flat tire, and he was going to help her.

His face was familiar from the AA meeting, but her gut steeled as she envisioned the tire iron swinging at his side. She should have listened to her gut, jumped in the car, and locked the door. She scratched at her arms. God, she needed a drink and a snort of something.

"Hello?" she cried out. "Is there anybody there?"

A cough barked and a sniffle sounded nearby.

Rebekka rolled off the bed and crawled toward the wire ropes covering her cell. The wires attached to a frame next to the wooden door. She tried to open the door by tugging the handle, but it wouldn't budge.

"Somebody help me!" she screamed.

Another cough sounded to her right.

She pounded her fists on the wood, the denseness of the door pushing back against her. Her thumps barely registered a sound. She screamed again, her voice cracking from the effort.

The harsh whisper of a female voice sounded. "Shut the hell up."

Rebekka darted to her right toward the voice before the wire rope attached to her ankle caught and jerked her off her feet. She face-planted on the dirt floor and tasted blood from where she bit her lip in the fall.

"Who's there?" she cried. "Is somebody there?"

The voice whispered again. "You're gonna bring him down if you don't shut the fuck up, lady."

"Bring who down?" Rebekka tried to lower her volume, though her pounding heart made it difficult. "Where are we?"

The voice went quiet for a moment before it answered. "In hell."

She reached forward and tried to pull herself up with the wire ropes. The hair on her arms rose as they closed in on the wires. Her brain registered the danger a millisecond too late. She screamed as she grasped them, electric pain radiating through her body. She fell back to the ground crying, rubbing the pain away from her hands. A thin sheen of sweat covered her body, her heart rate hammering.

"Don't touch the wires," the woman whisper-shouted. "Don't scream. And do what he tells you."

Rebekka clutched her chest. "What who tells me?"

"Stop asking questions and—"

Down the hall, a door thumped open, and light spilled across the hallway floor. In the faint glow across the hall, she spotted a half-dozen other cells like hers, all dark except for one where a dirty face peeked out from under a blanket. At the approach of heavy feet, the face disappeared.

The footsteps clomped toward Rebekka, each step causing her heart to pound in time with her head. Her vision blurred with tears.

What is happening?

A shadow spilled over her. She looked up into the smiling face of the man from the highway, jagged teeth jutting out from an unkept, wild beard. Rat eyes below a bald head, unnaturally small on his broad shoulders.

"Hey there, pretty girl," he said, his voice low, growling. "Welcome to Last Chance Road."

Rebekka whimpered and scrambled back against the wall, the rough concrete seams between the cold cinderblocks snagging her shirt. She pressed her head against the door so she couldn't see the man, her mind racing to imagined dark places, of him on top of her on the mattress, of his hands around her neck, of the tire iron beating her bloody.

The man's shadow disappeared as he moved to the door of her cell. Keys clinked together, metal scraped against metal, and a bolt thumped back.

The voice of the woman in the next cell echoed in Rebekka's head.

Do what he tells you. Don't scream.

Rebekka bit her bottom lip, choking back the scream demanding to be heard, a scream demanding to know what he wanted with her. As the door swung open, the man stepped in with a battery-powered camping lantern swinging from his side. He lingered at her feet, and she focused on his mud-crusted boots, unwilling to look him in the eye. After a minute, the man pulled the door closed behind him, and the light from the lantern bounced against the wood. That's when she saw the claw marks gouged in the door. Bloody scratches and broken nails buried into the wood.

That's when she screamed.

CHAPTER FIVE

"WE'LL GET THE DISHES," JAKE SAID. "YOU LADIES relax."

Jake and Bear stood and picked up empty plates from Bear's dining room table.

Their wives threw out a half-hearted plea to let them do it as they lounged in their chairs swirling the wine in their glasses. "No, please. We cooked. Let us do the dishes."

"Very funny," Bear said, kissing Audrey on the top of the head. "Grab another glass of wine, and we'll meet you on the front porch."

The ladies grabbed the bottle of wine and bolted from the table before Bear could finish his sentence.

In his quaint kitchen, under a wallpapered border of chickens and ducks, Bear scraped remnants of the pot roast into the sink and handed Jake the plates to load in the dishwasher.

"What'd you think of the pot roast?" Bear asked.

Jake cleared his throat. "It was...umm...fine."

Bear's nose wrinkled. "It was tough as shoe leather

and tasted like she dragged it through the dirt before she put it in the crockpot."

"Didn't stop you from eating it."

"You know how sensitive Audrey is about her cooking. After this many years I've learned to choke it down with a smile."

Jake stacked glasses in the rack. "I've had worse."

Bear cocked his head. "Where?"

Jake's eyes darted to the ceiling, thinking. "Last time we had dinner here?"

Bear chuckled and resumed scraping and rinsing dishes. "It's downright shocking how fat I am with the way she cooks. If you breathe a word of it to her, I'll break your legs."

"Your secret's safe with me." Jake's mind wandered to the girl in the Rusty Skillet as they finished the last of the dishes. "You know Daisy Everleigh?"

Bear froze before shutting off the water. The vein in his temple throbbed. "Sharla Babin's kid. Why?"

"She came into the Rusty Skillet after you left."

"I know. I felt the daggers in my back after I passed her."

Jake dried his hands on a dish towel and leaned against the counter. "What do you know about her?"

Bear crossed the kitchen to the refrigerator, extracting a couple beer bottles and twisting the tops off. He drained a third of his as he handed the other one to Jake. "I know I feel guilty every time I look into those sad, brown eyes. Her mom's been missing for four months, and we don't have a clue what happened. Her trail's as cold as the beer bottle in your hand."

"She wants to hire me to find her mom."

Bear's eyebrows shot up as he slugged back another

third of the bottle. He wiped his bearded mouth as he propped against the counter opposite of Jake. "What'd you tell her?"

"Said I'd check into it."

"What'd she say about me?"

Jake bit his bottom lip. "That you couldn't catch a cold."

The corner of Bear's mouth twitched. "She's a spitfire, isn't she?" The start of the smile disappeared. "And in the case of Sharla, I hate to say she's right. With the new jail, I'm seriously understaffed, and I don't have the money to hire and retain experienced employees. We can't even keep up with the emergency calls we're getting much less dig into cases like Sharla's the way we should. It's terrible. There's not a day that goes by I don't think about Sharla and that girl."

"You know the people Daisy's staying with?"

"The Wilkinsons? Kind of. Darla seems alright. Can't remember the husband's name but met him once. Think they have a son. She say something?"

"Sounds like she's a little ignored, and she's worried the dad is looking at her funny."

Bear set the bottle down. "I know the caseworker. I'll give her a call in the morning to check on them. What are you gonna do?"

"You care if I check Sharla's case file?"

"Come by in the morning. I'd love another set of eyes on it."

Jake breathed out. "Good. I was afraid you'd think I was stepping on your toes."

"I'm freaking drowning with the day-to-day shit around here, but I gotta warn you. There's not much to go on. The woman disappeared like a fart in the wind.

Left her wallet, her cell phone, and her purse on her dining room table. She was last seen by a neighbor in her front yard, her car's missing, and nobody's heard a word from her in four months. Honestly, a lot of people think she's just ran off with somebody."

"Without her wallet, purse, or cell?"

Bear pumped his shoulders. "She's an ex-con and didn't exactly hang around with Warsaw's high society."

"We have a high society?"

"Maybe three or four people. You definitely don't make the list."

Jake swallowed the rest of his beer. "You believe she ran off?"

Bear studied the floor. "No. I don't. Something happened to her. I don't know what, but there aren't any real leads. Let's grab another beer and meet the girls on the porch. We can talk about this tomorrow."

Bear turned on the water, reached to the wall near the sink, and flipped on the garbage disposal. A god-awful racket of grinding metal sounded.

Bear lashed out and hit the switch, peering into the sink as the gears wound down. "That didn't sound right."

Jake smirked. "Garbage disposals aren't meant to chew up shoe leather."

Bear ignored Jake's jab and answered his ringing cell phone. "Parley."

Bear's features changed from annoyance at Jake's jab to concern. He'd seen that look before and knew whoever was on the other end of the line wasn't delivering any good news.

"Secure the scene," Bear said. "Keep any prying eyes away. Oh, and Klages? Not a fucking word goes out over the air. Tell everyone there to keep their mouths shut. This is gonna get around fast enough as it is. Who else is there with you? Good, have him call the coroner. I'll be there in fifteen minutes."

Bear disconnected the call and tossed the phone on the counter. He raised the beer bottle to finish it off, paused, and set the bottle on the counter.

"What's up?" Jake asked.

"Guy walking his dog out by the visitor center found a body. Dog got loose and started digging around. Guy sees a decomposed hand and calls it in. Klages is out there, but it looks like a woman who's been there for a while."

"Jesus."

"Jesus is right. I hope she found Him before she met Him." Bear pushed off the counter and grabbed his wallet and keys. "I gotta get out there. You wanna come?"

"Sure. You want someone to hold your hand in the dark?"

Bear scowled. "No, you little dick. I'm afraid if I leave you here, there won't be any peanut butter lasagna left. Audrey won't want me to eat it, but I have a feeling I'm going to need to eat some feelings after this one."

CHAPTER SIX

FIFTEEN MINUTES LATER, THEY SWUNG INTO THE PARKING
lot of the Harry S. Truman Visitor Center. The flying-
saucer-shaped building sat atop Kaysinger Bluff over-
looking the Truman Dam and Reservoir. The building
housed exhibits detailing the history of the Osage Arm
of Lake of the Ozarks valley. It had been a while since
Jake was in there, but he'd found it interesting. The
complex included a nature trail along Kaysinger Bluff
with a log cabin complex, a general store, and an old
schoolhouse off the Hooper House Trail.

At this hour, the parking lot was empty, and Bear
turned his truck down a side road and drove along the
trail. A half-mile in, he spotted the flashing lights and
stopped short of Deputy Klages's squad car. Klages
rested against the car talking on her phone, hanging up
as Jake and Bear approached with flashlights in hand.

"Where is she?" Bear asked.

"Fifty yards off the trail," Klages said, waving at
them to follow. "She's wrapped in a heavy plastic. The
guy whose dog found the body almost couldn't lead us

back to it. To be honest, I don't blame him. I wouldn't want to see this twice either. The old guy said when he caught up to the dog, it'd pulled half her body clear and tore through part of the plastic."

Jake's eyebrows shot to the night sky. "Must've been a big ass dog."

"Rottweiler. Looks like it's on steroids. I'd kill for that kind of muscle definition."

They weaved their way around the trees, feet slipping down the natural slope on a bed of fallen leaves. Jake trailed behind Bear, ducking under branches Bear moved from his path and sent whipping back in Jake's direction. He gave his friend a few yards of distance so Jake didn't lose an eye.

Jake spotted flashlights moving around in the darkness ahead, the moon covered by clouds doing little to help light the way. They stopped in a circular clearing with a ten-foot radius.

"Jesus, Mary Mother, Joseph," Bear whispered, shining his light on a bone-white hand protruding from the dirt.

Jake moved his flashlight beam from the hand to the head, and a long-haired woman's skeletal face appeared —the Ozark dirt caking it on either side. Shoulder length dark hair, long face, slim nose, and a thin hoop lip ring made of silver on what was left of the bottom lip. Her upper torso was exposed to the waist. Jake recognized the top of the lettering of a shredded old Led Zeppelin T-shirt. Local wildlife had recently started feasting, not that there was much left for them.

"How long you think she's been here?" Jake asked.

Bear studied the corpse. "I'd have to guess twelve to

twenty-four months. Coroner should be able to give us a better timeframe. She look familiar to anyone?"

Jake, Klages, and a new deputy named Howard shook their heads.

Bear rubbed his hand across his beard. "Howard, I know there's not much to go on, but check missing persons reports when you get back to the office and see if you can find a match."

"We might have to resort to dental records," Klages said.

"You guys photograph the scene?" Jake asked.

"Dozens of pics," Klages said.

Jake ran his light to her waist, drawing closer to the corpse. Audrey's pot roast rumbled in his stomach. He spotted the top of a clear baggie sticking out of her pocket. He glanced up and noticed Howard wore disposable gloves.

Jake pointed toward the pocket. "Howard, since you're gloved up, see what's sticking out of her pants."

Howard bent his hefty frame and gently worked the plastic bag from the dead woman's pocket. He held it up, and Jake shined his light on it. Jake's guess was an 8 ball of heroin, three grams worth.

"Anyone have extra gloves?" Jake asked.

Klages pulled a couple sets from her back pocket and handed them to Jake and Bear. Jake slid the plastic over his hands and took the baggie from Howard. On the back of the baggie was a sticker of a crudely drawn cartoon unicorn, white with bulbous cartoon eyes and a yellow horn. The unicorn looked familiar, but Jake couldn't place it.

"Haven't seen this in a while," Bear said, drawing

close. "They called this shit Charlie after the YouTube short film that was famous a long time ago."

Jake snapped his fingers. "That's where I saw it. Charlie the Unicorn looking for Candy Mountain. Those videos were funny as hell."

"There was nothing funny about this batch of smack. Had several overdoses with this it. Shane Langston sold it and cut it with fentanyl."

Fentanyl was a synthetic opioid that was nearly a hundred times stronger than morphine. Dealers sometimes added fentanyl to their heroin to increase its potency. Users don't know they're purchasing fentanyl and use too much, thus the overdoses. Deaths involving synthetic opioids like fentanyl had skyrocketed in Missouri, as well as across the country, over the last couple of years.

The image of the unicorn flashed across Jake's brain. Besides YouTube, he'd seen it somewhere before. The harder he tried to hold onto the image, the quicker it washed away.

"Wonder if she took some of it, OD'd and someone buried her here to hide the body," Klages said.

Jake bent down and fished in her pocket, drawing out five more Charlie the Unicorn bags. Bear checked her back pocket and found a wad of damp cash.

"More like she was a dealer," Bear said.

Jake pressed to his feet. "And whoever put her here wasn't some junkie. They would've cleared out the smack and the money before they dumped the body."

"If she was dealing for Langston, we might have something on her in the files."

Goddamn it, where else have I seen that unicorn before?

Bear swung his light back to what was left of her

face. His face crunched as he knelt by her head, nose wrinkling. "Jesus. God, this smells awful." Gently pushing the hair out of the way, he revealed a rock under her skull with jagged edges and deep maroon stains. "I'd bet if we move her, we'll find the back of her skull caved in."

"I'm not taking that bet," Jake said.

The unicorn image drew into focus. Jake thought back to a bar called The Asylum and Garvan Connelly, the head of an outlaw biker gang called the Blood Devils. The last time Jake saw Garvan, he'd bled out on the floor of The Asylum with a handful of Jake's bullets lodged in his body. Before that fateful meeting, Jake noticed a pile of baggies on top of a poker table in the bar with the same unicorn stamp. Since Shane Langston had been tied into the biker gang, it made sense they had some. They were probably a major part of his distribution network. Of course, they couldn't ask Shane. Like Garvan, Shane had a bullet in his head with Jake's name on it.

"The Blood Devils," Jake said. "You remember the first time we went to talk to Garvan? Bags like this were scattered on the poker table. The Blood Devils were probably dealing it for Langston."

"Are there any of them left we could ask?"

"Most are dead or scattered to the winds," Jake said.

He stepped back and let Bear and his crew process the scene. The woman in the shallow grave definitely wasn't Sharla Babin.

Jake scanned the area. Was she buried somewhere nearby?

CHAPTER SEVEN

MERLE SAT ON THE BENCH UNDER THE LARGE OAK TREE, staring absently at the ground as he slipped his wedding ring on and off his finger. Charlene read in a magazine one time this gesture meant a man wasn't happy with his home life. Every time she caught Merle playing with the ring, she'd ask him about it. Once it became just the two of them, the questions turned into ass chewings. He'd managed to kick the ring habit for a while but started back up after he killed the girl at the dam.

He turned his attention to the moon over the tree-tops, liquid silver streaming between the branches of the trees. It was beautiful, but Merle shot his gaze back to the ground. He was in no mood for beauty. He didn't deserve it. Not yet. Maybe not ever.

He should get to the house and start prepping dinner. But Charlene would be there waiting for him. He jammed the wedding ring back on his finger, ashamed he wasn't looking forward to seeing his wife. Ashamed he wished his mother was there with him.

She'd been his buffer, from Charlene and anyone else who came along.

But his mother had always been on his side. After a car crash killed his brother when Merle was ten, his mother wouldn't let him out of her sight. She'd pampered him and spent what little money they had on getting Merle whatever he wanted, within reason. It had been smothering at times, but she'd protected him from the kids at school. She threatened to kill one of them even though she knew Merle was the one who started the trouble. And Merle believed with his heart and soul that she would have followed through with the threat. Nobody messed with her boy.

"You're all I have left in this world," she said. "I'll do anything to protect you."

And that's what she did. Even through this maddening time, even when he tried to hide things and she found out. She disapproved of what Merle did, begged him not to do it, but was always there to help him clean up the mess he made.

She knew things but acted like she didn't.

She did things but seemed to forget she did them.

Like if she told herself enough times that it wasn't happening, it wouldn't be real.

He supposed he did the same thing.

What would happen to her if he was caught?

You're all I have left in this world.

"Then you've got more than I do, Momma," he whispered.

Maybe this time would be different. Maybe this time he'd found the one who would fill the empty void in his soul.

Merle stood and marched up the hill to the house,

glancing past the barn to the dark shadows of the trees. He hoped this time would be different. He was tired of digging graves.

CHAPTER EIGHT

THUNDER RUMBLED IN THE DISTANCE AS A BANK OF RAIN-soaked clouds worked their way north toward Jake's house. He stood on the porch, absorbing the early October morning chill and the musty smell of pending rain sweeping over the heavy trees across the driveway. He took a sip of coffee as Maggie's arm slipped around his waist.

"You're up early after a late night. How was it?" she asked.

"Rough. Girl's been dead for a long time."

"Who was she?"

Jake took another drink of coffee and tossed the rest over the porch rail. "Don't know yet. Had dope on her the Blood Devils and Shane Langston distributed."

Maggie shivered. "There's a name I hoped to never hear again."

"I know, babe. Not to worry. Most of the Blood Devils are dead or fled the area."

Maggie was silent, looking to the darkening skies. "Hope the rain holds off until I get to work."

Jake hugged her tight and kissed the top of her blonde head. "Maybe you should call in sick. We could crawl under the covers and fool around while the rain pounds on the roof. A little Friday morning delight?"

She groaned. "That sounds amazing. What about Connor?"

"I could chain him to the coffee table and turn on Paw Patrol."

Maggie smacked his stomach. "He's a baby, not a dog. We have two new patients coming in today, anyway. What's on your agenda?"

"Nothing exciting. I get to sit on Tommy Roundtree for a few hours."

"I thought he was still in jail."

"Got out," Jake said. "His wife thinks he's cheating on her with Kitty Montgomery, but I honestly can't think of a woman in Benton County who is that desperate."

"Kitty might be," Maggie said. "At least that's what I hear."

"Maybe. Then, I'm going to dig into the Sharla Babin case."

Maggie drew back and twirled her car keys around her finger. "That poor little girl, Daisy. They brought her grandmother into Hospice House a couple months ago. When she died, I watched Daisy and it was like watching an egg crack. Her spirit spilled out like an egg yolk in a pan. It was heartbreaking."

"We'll see what I can find out. You ready for your weekend with Halle?"

Their daughter, Halle, was a freshman at the University of Nebraska in Lincoln. Her sorority was holding their annual Mom's Weekend festivities.

"Hell, yes. Can't wait to hang with my baby for a couple of days. I'll be back early afternoon to grab my bags before I head up." She rose on her tiptoes and nibbled Jake's earlobe, sending a shiver down his spine. "If you want to meet me here before I go, maybe it'll still be raining."

He kissed her long, pulling her in close, not wanting to wait for the afternoon in the rain. Connor's crying wafting through the open front door killed the mood.

"Go get your son," Maggie said, planting one last soft kiss. "I'll see you around three."

Jake waved goodbye as Maggie's Fusion rolled down the driveway, and he returned to the house, staring down at his chestnut-haired son looking up at him with wide-eyed tears spilling down his chubby red cheeks.

Jake picked him up and kissed his almost one-year-old head, the tingle from Maggie's lips lingering on his. "Son, someday when you're older, we're going to have a discussion about being a buzzkill."

———

AFTER FUTILELY TRYING to feed Connor steamed carrots and watching his son squish the mushy chunks between his fists, Jake gave him a bath and dropped him off at Bear's house where Audrey squealed with delight, her plump arms plucking the boy from Jake's grasp.

"Maggie called and said you couldn't pick him up before three o'clock," Audrey said, stroking Connor's head. "You two have something special planned?"

"Something like that. Bear already at the office?"

She poked Connor in his belly. "Left an hour ago after catching a couple hours of sleep. If I was a bettin' woman, I'd say he's at the Rusty Skillet wolfing down a pound of bacon."

Jake grinned. "Probably a good bet. He say anything about the body at the dam?"

"He said don't ask, and I know enough to leave it alone."

"He's smarter than he looks. You don't want to hear the gory details."

Jake kissed Connor on the forehead and headed toward town. Five minutes later, he cruised past the Rusty Skillet but didn't find Bear's truck. He turned north toward his sister's house, but there were no cars in the driveway. He felt bad. He hadn't seen her in weeks. The boys were in school, and she must be at work. He drove another couple blocks and parked a few trailers down from Kitty Montgomery. Kitty was banging the husband of his client, Marsha Roundtree, and Marsha wanted Jake to break her husband's kneecaps. Jake said the best he could do was get some pictures to help with the eventual divorce. Honestly, he doubted it would do any good. Tommy Roundtree didn't have two plug nickels to rub together much less anything to give to his wife in the divorce proceedings.

After a couple hours of sitting with no sign of Kitty or Tommy, his coffee was empty and he needed to pee, so he called it quits. Jake fired up the truck and headed toward the new jail on Old Highway 65 where Bear kept his office. The new jail was needed after nine thousand bats took up residence in the space between the ceiling and the roof of the old location off Main Street.

Jake swung into the parking lot, passing a wall bookended with flagpoles with Benton County Sheriff's Office in large black letters atop the beige stone. Jake parked and walked under the awning covering the entrance. After a quick bathroom stop, he wound his way back toward Bear's office, sucking in the smell of new carpet and fresh paint.

Bear raised his head from behind a paper covered desk, pen in hand, a scowl peeking through his bearded face.

"It's too early to look that pissed off," Jake said.

"Pissed off or just exhausted?" Bear threw the pen across the room. "Renny Styles quit, and Jenny Young-blood broke her ankle last night arresting some dipshit out by the Roadhouse Bar. She's out of commission leaving me down six positions. You want a job?"

"Not at the wages you're paying."

"I'd love to pay everyone a lot more than they're making. Budgets suck."

"Anything on our body last night?"

"The news hit the airwaves. Springfield station reported it this morning. Don't know how the hell they found out and I'm gonna squeeze somebody's balls in a vice for leaking it. Anyway, Howard thinks he found a match. Pretty sure it's Bethany Sheets, but we'll need dental records to confirm. She was reported missing two years ago. Like we thought, she died from blunt force trauma to the head."

Jake picked up the tossed pen and dropped into the chair opposite Bear's desk. "Know anything about her?"

"Did a few days for possession a while back. You were right, she dealt for Shane Langston on the west side of town, which explains the stash she had on her. She was no angel, but she was young and didn't deserve to die the way she did. Keep it quiet, though. Still trying to track down her family. What are you up to?"

Jake twirled the pen around his fingers like Ice Man from *Top Gun*. "Trying to catch up to Tommy Roundtree."

"He still dickin' Miss Kitty?"

"Supposedly. I'm having trouble catching them in the act."

Bear stood and arched his back. "Those are pictures I do not want to see. You want to check out the Sharla Babin file now?"

Jake stood. "Thought about Daisy all night."

Bear led the way down a short hall into a room with file cabinets lining a wall. "I don't think you're gonna find anything useful, but then again, you're full of surprises."

Bear extracted a thick folder from a middle drawer and plopped it on the table. "File stays in here."

Jake thumbed the folder. "You know, this isn't 1940. They have these things called computers."

"It's in the computer. I have Wendy print it out since me and computers get along like you and Shane Langston did."

"Except I shot Shane."

"Believe me, I've considered shooting that contraption on my desk more than once. Take all the notes you want and come see me when you're done. I'm running out to Sterett Creek to follow up on a burglary, but I'll be back in an hour."

Jake flipped open the four-inch folder crammed with computer printouts, handwritten notes, reports, and pictures. This was going to take a while.

Sharla Marie Babin, age 32, disappeared from her house on Chantilly Lane. A neighbor, Lonnie Kincaid, was sitting on his front stoop having a smoke when he saw her at approximately 11:45 p.m. standing in her front yard talking on a cell phone. Kincaid reported he couldn't make out what she was saying, but the tone seemed conversational, and Sharla did not appear to be agitated. Daisy was in foster care at the Wilkinsons' where she'd been for a few weeks after Sharla did a brief stint in the county lockup for narcotics distribution and her grandmother died. Report said Sharla had stayed clean since her release and was employed at the local Walmart stocking shelves in the wee small hours of the morning.

Pictures of the interior of the house showed shabby, but neat conditions. A cheap orange couch circa any 70s Sears and Roebuck catalog, a beat-up coffee table with an ashtray and can of Diet Coke, a TV in the corner with an HD antenna box nailed to the wall, a compact kitchen with dishes drying in a rack by the sink, and two bedrooms with the beds made and drawers closed. Jake had tossed his fair share of places searching for money or valuables when he collected for the mob, and nothing in Sharla's home gave that indication. The one thing that appeared off was an overturned chair at a four-person collapsible card table in the kitchen.

The folder contained interviews with Sharla's parole officer who said she was doing well and looked forward to reuniting with Daisy, another with her Walmart co-workers who said she kept to herself and offered nothing of interest, and disinterested neighbors who hadn't seen or heard anything.

A voice sounded from the doorway. "Find anything interesting?"

Jake glanced up at a squat woman in her late-fifties with platinum blonde hair and caked-on makeup. Jake met her before but couldn't remember her name. Just that she'd worked for Bear for years. "Not yet."

"I brought you a water." The woman shuffled over and set a plastic bottle on the table. Her eyes swept over the file. An overpowering flowery perfume wafted along with her. "Sad case."

Jake nodded. "Sure is. I'm sorry, I know we've met before but—"

"Wendy Blackwell. I work with your sister Janey and Bear. I'm sorta a doer of all things around here."

Jake snapped his fingers. "That's right. Sorry, I suck with names."

She smiled. "I'm not great with them myself. I thought you might be thirsty."

"Appreciated."

She opened her mouth to say something, but instead pasted on a tight-lipped smile. She turned on her heels and headed toward the door. Instead of exiting, she stopped and turned to face Jake.

Jake leaned back in his chair. "Something on your mind, Wendy?"

She peeked out in the hall and stepped back inside. "I see that little girl, Daisy, wandering around town, and it breaks my heart. I was friends with her grandmother, Doris. Wonderful woman."

"Did you know Sharla?"

"Not really. Just stories Doris told me. None of them portrayed Sharla in a good light, but Doris was hopeful she'd turn things around. For Daisy's sake. I hope you find out what happened to her. If you need any help with anything, let me know."

She pressed her lips together and left the room.

Jake spent another hour reviewing the file before

closing the folder and setting it on top of the cabinet. He headed back toward Bear's office. Bear wasn't back yet.

Jake's cell rang. The ID said Marsha Roundtree, his temporary employer. "Good morning, Marsha."

Her sharp tone knifed through Jake's skull. "The son of a bitch just left the house heading to that slut's place. I'd follow him but I gotta take care of the baby."

The baby was eight years old, but Jake let it slide. "How do you know he's going to see Kitty?"

"He actually showered and put on cologne. What else would he be doin' that for, because it sure weren't for me."

"I'll head over there now," Jake said. "Stay put and I'll call you later."

She growled. "Stay put? Where the hell else am I gonna go?"

CHAPTER NINE

"You see the news? They found a body out by the dam. Gotta be Bethany," Charlene said. "I told you to bury her deeper. Good thing you never listen to me. What the hell do I know?"

Merle ground his teeth together as he scraped the eggs out of the pan into a bowl, his hand trembling, hating the condescension in his wife's voice. News spread like lightning in a small town. That girl was the first, and she deserved everything she got for what she did. Still, there could be a trail which would lead to him. He couldn't let everything get wrecked before he finished.

"They're gonna find you, Merle, and God help you when they do."

He covered the bowl of eggs with cellophane and set them into a tub next to the biscuits. "They find me, they find you."

Charlene laughed. The grating sound made him want to strangle her. "What are they gonna do to me? It's your fuckin' mess. You deal with it."

It's what she always said. Everything was his mess, no matter whose hand was involved in making it.

Merle lugged the tub of clothes and food to the barn and down the creaking cellar stairs, wishing Charlene could help instead of chewing on his ass about everything under the sun. She left the dirty work for him. She didn't used to be this way. She used to be sweet and funny. After their daughter started using, everything went bad.

With his fingers hooked under the handles of the tub, he raked his elbow along the wall at the bottom feeling for a light switch. He softly sang *Angel of the Morning* by Juice Newton—*her* favorite song. She'd played it over and over until he and Charlene were sick enough of it to vomit. Now he'd give everything to hear her sing it one more time.

Merle found the switch and flipped it up with his rough elbow. Seconds after the light slammed through the darkness, scurrying sounds scraped the floors of the cells. The uninitiated would think there were rats, but Merle knew it was the women.

He set three identical blue dresses, fresh washcloths, motel-sized bars of soap, and white plastic combs outside each of the three doors. Charlene made him take the extra time to iron the dresses, which he hated, because he wasn't any good at it and it seemed pointless in this case. But, he'd learned long ago that arguing with his wife was an exercise in futility. Grabbing the silver pails, he filled each halfway with lukewarm water and deposited them outside the doors.

He stepped in front of the new girl's cell first, watching Rebekka through the electric wires, tilting his head from side to side, trying to see her better as she hunkered in the shadows on top of the bed, back against the wall. She looked so much like her that he could picture his angel lying on the cot. His heart ached.

"Good mornin'. Hope you slept well," he said. The whites of her eyes shone through the dark, and while they were fearful, they hadn't yet been robbed of the fire. Clutching the remote in one hand, he unlocked the cell door with the other and swung it open, finger hovering over the button which would shock the girl if she made a move. She didn't.

"Good girl," Merle whispered. "I got somethin' for ya."

He dipped to the floor and grabbed the clothing with one big hand and tossed it on the bed along with the soap and comb. He set the pail of water at the end of the bed frame.

He stood again and wrinkled his nose. Pulling a flashlight from his pocket, he shined the beam in the corner to the half-full waste bucket.

"Oh, darlin'," he said. "I apologize you had to sit in here with that foul smell this whole time." He directed the beam to the corner of the cell next to the bucket where a six-inch circular steel lid with a thick ring on top sat. "Just dump your bucket in the hole when you're done. It still won't smell like no bed of roses, but it'll be better."

"Let me out of here. Please," Rebekka said from the shadows.

Merle raised the remote. "Good girls don't speak unless spoken to. You get the first one free since you didn't know. The next one'll cost ya."

She jerked her upper body off the wall. "Go to hell, you fuc—"

Merle pressed the button on the remote, and the girl's body stiffened and shook. Grunts that wanted to turn into a scream lay trapped in her throat, eeking over her spittle-covered lips as her eyes rolled over white. After a few seconds, he released the button and watched as she drew herself up into a silent little ball.

Merle gritted his teeth. "Don't make me do that again, little girl. That was a middlin' setting. Don't make me turn it up. Now, I'm gonna unlock your ankle so you can get cleaned up. Use the soap, run the comb through your hair, and put on the clothes. I want you to look presentable. Trust me when I tell you if you try anything, you will be punished. Cooperate and we'll have a nice little meal together. Understand?"

The girl dipped her chin down and back, the fire still flickering in her eyes. Diminished, but still there.

Merle bent over and unlocked the anklet tethering her to the bed and its electrical source. Standing slowly, he backed toward the door, his voice and face softening. "You got twenty minutes till breakfast. Made your favorite scrambled eggs and homemade biscuits. Don't dawdle."

———

Rebekka's fingers dug into the cinderblock wall behind her as the man swung the door closed. He moved away before stopping in front of the wire ropes crossing the opening of her cell.

He smiled a terrifying mess of gnarled, yellowed teeth. "I'm really glad you decided to come stay with us for a spell. I got high hopes things are gonna work out just fine."

She bit her bottom lip to keep from screaming. She wasn't hooked up to the electrical current any longer, but memory of the two shocks rolling through her body kept the sounds at bay. It was the most excruciating and terrifying physical pain she'd ever experienced and had no desire to go through it again.

Leaning forward, she probed what the man left behind. A thick-toothed comb you'd get at a Dollar General—maybe she could break it and use it as a weapon. Broken just right, it would make a decent dagger. The cheap fabric of the plain blue dress scratched against her palm. Searching the pockets, she found nothing. A full two sizes too small, it looked like it would hit her mid-thigh. The cotton underwear was a grungy white, and she shivered at the thought of wearing them.

The man's muffled voice rolled across the expanse between Rebekka's cell and the mystery girl across the way. As he stood outside the cell, the man raised the remote and pressed the button. A garbled scream from the girl followed, and Rebekka jammed her hands against her ears to muffle it. The man entered the cell, jabbed a finger at the figure hidden in the darkness, and said something with a razor-sharp edge to it. Stomping out, he locked the door and disappeared.

Rebekka moved to the edge of her bed, dipping her fingers in the lukewarm water in the rusty silver pail. As tears rolled down her grimy cheeks, she wondered how she ended up here. She thought she'd hit rock bottom when her mother confronted her about her empty jewelry box. Rebekka claimed to know nothing despite the fact the Oxy she bought with the pawn shop money still coursed through her veins. The look on her mother's face had been soul crushing, even through the euphoric haze of the drug. What spurred her to rehab and AA meetings was waking up behind the Walmart next to a dumpster three months ago with sticky thighs and a crushed twenty-dollar bill in her hand with no recollection of the earning experience.

But she'd been clean since that new rock bottom. Ninety-two days. The man said it was breakfast time. So ninety-two days and sixteen hours give or take. She had a job. Her anger issues were more or less under control. She was beginning to earn the trust of her parents and friends again. Now this. Fucking life was cruel.

A tear plopped in the pail at her feet, and a tapping sounded from across the hall. A pencil-thin brunette with wide eyes plinked her comb against her own pail, her eyes locked on Rebekka's. She jabbed a finger at the pail and ran a washcloth over her dirty, thin arms. She ticked her head toward the man's direction and back at the pail. Her message was clear. Get busy.

Twenty minutes later, the door to her cell groaned open. The man stepped back with the keys in one hand and a raised taser in the other. Rebekka's eyes locked on the device—damn sure she didn't want any part of it. As she stepped through the opening into the dark and musty chamber, her two other fellow prisoners emerged, dressed in matching, cheap blue dresses. The other two automatically plodded forward toward a four-person table set in the middle of the low-ceilinged room. They'd done this before. The man gently prodded Rebekka forward.

The other two women sat meekly at either side of the table, hands folded in their laps and eyes locked on the empty plates in front of them. The man pulled out a chair and waited for Rebekka to take a seat. Her eyes swept the room—a half-dozen cell doors, a bench and sink on the far wall in front of her, and a set of wooden stairs leading up. Could she grab the back of the folding chair, knock the bastard down, and make her escape? Her body trembled, but she wasn't sure if it was from fear or anger.

The man killed the possibility of escape by pressing her down into the chair and shoving her forward into the table. In front of her was a paper plate, flimsy plastic fork and spoon, and a paper cup. Nothing that could be used as a weapon. Bowls of scrambled eggs and hash browns steamed in the center of the table in between paper cups filled with orange juice. Despite the terror flooding her system, her stomach growled in anticipation.

The man stepped to the other side of the table, sat, folded his hands, and bowed his head.

"Lord, we thank you for this bounty before us," the man said, his voice low and gravelly. "We thank you for our three guests, and we ask for your guidance."

Rebekka bristled. *Guests? Guidance for what? What the hell was going on?* She snuck a peek at the other two women. The woman to her right was pale with stringy auburn hair. She returned Rebekka's stare and shook her head with two quick jerks before dropping her eyes back to her plate. The message was *"Whatever you're thinking, don't."* The skinny woman from across the hall sat on her left, eyes squeezed so tight her cheek bones nearly met her eyebrows as a tear leaked from her eye. From her haggard appearance, she'd likely been here the longest. Rebekka wondered if there were or had been others in the additional cells. She fought back trembles, too terrified to look around for any other women—afraid it might set off the man and afraid of what she'd find if she did.

"We eat this food for the nourishment of our bodies and in tribute to you," the man continued. "Bless the souls of those we've lost and forgive the righteous hand that sent them on their way. Amen."

The righteous hand that sent them on their way? Rebekka wanted to say it was the most fucked up prayer she'd ever heard, but she had a feeling it wouldn't go over well with the man before her. Her smart mouth landed her into trouble in life more than once—expelled from high school for a time, kicked out of her childhood home by her father, smacked in the mouth by the criminal ex-boyfriend who hooked her on Oxy and heroin. The man across from her had cruel features, like he enjoyed dispensing a little torture as he spooned food onto their plate, all the while wearing that plastic smile. So, she kept her mouth shut.

The man chewed on a mouthful of eggs, a chunk falling into his mangy beard. He turned his head to the emaciated girl on Rebekka's left. "Chloe, tell me one thing you're thankful for today."

Chloe. At least Rebekka had a name to work with.

The girl picked up a plastic fork and moved the eggs on her plate around. Her voice trembled with fear. "This food."

"This food what?" the man asked, leaning forward.

Chloe's bottom lip trembled, her petite figure shivering like an icy breeze rolled through the chamber. "This food...Daddy."

"There ya go, sweetheart." He turned to the girl on

Rebekka's right. "How about you, little Chloe? Whatcha thankful for today?"

Two girls named Chloe? And Daddy? What in the actual hell?

The woman who occupied the cell next to Rebekka's stared at her plate, showing as much emotion as the stone walls of their cells. "You for taking such good care of us, Daddy."

Goosebumps exploded over Rebekka's arms. Chloe. Daddy. The same blue dresses.

"And last but not least," the man sighed from across the table, his thin lips parting as a crooked smile rose, revealing those jagged, broken, stained teeth. "Our newest guest. Tell me, Chloe. What are you thankful for today?"

A familiar anger boiled inside Rebekka. She didn't like to be scared, and right now she was terrified. She learned long ago to turn the terror into rage and to strike out at whatever tormented her. It served her well at times and not so well in others.

"I...ummm," she stammered before dropping her head.

"Look at me." His eyes bore a hole in her soul, the playful edge in his voice turning into a razor. "Chloe? What are you thankful for?"

She should keep her emotions in check and make something up. But, if she had any semblance of self-control, she probably wouldn't be in this basement dungeon in the first place. God, she needed a fix to wash away this nightmare.

"What in the hell do I have to be thankful for?" Rebekka spat.

The plastic smile melted as the man stood. "You got

plenty, young lady. A roof over your head. Food on the table and a daddy who loves you."

"My name ain't Chloe, and you ain't my daddy, you sick son of a bitch."

The man advanced around the table, shoving the taser in his pocket. As he moved, he unbuckled his belt, slapping the leather free from his belt loops in a second like a gunslinger on the draw. Chloe 1, the girl across the hall, whimpered as she pressed her eyes shut. Chloe 2, her neighbor, drew her limbs tight, turning away. The man stopped in front of Rebekka's chair, the anger radiating off him like a furnace as he towered over her.

"You take that back, young lady, or I'll make you wish you had."

Rebekka knew she should obey—knew she should comply until she found a way out of this. But it wasn't in her nature. She wasn't going to turn into one of the terrified zombies who sat on either side of her. "Fuck y—"

She never saw the hand lash out, just felt her body flying back and her head smacking against the hard dirt floor. Stars filled her eyes as the belt bit into her skin until the fog cleared enough to raise her arms to try to ward off the blows. The man's face twisted with rage, spittle flying from his mouth as he swung the belt. Chloe 1 began to wail. The wails turned to screams.

The man stopped beating Rebekka and turned as Chloe 1's anguished cries echoed off the stone walls. He held his hands to his ears, as if the screams caused him physical pain.

"Stop it, Chloe," the man said, glancing to the ceiling, trench lines creasing his Neanderthal forehead.

Chloe 1 continued to wail.

The lines deepened away as the man's face morphed into a mask of anger and he advanced on her, raising his belt from his waist. "I said stop it right now!"

Chloe 1's tiny fists scratched and swung as she scrambled back. He whipped the belt and cracked it across her face. Every time he yelled at her to stop it, he followed it up with another swing of leather. Chloe 1's volume impossibly rose, and she flailed her stick arms as if possessed.

"Damn it, Chloe," the man yelled as he tried to control the Tasmanian devil in front of him.

"My name is not fucking Chloe," she screamed, thrashing with a clawed fist and drawing a line of crimson across the man's face. The man stepped back, jaw ajar, eyes wide. He touched his face with his fingers and drew back blood. "My name is Jenny King, you sick fuck."

The man's face bloomed red, his teeth baring in a snarl. He clamped his hands around her face and violently jerked her head to the left. A crack silenced her screams, and her lifeless body clumped to the dirt floor.

The man stood over her, chest heaving, belt dangling from a ham-sized fist. Rebekka shot her eyes to Chloe 2 who hunkered silently in her chair with hands clamped over her ears. The man turned and wide, sad eyes flickered between the two remaining women.

"Look what you made me do," he whispered.

A high-pitched, low-volume whimper slipped from Chloe 2's lips as she drew herself tighter into a ball, turning away from the man.

Rebekka slid back along the dirt, wanting nothing more than to get away from this lunatic.

"Look. At. What. You. Made. Me. Do," the man repeated, his eyes turning hard, each word a sentence unto itself.

He stepped toward Rebekka, dropping the belt and pulling out the taser.

Rebekka scrambled until her back pressed against the door of her cell, hard enough to feel each grain through the cheap cotton fabric, eyes darting around searching for anything to ward off the advancing giant.

"Look at what you made me do!" the man howled, lunging forward.

Rebekka screamed as the electricity arced through her body, turning everything to black.

CHAPTER TEN

THE FRIDAY MORNING SUN CLIMBED TOWARD ITS APEX AS Daisy kicked an empty beer can down the shoulder of Old Castle Road. Occasionally, she'd pick up the drone of tires on the cracked asphalt and would scamper to the thick brush on either side to hide until the car passed. She supposed nobody would probably care much that she skipped school. But she was smart enough to know a ten-year-old girl wandering the backwoods roads alone could end up in a whole heap of trouble if the wrong person came along.

Mrs. Wilkinson was probably having a hissy fit, wondering where she was after the school called her telling her Daisy didn't show up. Again. Daisy thought the old bitch would probably be more mad that her hell-spawned foster kid made her look bad than the fact she didn't know where Daisy was.

She slammed the toe of her second-hand Converse into the can, sending it scraping and spinning across the road. She was mad at herself for making Mrs. Wilkinson feel bad. She called her an old bitch, but at least the lady made an effort to connect with her. Daisy knew she didn't make it easy. Fiery energy just radiated through her skinny frame whenever Mrs. Wilkinson tried to connect, to act like her mom. Not that Sharla Babin was a candidate for mother of the year. But, despite her many shortcomings, she was still Mom, and Daisy missed her which only made her madder. She booted the can again and choked back the tears pressing against her eyes.

Her gramma's house came into view through a copse of trees a quarter mile down the road. From the sparse brown weeds growing along the rough edges of the asphalt, something glimmered by the mile marker sign, catching her eye. Stepping closer, she bent and picked up a cheap, gold locket shaped like a heart. Daisy knew by the weight of it that it was all but worthless. It was something you'd get on sale at Walmart, but still nicer than anything she had. She slipped it in her pocket as the rumbling of an engine neared.

As she darted for cover on the side of the road, she hissed as a thorn in a bush drew a thin scratch of blood across her shin. A rusted green truck belching black smoke rolled past, heading toward town. She licked her thumb and wiped the blood from her leg before emerging and running the last stretch to her gramma's driveway.

What remained of the old house sat fifty yards back from the road amid overgrown weeds and trees hugging the partially burned husk. She dragged her feet up the sparse gravel driveway as a heaviness settled in her heart. She paused at the sagging front porch, taking in the jagged cuts of wood and the peeling white paint charred by the fire which took out the living room on the right and the back of the house.

Daisy stared at the living room window, almost able to see Gramma there. Daisy had managed to drag the old woman out of the thick smoke after she'd fallen asleep with a lit cigarette in her hand. Daisy's mom had been in jail for meth and, by then, Gramma didn't even know who Daisy was half the time. The dementia had clawed its way into her brain and ripped away the memories. Daisy shot daggers at the sky and at God for allowing anyone to suffer such a cruel fate.

Daisy kicked aside a needle and a rusty spoon and climbed up the creaking front steps, sliding through the front entrance where the door used to be, hoping nobody was inside. Last time she visited, a grungy couple was passed out in the husk of the dining room on sleeping bags and using stuffed garbage bags for pillows. Daisy had called Sheriff Bear to clear them out, and there was nobody there today. Just a few extra beer cans and trash.

"At least the fat bastard did something right," she muttered.

Daisy climbed the dilapidated staircase, stepping close to the wall where the wood felt marginally secure, intentionally not looking at the burned-out circle in the living room where Gramma used to sit watching her soaps.

At the top of the stairs, she glanced down the hall to the door covered in magic marker where her two brothers stayed for a week before Mom whisked them all away to live with some dirt ball drug dealer in Kansas City she'd fallen in love with. Daisy twirled the cheap gold chain of the locket she found as she remembered the drug dealer's scraggly dark beard over sunken cheeks, yellow eyes, and a poorly drawn dragon tattoo on his right arm peppered with needle marks. Daisy was happy when the man went to jail, because she thought they could come back and live together in Gramma's house. Instead, Mom joined the dealer in jail, her brothers were sent to foster care somewhere in Kansas City, and Daisy was sent back to Gramma's house. She hadn't seen or talked to her brothers in two years.

She entered her old bedroom, keeping her feet on the charred boards she knew were still good. An iron bedframe sat next to an empty dresser. Black char marks chewed their way up one wall as the morning sun broke through the burned-out hole in the roof. The fact nobody tore down the house was a miracle. If they did, it would kill her. It was the last tie holding her family together, the only real home she'd ever known, and the one place she felt safe. All the reasons she kept coming back.

She sat on an old bucket she'd found a few weeks ago and propped her elbows on the windowsill, watching the road through the trees. She liked to come here and remember a time where life was bearable, even nice in moments. Where she had someone who cared. Where she played hide-and-seek with her brothers while the smells of dinner cooking seeped through the floorboard. She wiped a film of dust from the window as a tear spilled down her cheek. Her mom, gramma and brothers weren't perfect, but they'd been family.

Gramma was dead, though. Probably her mom, too, as much as she hated to admit it. But part of her still held out hope she was alive. Part of her came to this house, waiting for the day when her mom would stroll up the driveway, shiny and clean with a perfect smile reserved only for her little Daisy Dawn.

Daisy rested her chin on her hands, the locket swinging beneath her clenched fists, and dreamed a little dream. And though she and God had their differences, and she cursed Him more than she probably should, she said a prayer for Jake Caldwell to bring her mom back to her.

CHAPTER ELEVEN

Jake leaned against a ramshackle mobile home across a narrow dirt road as he watched Kitty's trailer gently rocking. Sounds from a TV or radio drifted from an open window of a nearby home. He'd debated busting in and nabbing Tommy while he was in the throes of passion but decided he couldn't stomach the image of those two slapping against each other. He carried enough mental baggage as it was. He fingered the zip ties in his jacket pocket from his glove compartment in case Tommy wanted to get feisty.

Kitty's trailer was arguably the nicest one in the trailer park, but it wasn't saying much. Kitty's yellow siding was at least free from dirt and reflected the midmorning sun. Flowery curtains trimmed the windows, and a set of decent plastic lawn furniture surrounded a homemade firepit made from haphazardly arranged rocks and stones.

A pair of synchronized moans drifted across the morning breeze through a cracked window. Jake hoped it meant they were wrapping things up. His cell phone dinged with a text from Maggie. It was a picture of a digital clock displaying 3:00 PM. Jake felt a stirring, anxious to wrap this up and get home to her so the next moans he heard were Maggie's.

A hulking figure in jeans and a black T-shirt darted across Jake's peripheral vision, snapping him from the daydream. The male figure threw open the door to Kitty's trailer. Based on the size and the shitty ponytail, it was Gunner Jacobson—one of the last remaining members of the Blood Devil bikers. While Jake, Bear, and the FBI wiped out most of the gang in a massive shootout at The Asylum, Gunner had been smart enough to disappear. Guess he wasn't smart enough to stay gone. Jake made a mental note to ask him about the Charlie the Unicorn heroin bags.

Jake slipped out his phone and dialed the number of FBI Agent Victoria Snell, his sometimes partner over the years.

Snell answered on the second ring. "Please don't tell me you've uncovered some plot to assassinate the President or something else that's going to drag me through the muck. I'm still digging out from under your last mess."

"Well, good morning to you, too, Victoria. This one is easy. Gunner Jacobson still on your FBI Most Wanted list?"

"Jacobson? One of those Blood Devils?"

"That's him."

"Hold on." Computer keys clicked. "Twenty-thousand-dollar reward for information leading to his capture. Why?"

Jake did the mental math. It'd be equal to a semester of tuition, room, and board at Nebraska for Halle.

Jake stiffened as Kitty screamed and a deep-throated voice barked from within the trailer which bounced and rocked. Something shattered.

Jake pushed off from his perch. "Get the checkbook out. I'll call you back later."

"Jake, what are you—"

Jake clicked off and started across the road. Seconds later, Tommy flew out the front door, naked as a jaybird. He sprawled face down in the dirt next to the plastic lawn furniture, and Jake hoped Tommy lost his erection from his encounter with Kitty, or he would be in a world of hurt.

Jake turned his attention to his new paycheck as Gunner bounded out after Tommy, face screwed with anger and a stringy ponytail flopping back and forth as he buried the toe of his boot in Tommy's ribs.

Jake felt no obligation on a moral level to protect Tommy, but if Gunner beat Tommy to death, Tommy would have no money to pay his wife, and Jake wouldn't get paid. Shitheads like Tommy didn't carry insurance policies. The paycheck from nabbing Gunner would dwarf what Jake would get from getting the dirt on Tommy, but he was hired to do a job and he intended to see it through. Jake slipped his Sig Sauer from his waist holster and crossed the road. Before he arrived, Kitty flew through the door in a satin pink kimono which failed to cover up anything it should.

"Stop it. Leave him alone, Gunnie," she screamed, throwing worthless fists against Gunner's back.

Gunner whipped a ham-sized fist behind him, and Kitty toppled over the lawn furniture and lay in a ball.

Pointing the gun at Gunner's head, Jake whistled.

Gunner's eyes shot up, his leg drawn back to deliver another blow.

Gunner's lip curled. "Caldwell? What the fuck are you doing here?"

Jake stopped fifteen feet away, dropping the gun angle to forty-five degrees. Not exactly in firing position, but less confrontational and close enough that Gunner would know what waited for him if he tried anything. "I'm gonna need you to stop kicking Tommy's ass for a minute, Gunner."

"Fuck you," Gunner spat, launching his foot into Tommy's ribs hard enough to launch the man a half foot. "He's bangin' my old lady."

"I said stop," Jake yelled.

"I ain't your goddamn old lady, you asshole," Kitty screamed. She'd worked herself into a sitting position, knees drawn up. While she'd managed to throw on the kimono, she'd failed to don any other stitch of clothing, and her untrimmed shrubbery was on eye-searing display, like a seventies porn movie. Jake blinked away the horror before it burned into his retinas.

Jake raised his gun and swung it toward Gunner, his finger resting on the trigger guard. "Come on, Gunner. Take a step back."

"How'd you find me?" Gunner asked.

"Happy coincidence. I haven't thought of you since I blew a half-dozen holes in your old boss at The Asylum."

"Then who are you here for?"

Jake ticked his head toward the lump at Gunner's feet. "Tommy boy. He owes my client child support."

Gunner's eyes narrowed. Jake could practically visualize the hamster turning the wheel in his peabrain as the hulk considered his alternatives. Jake already kicked his ass once before, and Gunner ended up with a knife buried in his shoulder. Gunner's chest heaved as he took a step back.

Tommy groaned and spat a wad of blood on the ground. "My wife hired you?"

"Shut up," Jake ordered. "She called me when you left the house this morning. You're lucky I don't let Gunner here finish you off."

"I ain't got no money."

"We'll see about that."

Kitty climbed to her feet. "He's lyin'. He's got a stash in his pocket right now."

Tommy's eyes shot wide. "Kitty! Why in the hell would you—"

She stomped toward them. "Cuz you're a lyin' piece of shit! You said you left her. I ain't no homewrecker."

"Speaking of lying pieces of shit," Gunner said, his lip curled. "I suppose all that missing me talk was a lie."

Jake sighed. He was in the middle of a bad Jerry Springer episode. The only thing missing was the crowd chanting "Jerry! Jerry! Jerry!" Now came the tricky part. There were three of them and one of him. Gunner was obviously the biggest concern, and if he figured out Jake was going to haul his ass in, there would be a fight, and who knew what Tommy or Kitty would do.

Jake pointed toward the woman. "Kitty, while I take care of this mess, you want to go sit in a chair over there?"

"Hell no," she sneered. "This here's my property and you don't give me orders."

"I didn't give you orders," Jake said, keeping his voice smooth. "I asked you nicely. There's a lot of bodies here, and I'd hate for my trigger finger to slip. Pretty please, with sugar on top, go sit in the fucking chair."

Kitty threw up her hands as if in disgusted resignation, but complied, plopping down in a cloud of dust on one of the firepit chairs.

Jake slipped the zip ties from his pocket and tossed them to Gunner, keeping the gun trained in his direction. "Gunner, do me a favor and zip Tommy's wrists together for me."

"Screw you. Do it yourself."

Jake set his jaw hard and pushed the gun forward, setting the sights on Gunner's chest. "You came at me with a knife last time we tangled, so forgive me if I don't wanna turn my back on you. Just do it, please, and we can be on our merry way."

Gunner's eyes narrowed and the muscles in his forearms rippled. If he took off running, Jake wasn't sure what he would do. He didn't have cause to shoot him, and Maggie was one unnecessary brawl away from Jake spending a month on the couch. He'd probably have to run the man down because twenty grand was nothing to spit at.

"Toss a few of his bucks my way for the effort?" Gunner asked.

Jake gave it a moment's thought. "Sure. That'd work. I hear Tommy has some cash on hand."

Jake had zero intention of giving Gunner anything but burns on his wrists from a set of tight handcuffs.

Gunner stooped, grabbed the zip ties, and latched them onto a protesting Tommy's wrists. Tommy howled during the process, probably because Gunner dislocated his shoulder wrenching the man's arms back.

Gunner stood and wiped his hands on his grungy jeans. "Now what?"

Jake stepped forward. Ten feet away. "Now turn around, lean your head against the trailer and put your hands behind your back. Don't even think about running, because you know I'll plug you in the back without a second thought."

Gunner's jaw dropped. "What the hell, man? I thought you—"

Jake held a hand up. "Chill out. I just wanna secure you while I search Tommy and get him in my truck. After that, I'll let you and Miss Kitty get back to your lover's quarrel."

Gunner didn't move. His eyes darted around as if scanning for a weapon or an escape route.

"Or I could shoot you in the kneecap," Jake offered. "Don't make an easy situation difficult, Gunner. A couple minutes in cuffs is all I'm askin'. You'll have a little cash in your pocket and won't have to see me again."

Gunner chewed on the idea and his upper lip for a minute, then moved toward the trailer.

"You're a fuckin' idiot," Kitty cackled from the chair.

"Shut up, bitch," Gunner said. "I'll deal with you later."

When Gunner's head touched the yellowed side of the trailer, Jake stepped up and pressed the barrel of his Sig Sauer against the back of his neck. With his free hand, he slapped the cuffs on Gunner's raised left hand and pulled it around to his back, cranking it up high enough to cause a little tension, but no pain. He didn't want Gunner to panic.

Once he secured Gunner, Jake spun him around

against the trailer and showed a picture of the heroin bag they'd found out by the dam. "Since we're talking all friendly-like, do you recognize this?"

"It's Charlie. Haven't seen that in a long time. Where'd you find it?"

"In a dead girl's pocket."

Gunner drew back. "Then I definitely ain't sayin' shit. I don't know nothin' about a dead girl."

"If I showed you a picture of the girl we found with it, would you tell me who she was?"

Gunner snarled. "Not even if it was my fuckin' sister. Next thing I know, you'd be pinning her death on me. I ain't even been in the state for months."

"I know you didn't kill her. Just trying to solve a mystery here."

"Then hire Scooby fuckin' Doo."

"I'll throw in a C-note if you can tell me who she is." Jake held up a picture of the remains of the dead girl from his phone. "Found her last night buried in the woods out by the visitor center."

Gunner squinted at the phone and his mouth twisted. "Looks kinda like Bethany Sheets. She wore that Zeppelin T-shirt seven days a week. Wondered what happened to her. She's looked better."

That confirmed what Bear suspected. "She deal for you guys?"

Gunner shook his head. "For Shane. Saw her a couple times at The Asylum. Can we get this over with? I don't like cuffs."

"You should be used to it by now," Kitty sneered.

Gunner moved in her direction, and Jake pushed him back against the trailer. "Any idea who would've killed her?"

Gunner spat on the ground. "Could've been anybody. Drug dealers don't exactly hang around with good people, you know."

"But nobody specific comes to mind?"

"Shane is the only one who jumps up," Gunner said. "But if he did it, he wouldn't have buried her in the middle of the woods. If he killed her, he'd do it to send a message, and that'd mean something public. Maybe you should ask him."

"Can't ask a dead man. I blew his head off."

"No shit? Good for you. Guy was a fucking psychopath."

"Where'd you go after the gunfight anyway?" Jake asked.

"Escaped out the back through the woods once the shooting started. Nabbed a buddy's boat at Forthview and hauled ass across the lake before all hell broke loose."

"That was over a year ago. Where after that?"

"Iowa, Nebraska, Colorado for a bit. Couldn't stay away from Kitty anymore."

Jake flicked his eyes between the two. "You came back for *her*?"

Gunner shrugged. "Love makes you do dumb shit, you know?"

"Indeed, it does," Jake said, jabbing the pistol barrel in Gunner's side and pushing him toward his truck on the other side of the road. "Like letting me cuff you. Don't move Gunner, or I'll break the rest of your ribs."

"What the fuck, man?" Gunner tugged, trying to run, but Jake held firm. "We had a deal."

"I lied. Don't worry, I'm sure the feds will kick you loose after a little time in their care."

"Caldwell, you son of a—"

"Now, don't say anything you'll regret, Gunner."

———

"Holy shit," Bear said, jaw hanging open. "Where did you find him?"

Jake let a couple deputies haul Gunner back toward the cells and told Bear the story. "I might go buy a lottery ticket."

"Buy me one too. With twenty grand, you can buy a mess of scratchers."

Jake flashed a wad of bills he took off Tommy. "And I got Marsha Roundtree's money. I'm battin' a thousand today."

"Knowing Tommy, I'd have the money sterilized."

Jake shoved the money in his pocket. "Hey, Gunner confirmed our dead girl was Bethany Sheets. Said she dealt for Langston but doubted Shane did it."

"We're still trying to track down her family. It's like they don't want to be found." Bear checked his watch. "Since you're Mr. Moneybags, how 'bout you buy me lunch?"

"I'll pass," Jake said. "I'm going to take a run out to Forthview and talk to your dipshit ex-deputy Wyatt Corkins."

"That idiot couldn't generate enough brainpower to lightly toast a piece of bread. Why talk to him?"

"He talked to the last dude that saw Sharla. I want to pick his brain before I pop over to Sharla's house and poke around. After I deliver Marsha her share of Tommy's dough, of course. I have to be back at the house by three."

"What's at three?"

Jake shucked his eyebrows and sang, "Skyrockets in flight."

Bear groaned. "Afternoon delight. I've forgotten what that's like, you lucky SOB. If you find anything interesting with Corkins, let me know. And don't do anything stupid."

Jake feigned shock. "Now when have I ever done anything stupid?"

"Hardly ever," Bear said, turning toward his office. "Just on the days ending in the letter *y*."

CHAPTER TWELVE

Forthview was a small lakeside community located off Highway M. It was twenty-five miles of narrow, winding roads east of Warsaw. There was no actual town by the name of Forthview, but that's what everyone called it long before Jake was ever born.

Jake hadn't returned to the area since his adventures at The Asylum, the ass-kicking biker bar which used to be run by the outlaw Blood Devils. Jake, Bear, and a squad of FBI agents wiped out most of the Blood Devils in a fire fight over a year ago. The Asylum rolled by on his right. He'd heard someone else took it over and tried turning it into a roadhouse featuring local bands. They'd painted the black building white and named it The Coop, but it still looked like a dive.

As he rolled into the community on Forthview Road, cottages dotted the landscape with boat docks spilling into the sprawling lake. Wyatt Corkins lived on the Deer Creek Arm side of the community. His dirt-crusted, vinyl-sided house slumped underneath an overgrowth of trees whose branches would scrape off the shingles given a strong wind. There were some nice homes in Forthview, but Wyatt's definitely wasn't one of them.

Jake dropped his boots to the graveled driveway, peeking around either side of the house. No dock leading to the water, just scrub brush and metal debris Wyatt must have chucked out his back door. Judging from the metal parts—empty beer cans and other trash strewn on either side of Wyatt's front steps—the man wasn't overly particular on where he threw anything. If this is what the outside of the house looked like, Jake was concerned with the inside and hoped he didn't get invited in.

He knocked hard three times on the smudged glass of the screen door. A muffled cough emanated from inside and something clinked. A few seconds later, the door opened enough for Wyatt Corkins's stubbled face to squint against the daylight. The waft of booze and cigarette smoke hit Jake hard.

"Caldwell? What do you want?"

Jake slid his boot up into the door opening. He had a feeling Wyatt was going to attempt to slam the door in his face. "I need to talk to you for a minute."

"Ain't got nothin' to say about nothin'. I quit the sheriff's department."

"Quit or were fired?"

Wyatt sucked on his teeth. "That sumbitch Bear knew I was quittin' when I walked up, and he fired me before I could open my mouth. Made himself feel superior and shit."

"Whatever you want to believe, man. Give me a few minutes and I'll get out of your hair."

"I'm busy."

"I can tell. I'll let you get back to it after you answer a

couple of simple questions about Sharla Babin. You did the last report on her."

Wyatt sneered, his eyes brightening. "You deaf, Caldwell? Fuck you and your buddy Bear. I ain't got nothin' to say to either of you."

As predicted Wyatt tried to slam the door shut, and it bounced off Jake's boot.

"Two minutes, Wyatt. That's all I'm askin'. Please."

Wyatt opened the door wider and kicked at Jake's foot. "Move your goddamn foot. I got rights."

Jake set his jaw. "You kick my foot one more time and I'm going to put it so far up your ass you'll be tasting leather. Two minutes."

Wyatt stopped kicking, smoldered for a ten-count and swung the door open. "Fine. Come on in. You got your two minutes."

Jake stepped across the threshold, and the smell of old grease and smoke hit him. A threadbare sky-blue corduroy couch sat along one wall with a cheap, generic cowboy on a horse painting hanging above it. An off-brand television rested on a milk crate in front of a scarred coffee table littered with empty bottles of Old Crow whiskey and an overflowing ashtray. That brand of whiskey was better suited for stripping grease from parts than drinking. Jake left the door open behind him to air the place out.

"You wanna sit?" Wyatt asked.

"No, thanks. I don't wanna stick to anything."

Wyatt's lip curled up as he grabbed a nearly empty bottle of the Old Crow and fell back onto the couch. "You always were a smart ass."

"Better than being a dumb ass."

"You gonna insult me or ask your questions so you can get the hell out?"

Jake leaned against the doorframe. "You responded to Sharla Babin's disappearance, did the report."

"That ain't a question."

"You questioned the neighbors and didn't find anything of interest."

Wyatt lit a cigarette and lounged back, blowing smoke to the ceiling. "Still not a question. Tick tock, Caldwell."

Jake resisted the urge to cross the room and separate Wyatt's jaw from his body. "I'm looking for anything you can think of that's not in the report."

Wyatt's eyes turned to slits. "Like what?"

"I don't know, something that maybe tripped your cop trigger but didn't amount to anything."

"If anything did that, I woulda put it in the report."

"It's just that you wrote about the house and interviewed a couple of neighbors and that was it. There had to be more."

Wyatt took another slug off the whiskey bottle. "You sayin' I did a shitty job investigating the scene."

"I'm wondering if there's anything you can think of now that—"

"I did a good job. I covered the house, the neighbors, the tent behind the house, the—"

Jake stiffened. "What tent?"

"There was a tent on the other side of the road behind the house. Nobody was in it when I checked. I was gonna go back later to check it out before the afore-motioned...mution—"

"Aforementioned. Don't try to talk like a smart person, Wyatt."

"Before he fired me."

"You see anything suspicious in the tent?"

Wyatt's eyes explored the ceiling. "Naw, at first I figured it was some homeless dude, but the area was really neat. Like someone was campin' there. Homeless people ain't that neat."

"Why didn't you put anything about this tent in your report?"

Wyatt blinked. "I did."

"No, you didn't. I read the report and there's nothing in there on the tent."

Wyatt jabbed the cigarette in Jake's direction. "I abso-fuckin'-lutely put that in the report. If you didn't see it, maybe you didn't look hard enough."

Wyatt was a scumbag and apparently incompetent at living based on his immediate surroundings, but Jake believed him. There was no hesitation, and he was forceful in his declaration.

"Wonder why it's not there now?" Jake asked.

"You're the big shot private investigator," Wyatt said, leaning back and sucking the rest of the Old Crow bottle dry. "You figure it out as you find your way out of my house."

CHAPTER THIRTEEN

JAKE DROVE BACK TO WARSAW, FINGERS DRUMMING ON the steering wheel. *Why would someone remove details from the report?* He'd have to ask Bear.

He cruised through town and stopped off at Marsha Roundtree's house, slapping most of Tommy's money in her palm. For getting a wad of cash, she offered more curses toward her husband than thanks to Jake. Even though they'd agreed on his cut, she wanted to renegotiate his fee once she held the stack of bills. Jake already took his fee out of the wad before he gave it to her and left her spewing profanities from her front porch.

The Friday lunchtime crowds packed the few restaurants around town, so Jake skipped the wait and would come back later. He cruised past the Wilkinsons' house, part of him hoping to see Daisy and check in on her and the other part hoping she wasn't there, because he didn't have a thing to tell her.

Leaving Warsaw proper in his rearview mirror, he made his way along a shoulder-less road shaded by a canopy of oak trees, admiring the turning leaves. Jake thought there wasn't a better place to be than the Ozarks once those leaves exploded in vibrant shades of orange and red. Chantilly Lane rolled up on his left and he made the turn. Quaint ranch houses popped up on either side of the road, most needed new paint, siding, and roof work. An entrepreneurial kid with a lawn mower could make some decent cash.

Sharla Babin's house crept up on his right—yellow siding, two windows on either side of a weathered, brown door covered by a screen hanging on for dear life by the top hinge. Knee-high weeds bordered a broken sidewalk leading to a pair of crumbling concrete steps. To the left of the house sat an empty carport, its tin roof collapsing under the weight of massive branches of a large oak tree.

Jake stopped his truck, letting the engine rumble as he scanned the area. No signs of life in the house, which wasn't surprising. He stepped onto the road and made his way up the sidewalk. A dog barked nearby as a breeze rattled the leaves in the trees overhead.

Jake peered in the living room window. It looked exactly like the photos from Bear's files. He checked the other window, but the shades were drawn.

"Help you?" a voice drawled to his left.

Jake turned and a rail-thin man in his forties eyed him from a wired fence splitting the properties. He took a drink from an oversized can of Bud Light and wiped the suds from his bristly, red beard.

Jake stepped toward him, trying to recall the man's name from Bear's file. "Afternoon. I'm just lookin' at—"

"Sharla's gone and she probably ain't comin' back. Assumin' that's who yer lookin' for."

Jake stopped a few feet from the fence. "I know. Her daughter asked me to help find her."

The man squinted and shook loose a Marlboro from a crumpled pack in his shirt pocket. With grimy fingers, he flicked a Bic and sucked in a lungful of smoke. "Daisy, eh? How's she doin'?"

"Alright, I guess. Given the circumstances."

"She's a handful. Fulla piss 'n vinegar."

"I'm Jake Caldwell."

"I've heard of ya," the man said.

"Anything good?"

He slurped a drink and sucked a drag, flicking the ashes to the wind. "Depends on who's talkin'. The bad stuff comes from shitheads who couldn't find their asses with both hands and a flashlight, so I reckon you're prolly a'right."

"Good to know."

"I'm Lonnie Kincaid. I used to drink at the Horseshoe with your old man. Stony."

Jake's father died of lung cancer a few years back and wasn't missed by anyone as far as Jake knew. "Hope you won't hold it against me."

Lonnie sniffed. "Kinda hard not to. Your dad was mean as a snake. Once broke my nose for askin' how he was doin'. Stood over me waving his knuckles in my face." Lonnie dropped his voice to a low growl in an impressive Stony Caldwell imitation. "That's how I'm doin'. You got anymore fuckin' questions?"

Jake shifted on his feet. Sounds like something his father would do, especially if he'd gotten his drink on that day. Which was most days. Still, it didn't help Jake here.

"Sorry about that and I can relate. He wasn't much

different at home." Jake ticked his head toward the house. "You know Sharla well?"

Lonnie drained the rest of his beer and chucked the can over his shoulder. "Well 'nough to say hello. She was a nice enough lookin' gal, but I was told to keep my distance."

"By Sharla?"

"By Daisy." Lonnie curled his lip. "She told me God put that fence there for a reason, and I should stay on my side of it. Like I don't take enough shit from people. I gotta hear it from an eight-year-old."

Sounded like something Daisy would say.

"I heard you were the last one to see Sharla the night she disappeared."

Lonnie stiffened. "Aw, c'mon man. I didn't have nothin' to do with that. Didn't care much for her little girl, but that ain't how I roll."

"Didn't think you did. Could you tell me about it?"

"I told the cops."

"I know. I read the file, but the cop who interviewed you was kind of a moron."

Lonnie snorted. "Corkins? That's puttin' it mildly. He was a dumb, snot-nosed little kid. Didn't get much smarter as an adult."

"If you could tell me, it might help me find out what happened to Sharla. It'd help out Daisy to know someone's trying."

Lonnie took a last drag of the cigarette as he considered Jake's request, flicking the butt into his yard near a patch of weeds springing from bare dirt. "Yeah, but who's gonna help *me*?"

"That would assume you have a story to tell."

"I believe I do. Scratch my back, I scratch yers. Squid pro quo."

Jake pinched the bridge of his nose. He knew where this was going. Nobody seemed to want to do anything these days without getting something in return, and it depressed Jake to his core. "You need something in particular, Lonnie?"

Lonnie bared tobacco-stained teeth. "Well, since your askin'."

"I'm really not, but I have a feeling you're going to anyway."

Lonnie cranked his head over his shoulder. "See the blue house down the street? The one with all the shit in the yard? Guy named Willie Dykes lives there."

Jake nodded. "I'm familiar with Willie."

Willie Dykes was a problem child for the law enforcement community in Warsaw. He wasn't violent or a drug pusher, just a lowlife with sticky fingers whether it be gum, liquor, or the occasional car. Jake caught Willie with his hand on the door handle of Jake's truck last year and let the man weasel his way out of a beating.

"Well, he's a fuckin' thief."

"Tell me something I don't know," Jake said.

"He stole my stereo outta my garage in broad daylight. My ex-wife gave me the stereo, and it's the only thing she let me keep. It has value to me. Sentimonious...sentitismal..."

"Sentimental."

Lonnie snapped his fingers and pointed. "That be it. You get my stereo back, I'll tell ya everything you want to know about that night with Sharla."

Jake ran a hand over the stubble on his cheek. "How do you know Willie took it?"

"I saw him runnin' down the street with it. But my leg ain't so good, and I couldn't chase after him."

"You tell the cops?"

"Same dipshit cop who took my statement. But he ain't done nothin' about it. Like I said, you scratch my back, I scratch yours."

"What's the stereo look like?"

Lonnie shaped a three-foot by two-foot box with his hands. "Panasonic. Yea big. Black. CD player above a double tape deck. Speakers on either side."

"Tape deck? How old is this thing? You could probably buy a new one for twenty bucks at Walmart."

"Sentimental value, like I says."

Jake started toward Willie's house. He stopped and turned. "You better have something worth telling me, Lonnie. You blow smoke up my ass and you'll have *two* bad legs. Got it?"

Lonnie ticked his chin, and Jake headed down the street, his boots crunching the sandy grit covering the street. Willie's house slumped fifty yards away, a mess of haphazardly-applied siding surrounding a broken front window with cardboard covering the opening. A menagerie of rusted lawn ornaments dotted the weed-infested front yard. Jake half expected to see a condemned sign nailed to the cheap front door. There were some really nice houses in Warsaw. Jake questioned why he got stuck knocking on the doors of the shitty ones.

He pulled out his cell and called Bear. "I'm getting ready to pound on the front door of Willie Dykes."

Bear chuckled. "What for?"

"Long story. Anything I should be worried about or any outstanding warrants to serve while I'm here?"

"No warrants and don't touch anything. You might end up with lice or fleas if you go inside. Other than that, you should be good. Anything I need to know?"

"I'll fill you in later. Thanks."

Jake stepped along pavers leading to what was left of the front door. He pounded three times, stepped back, and waited. After a minute, Willie yanked open the door clad in a grungy wifebeater and gray sweatpants.

Willie's frazzled mane of stringy hair shot out in all directions above a scraggly beard streaked with gray. His sleepy eyes scanned Jake up and down. "Caldwell? Whatcha want?"

Jake wrinkled his nose. "Hey, Willie. I need the Panasonic."

"What's a Panasonic?"

"Lonnie's stereo you stole. I don't have time to dick around, so give it to me and I'll let you get back to whatever nasty shit you were doing."

Willie's eyes darted to the ground. "I don't have Willie's stereo. Did that fucker tell you that?"

Over Willie's shoulder, Jake spotted the Panasonic on a sagging shelf under a spiderweb crusted window. "I can see it right there. Just give it to me. Besides, you owe me."

"The hell I do. Fer what?"

"For not breaking your hands as you were getting ready to steal my truck."

Willie shuffled. "I wasn't gonna take it. I didn't even know it was yours or I wouldn't have tried. For reals."

Jake drew in close, tightening his jaw. "Last chance before I do what I should've done in the parking lot."

Willie groaned. "Fine. But I'm keepin' the CDs that were in it."

"Like I give a damn. Go get it and don't make me cross this threshold."

Willie shuffled across the chipped hardwood floors, tripping over a half-full trash bag of debris. Yanking out the stereo's plug, he hefted the unit in his skinny arms and brought it to Jake, shoving it into his chest.

"I hope that sumbitch blows the speakers out," Willie grumbled.

Jake did a doubletake. "You already blew 'em out, didn't you?"

"Just the right one."

Jake turned to leave.

"Why you doin' this for Lonnie, anyways?" Willie asked.

Jake turned back. "He's the last one to see Sharla Babin alive. Says he has info."

Willie scratched his beard. "Ayuh. He'll probly tell you about the truck."

"What truck?"

"The one cruisin' around Sharla's house the day she disappeared."

Jake cruised through his mental notes from the files. There wasn't a mention of any truck in the neighborhood on the day of the disappearance. He set the stereo down on the rickety steps. "Tell me about the truck."

Willie rubbed his thumb and forefinger together in the universal money sign, his rheumy eyes scanning the sky.

"Fuck you, Willie. What'd you see?"

Willie grabbed the side of his front door and tried to swing it closed. "You don't wanna know. That's fine."

Jake jammed his boot in the opening and pushed it back open. Reaching into his wallet, he extracted a twenty and held it up in the air between his index and middle finger. "What truck?"

"I only seen it once. Big 'un. Tan. Parked down from Sharla's that afternoon."

"What kind of truck?"

Willie pumped his shoulders. "Beats the hell outta me. F-750, 850? I'm not so good with makes and models. It was older, not one of them fancy new ones with the special tailgates that fold out like a fuckin' jigsaw puzzle like I seen on TV."

"Anything distinguishing about that particular truck?"

"Disting-what?"

"Special. Remarkable. Something you remember other than it being old and tan."

Willie scratched his scalp like a dog, causing a disgusting avalanche of dandruff to fall onto his bony shoulders. "Not really. I do 'member was a white sticker in the back window on the driver's side. Like a cross with some writin'. Couldn't tell ya what it said. I ain't so good with letters."

"Looks to me like you're not so good at a lot of things."

Willie winked and held out his grimy palm. "I scored the stereo plus twenty bucks, didn't I?"

Jake dropped the twenty onto the ground. "Don't spend it all in one place."

Jake picked up the stereo unit and headed back to Lonnie's. *Big tan truck. Sticker in the back window.* Didn't ring an immediate bell in terms of seeing it around town. Maybe Lonnie could shed some light on it.

Lonnie's big, earthshattering news was also the presence of the truck. Lonnie saw a figure sitting in it, a large man, but couldn't identify anything specific because the window was tinted. He didn't notice a sticker in the window but mentioned the truck's rumbling exhaust when the person left before sundown. Everything else he told Jake was non-truck related and covered in the police report.

"Did you tell this to Wyatt Corkins?"

"Yup. Said he'd make a note of it, but he never wrote nothin' down, and that son of a bitch was too stupid to remember anythin'. Either that or he didn't believe me."

Jake silently agreed about Corkins's intellectual abilities. Still, another fact that didn't make it in the police report. Weird. Jake wished he would have come here first so he could have asked Wyatt about it.

Jake left Lonnie to polish his worthless stereo. Passing along the side of Sharla's house and into the overgrown backyard, Jake spotted a large oak with an empty bird feeder attached to a low branch. A frayed hammock stretched from the oak across the sparse grass. Beyond the backyard, he caught a glimpse of the back road Corkins mentioned. He stepped through an open gate and stood by the dirt road running east to west, swallowed by trees and shadows on either end. The road was narrow but wide enough for a car and maybe a motorcycle running alongside of it. A strip of dead grass ran down the middle.

No mention of the road on the police report. There also wasn't a mention of a weather-beaten tent hiding along the tree line twenty yards back from the road, directly across from Sharla Babin's gate. The tent fabric rustled as someone inside moved around.

A homeless person or a camper with a shitty sense of scenery camped directly across from a missing person's house raised a number of questions. But the biggest question was, did its occupant know anything about Sharla's case? One way to find out.

Jake stepped across the road, heading for the tent—the hair on his neck prickling.

CHAPTER FOURTEEN

REBEKKA SAT CHAINED TO THE BED IN HER CELL, UNABLE to break her gaze from the broken body of Chloe 1. Her body remained on the ground where it fell after the man snapped her neck. It'd been at least an hour since Rebekka woke from her latest shock treatment. Her ribs hurt and head throbbed, but she otherwise seemed unharmed. Physically, anyway.

A door creaked open in the distance, and the lights flooded the hallway between the cells. The man clomped across the floor, stepping over Chloe 1's dead body like it was a piece of trash.

Not Chloe, Jenny. Jenny King, she thought.

Rebekka inched toward the far wall, peering through the electrified cables to track the man, seeing him squat down onto a stool facing the empty corner of the hall. He bowed his head as he pressed his elbows to his knees. After a moment, he spoke, too low in volume to make out what he said, but there were questions in his tone, and it sent shivers down her spine.

Jesus, this crazy bastard's talking to walls.

After a few minutes, the man climbed to his feet, stepped over Jenny's body and into her cell. He gathered the blankets and sheets from her bed and left the cell, dropping them on the floor. He spread the sheet and gingerly rolled the dead girl onto it. As she lay on her back, he gently turned her head square and placed her hands over her stomach. The corners of his mouth turned down as he studied his handiwork.

The man's eyes drifted to Rebekka. "You have anything to say for yourself?"

Go fuck yourself was at the tip of her tongue, but Rebekka spotted the remote on his hip. She didn't want to risk another shock. Her mother had said, "You get more flies with honey than vinegar."

"I'm sorry," Rebekka choked, barely able to get the lie past her lips.

The man took two steps toward her cell, his lips drawn tight. His hand drifted to the remote. "I'm sorry, what?"

Rebekka swallowed. "I'm sorry...Daddy."

The corner of the man's mouth curled toward his ears. "That's better, Chloe. See? It's not so hard to be a decent human being. I don't want to hurt you, so don't give me a reason. I brought you here for a reason. Sure hope you don't make me regret it."

Rebekka ground her teeth, every fiber in her body wanting to scream, but she kept her silence.

The man turned his attention back to Jenny, wrapped the sheets around her with care, and hoisted her over his shoulder. With a final withering glare to the two women in their cells, he stomped back toward the stairs and thudded out of sight.

When the light disappeared and the sound of the

door closing echoed in the basement, Rebekka crawled to the front of her cell, careful not to touch the thick wire ropes. Even if she wasn't shackled to the bed, there was no way she'd be able to squeeze through the narrow openings.

"Hey," Rebekka whispered, hand pressed against the opposite wall closest to her only ally. "You awake over there?"

There was no response.

Was she asleep? Was she dead? *Or is she ignoring me?*

Rebekka licked her chapped lips. Her pulse thumped, desperate for some contact, some kind of information, some semblance of normalcy in this horrific situation. "Chloe? You there? Jesus Christ, please talk to me. I'm losing my mind."

From the next cell over, feet scraped across the floor. Her neighbor's breathing rattled. She was close, separated by a cinderblock layer of concrete.

"What's your name?" Rebekka asked.

"Does it really matter at this point?" the woman said, her voice slow and heavy, like her despair dragged the words to the floor.

Rebekka's pulse quickened, ecstatic the woman was at least talking to her. "I'm Rebekka. Rebekka Hammill. I'm from Springfield."

"Goody for you. So was Eve."

"Who was Eve?"

"The girl who was in your cell before you."

Rebekka's eyes darted to the base of the door. Were those Eve's bloody claw marks in the wood? She shivered. "What happened to her?"

"Haven't seen her in a while. She's probably dead. Just like Jenny. Just like we're gonna be."

Rebekka licked her cracked lips. Her mind raced, wondering how many there'd been before her. "How long have you been here?"

A protracted, phlegmy cough rattled. "No idea. Weeks, months?"

Rebekka rubbed the concrete wall. "Are you okay?"

"I hope I'm dying."

"Don't say that."

The woman huffed. "Wait a while. You will too."

"Why does he keep calling us Chloe?"

No response, just labored breathing sounded.

"And the creepy daddy stuff?" Rebekka pressed.

"You'll find out soon enough," the woman said. "If I spoil the surprise, he really will kill me."

Rebekka peeled her attention from the wall where she imagined the woman sat and peered down the hall. No sign of Mr. Wonderful. "Where are you from?"

"Warsaw. Kansas City. Lincoln. All over. Not that it matters now."

Rebekka's broken nails scratched at the concrete wall, wishing she could dig through the concrete and touch the woman, to feel some reassuring contact with another person's skin. She was scared and alone, and my God what she wouldn't give for some Oxy or a Xanax, anything to take the edge off and numb her racing mind.

Rebekka offered a half-hearted laugh. "I don't suppose you have any pharmaceuticals over there?"

The woman snickered. "I wish. If there was a time to relapse, now'd be the time."

"Did you know the other woman? Jenny?"

The question lingered in the air for a good fifteen

seconds. "No. She was here when I got here. Bein' across the way, we never talked."

"Are there others besides her?"

Another silent beat followed by a long exhale. "There was. I don't wanna talk about it."

"Who is this guy?"

"All you need to know is to do what he says. You're lucky to still be upright after talkin' to him that way. Don't push your luck. He can snap at the drop of a hat. Just like he did Jenny."

There was a dead girl and others before her. She flashed back to the bloody claw marks at her own door. *Jesus, how many of these cells have been occupied? What kind of hell have I been thrown into?*

"Anyway," the woman whispered. "I'm done talking. He catches us, there'll be consequences."

The woman shuffled away from the wall, her chain scraping along the floor.

"Wait!" Rebekka said, wincing at the volume she used. "What's your name?"

The woman released a sad sigh. "Chloe. My name's fuckin' Chloe. Same as yours."

"No, your real name."

"It don't matter. We all die a Chloe."

Rebekka smacked the wall, heat creeping up her neck at the resignation in the woman's voice. "Don't give up hope. If you give up, you're already dead."

The woman barked a cough. "I gave up long before I landed in this cell. *Chloe.*"

In the cell on the other side of an impenetrable, cold stone wall, the groan of the bedframe sounded, followed by muffled cries. Rebekka had cried enough into her own pillow in her life to recognize the sound.

Scanning her dank surroundings, sucking in the stale air of the dungeon, she crawled back to her bed and followed Chloe's example, pressing the lumpy pillow to her face until her tears ran dry and she fell asleep.

CHAPTER FIFTEEN

After the midday sun swung past its highpoint and began its descent, Daisy climbed down from her perch at her bedroom window of her gramma's house. She resigned herself to the fact that an ass beating or at least an ass chewing was waiting when she went back to the Wilkinsons' house for skipping school.

Daisy hugged the wall as she walked down the half-burned-out stairs toward the front door. Her mom wouldn't have liked her skipping school...if her mom was sober. When Sharla hadn't been hopped up on whatever it was she drank or smoked or popped, she was a good mom. She'd made sure Daisy did her chores and homework, though she was of no help with the schoolwork, especially math.

"Do better than me, Daisy," her mom would say when Daisy would protest. "I didn't learn what I shoulda in school early on, and once you get behind, you're screwed. Do better than me."

Daisy thought of reading to her mom as she perched on her lap on the porch in her old rocking chair, sneaking glances to see if her mom was paying attention. Daisy loved the smile that would cross her pretty face when her mom told her how proud she was of her. Cooking dinner side by side in Gramma's kitchen, chopping up onions and carrots for her homemade chicken noodle soup. Playing hide-and-seek in the crappy Kansas City apartment, giggling when Sharla couldn't find her and giving up her hiding spot. Would she ever do any of those things again?

She crossed the knee-high grass in the yard that bent south with the breeze, the musty smell of fall and the hint of something burning. Whether it came from someone down the road burning brush or the air sweeping over the charred husk of her gramma's house, she didn't know.

She shivered despite the sun shining bright overhead in a cloudless blue sky. Ever since her mom disappeared, she couldn't seem to get warm. An emptiness raked at her insides, wondering if the rest of her childhood would be like this, wandering around questioning where her mom was, if she was alive. Wondering if she would be shuffled from foster home to foster home until she reached adulthood where she'd be tossed to the side, because nobody gave a shit once you got older. Forget adoption. She couldn't paste on a fake smile or keep a curse word out of her mouth long enough to charm anyone into taking her in.

She turned left at the main road, kicking a large chunk of gravel and watching it bounce its way along the cracked asphalt. In the ditch to her right, she spotted an empty vodka bottle. Not her mom's favorite brand, but there were times where Sharla wasn't that picky. The tears leaked silently from her fawn eyes, and she let them drop without wiping them away. Nobody was around to see them, and she was too damn tired to wipe them away.

Flashes of her mom beat away at the edges of the fairy tale. The nights Daisy couldn't wake her up from a stupor on the couch. Cleaning up her puke. Changing her bedsheets. Being screamed at for making too much noise. Getting locked in the closet and forgotten for two days for some unknown crime other than being an anchor on a good time. Turning a blind eye when some guy Sharla brought home would darken Daisy's door, wanting something Sharla couldn't provide.

Daisy pulled the locket from her pocket and twirled the jewelry on the thin chain until it blurred. It looked like the locket her gramma gave her. The one Sharla pawned a couple of years ago. Daisy knew it wasn't the same one, but a flicker of hope stirred as she palmed the cheap gold.

A car honked behind her, and Daisy stepped to the side onto the narrow shoulder, waiting for it to pass.

"Daisy?" a voice sounded.

Daisy turned and spotted Mrs. Blackwell, one of her gramma's friends. She was a nice lady, though she smelled of Ben Gay.

"Hello, Mrs. B," Daisy said.

The older woman hoisted her girth out of the car, her head barely crossing the top of the door. "Visiting your grandmother's house again?"

Daisy nodded.

"Aren't you supposed to be in school right now?"

Daisy nodded again, cursing herself for not paying attention and jumping off the road when the car approached.

"Well, climb on in," Mrs. B said, the sunlight glinting off her silver hair. "I'll give you a ride to the Wilkinsons'. And don't tell me you're fine and can walk. Come on."

Daisy climbed in the passenger seat of Mrs. B's Buick, snapping the seatbelt into place and holding down the strap where it tried to rise into her neck. The car smelled like pine from a Christmas tree attached to the air vent.

Mrs. B put the car in drive and rolled toward town, asking questions and reminiscing about Daisy's gramma. Daisy answered the questions politely and lied that she was fine. She figured Mrs. B wouldn't want to hear her sob story anyway, and Daisy liked to hear tales about her gramma.

As they approached her street, Daisy pried the locket open with a dirty thumbnail and noticed there was a picture inside. She studied the picture—an older woman on one side and a similar, but younger version of her on the other. They both had big hair and wide smiles. Daisy didn't recognize the older woman but thought the younger one looked familiar. Blond hair, thin nose, plain but pretty.

"What do you have there?" Mrs. B asked as she pulled in front of the Wilkinsons'.

Daisy snapped the locket shut and shoved it in her pocket. "A locket. Found it on the side of the road near my gramma's house. Thanks for the ride, Mrs. B."

"My pleasure, dear," she replied, as Daisy opened the door. She placed a hand on Daisy's arm, freezing her in place. "I want you to know I pray for your mother every night."

Daisy stared at her scuffed shoes, perched halfway out the door. "Thank you. So do I."

Mrs. Wilkinson waited at the door, her fat arms crossed and a scowl adorning her makeup-laden face. At that moment, the sadness melted through Daisy's shoes and the anger in her heart took its place, radiating through her thin body, steeling itself against the tongue lashing that was sure to come.

Twenty minutes later she sat alone on the floor in the corner of her room, scowling at the ugly flower wallpaper and the stupid pink lampshade on her nightstand and baby unicorn and rainbow bedspread. She hated it all. Mrs. Wilkinson didn't lay a hand on her, but her words cut deeper than any belt would have. *Your mother isn't coming back, young lady. Your mother isn't coming back.*

Daisy stood, wanting to run, to burn off the ball of hate churning inside her chest. Hate at the Wilkinsons, hate of this room, hate of her life, and hate of her mom for leaving her this way. She threw the locket across the room and shoved her trembling hands in her pockets before she could lash out and break something, landing herself in more trouble than she was already in.

Pulling out the card, she read the print. *Jake Caldwell, Private Investigator.*

She was frustrated she hadn't heard from Jake. Did she make a mistake trusting him? Trust didn't come easy, but there was something familiar in his eyes, the way he looked at her. Not with pity or sympathy but understanding.

But that didn't mean he was doing anything to find her mom.

She cracked open her bedroom door. Mrs. Wilkinson was downstairs talking to someone at the front door, relating the woe Daisy caused on whatever poor soul stood on their porch. Mrs. Wilkinson had lots of friends and visitors were frequent.

The television in Mrs. Wilkinson's room played the news out of Springfield on low volume, the room smelling like the god-awful rose perfume she wore too much of. Daisy tiptoed in her socks across the bedroom and picked up the phone. She hoped Jake Caldwell had some news to tell her because she needed something.

Before she could dial, a face on the television caught her breath in her throat. The phone receiver dropped to the nightstand as Daisy took several steps toward the screen. The volume was too low to pick up the murmurs of the anchor man, but red ribbon emblazoned the caption along the bottom in bold white letters.

SPRINGFIELD WOMAN MISSING SINCE WEDNESDAY

Daisy's mouth went dry.

The picture on the screen was the same woman in the locket Daisy picked up from the side of the road. She was sure of it.

With goosebumps dotting her arms, she darted back to her room, snatched the locket from the floor, and pried open the cheap gold. It was definitely her.

Daisy ran back to Mrs. Wilkinson's room and pounded the number pads to call Jake Caldwell.

As the phone rang, she studied the woman's picture still emblazoned on the screen. It was eerie how much the woman looked like her mom.

CHAPTER SIXTEEN

THE TENT WAS NESTLED AMONG THE TREES IN A SMALL clearing twenty yards from the road. The cheap green fabric rustled in the breeze, and Jake hoped whoever the occupant was had plans when the harsh Missouri winter months hit, because the tent wouldn't protect them from shit. Next to the tent, a rusty lawn chair with frayed red fabric set in a checkerboard pattern faced the road.

He stepped on leaves and twigs as he made his way, purposefully alerting whoever was in the tent about his approach. He slipped his jacket over the edge of the Sig Sauer in his waist holster just in case.

Someone moved around inside the tent, and Jake stopped fifteen feet away, clearing his throat to officially announce his presence.

A thick head of black hair peppered with silver poked from the flap. A pair of beady eyes squinted against the sun as a lean body followed clad in dirty jeans and an untucked red flannel button-up shirt with the sleeves rolled to the elbows. He stood shoeless beside the tent with a weathered, wooden baseball bat raised to his chest, striations of muscles twitching in his forearms.

"Afternoon," Jake said. "Hope you're not planning on taking a swing at me with that thing."

"Depends on your intentions," the man answered. "I don't have much, but I suppose I'll fight for it."

"I have no intentions of taking anything. I'm looking for some information."

"Regarding what?"

The man's eyes were small and bloodshot but intelligent. The way he spoke relayed an education. How he ended up in a tent off some backwoods road in Warsaw would be an interesting tale.

"What's your name?" Jake asked.

"Who's asking?"

"Jake Caldwell."

"You're not a cop."

"Nope. Private investigator."

The man lowered the bat, letting it drop by the tent. "Caldwell. I've heard of you."

Jake couldn't get used to the fact he had a reputation. It was unnerving. "That a good thing or a bad thing?"

"I dropped the bat, didn't I?" The man smiled, displaying straight teeth. "From what I hear from the few friends I have left, it wouldn't do me much good against you. My name's Jeff Osgood. Oz to my friends."

"Hello, Oz. Nice to meet you. What are you doing back here?"

Oz spread his arms wide toward the woods, wobbling a little from the effort. "Living the good life or enduring the tragic results of some questionable life choices, depending on which way the wind is blowing."

Jake figured the guy wasn't drunk but definitely had a good buzz on. "Which way is it blowing today?"

Oz stuck his thumb in his mouth and raised it in the air, smiling again. "The good life is a process, not a state of being. It is a direction not a destination."

"You just make that up?"

"Nope, Carl Rogers. A humanistic psychologist. Met the man once at a workshop in Brazil."

"You a psychologist?"

Oz extracted a pint of bourbon from his back pocket and took a healthy swig. He offered the half-empty bottle to Jake, who declined with a polite wave of the hand. Oz took another drink and studied the bottle's label. "I was until the stories laid at my feet drove me to drink. This bottle was a temporary respite from my occupation that offered comfort in the short term, but inevitably ended my practice once the drink took hold. But you didn't come to hear my sad story of self-destruction. What can I do for you?"

Jake took a few steps forward. "How long have you been camped out here?"

Oz tucked the bottle back in his pocket and sniffed. "Oh, off and on for six months. I don't mind the chill, but I'd die out here in the heart of our Midwest winters. I keep hoping I'll be able to kick this habit and get back to a regular life, but it hasn't happened yet. I have my doubts it ever will."

Jake studied the man's face and demeanor, wondering if he could have something to do with Sharla's disappearance. His gut said no, though he was certainly in the right vicinity with easy access to the house.

"Must make it tough to survive."

Oz swept his hands wide. "I opted out of society by choice. Saved some money from my practice to live on. I'm a drunk with little want or need except the drink."

Jake pointed at Sharla's house. "You know the woman who lives there?"

"Sharla? Not terribly well. Helped her with some yard work periodically for something to do and to bolster my exponentially waning altruistic notions. She'd leave some food outside her back gate for me, which saved me a trip to town. Nice lady. Cute little girl. She liked to climb that big oak."

"The mom went missing."

Oz's face fell. "I know. I heard the talk around town when I ventured in for supplies."

"You know anything about the night she disappeared?"

Oz extracted the bottle and took another long drink, his eyes locked on Sharla's house. A hangdog expression crossed his face. "I stare at their house every day hoping to see them again. Sharla would pop out on the back porch and smoke. She'd stare out in the dark and we'd smoke together, the cherries of our cigarettes glowing in the night like beacons. It was like a couple of lonely souls connecting from a distance. Probably sounds creepy, right?"

Jake shrugged. "A little stalkerish."

"That's why I didn't go to the police. I didn't do anything to her if that's the question you're dancing around, and if anyone tried while I was around, they would have met the working end of my bat. But nobody ever came to ask me anything, and I didn't volunteer anything because one of these Keystone-Warsaw cops would crack my skull with a nightstick and ask questions later."

"You didn't go to the cops, but you know something?"

Oz pulled out a cigarette, lit it and sucked in deep. "If my liver doesn't kill me, these things probably will, but goddamn I love them. I saw a truck that night back here on this road."

Jake bristled. "What kind of truck?"

"Sharla wasn't a stranger to people coming over. I saw them through her back windows." Jake's eyes widened, and Oz grinned. "Hey, you can only look so long at the stars, and you can only see into the kitchen. But I never saw anyone park back here until that night. I noticed because the truck blocked my view of her house."

"What kind of truck?" Jake repeated.

"Big, older model, light colored, but it was too dark to make out any particulars."

"You notice anything in the back windows?"

"This isn't the first you've heard about said truck, is it?" Oz asked. "No, I couldn't make out anything like that. A big man moved around the back end of the truck before closing the tailgate."

"What was he doing?"

"I have no idea," Oz said.

"Anything distinguishing about him?"

"You mean like the tattoo on his right arm?"

"Something like that," Jake said. "You see what it was?"

"Looked like a face, right on the bicep. But, like I said, it was dark. Couldn't make out whose face."

Jake's grin dropped and he narrowed his eyes. "If it was so dark, how could you see a tattoo?"

"The right rear taillight was broken out, and the bulb shined pretty bright in our Ozark darkness."

"What time was this?"

"Close to midnight, I'd say."

"Anything else?"

Oz stubbed his smoke in the ground. "Just drove off west with the lights off."

"It didn't strike you as suspicious?"

"Of course it did. But I was deep into a bottle and couldn't have done anything even if I wanted to. Didn't even make it back into the tent that night. Fell asleep in the chair and woke up hungover with a crippling crick in my neck."

"If you were so hammered, how can you be so certain on the tattoo?"

Oz shrugged. "I know what I saw. You can believe me or choose not to."

Jake crossed his arm, studying the man. This guy gave off a harmless vibe. Jake's assumption was the man had nothing to do with Sharla's disappearance, but his lack of action stuck in his craw.

"A woman's been missing for months, and you've said nothing about material information that's directly related to her disappearance. That's a whole lot of fucked up, Oz."

Oz stiffened. "I didn't do nothing, man. I sent an anonymous letter telling everything I told you to the sheriff's office."

"When was this?"

"Couple of days after she was declared missing. I packed up and left for a while when the search parties combed the woods, but I came back a couple months ago."

"There wasn't a note in the case file, but I'll ask the sheriff."

Oz shifted from side to side, rubbing his arms. "Maybe I should've made sure somebody acted on it, but I was afraid to link myself to it. Homeless drunk living right behind the missing lady's house screams likely suspect. Hell, they could railroad me six days from Sunday."

Jake cocked an eyebrow. "But you came back."

"Like I said, I keep staring at the house every day and hoping she shows back up."

"I hope so too," Jake said. "Thanks for the information."

As Oz disappeared back into his tent, Jake walked west down the road to see where it led. Once he passed the equivalent of a city block, the houses to his left grew more dilapidated and farther apart. The road narrowed as the trees on either side of the road closed in. He topped a rise and paused. The road continued a good half-mile before disappearing over another rise in elevation.

He'd need his truck to scope out the road further, so he turned and headed back toward Sharla's house. He mentally rolled through the geography of Warsaw, trying to visualize every vehicle he'd ever seen, trying to conjure an image of an older truck meeting the definition of his three witnesses, but nothing materialized. He reached his truck as his cell phone buzzed in his pocket.

He didn't recognize the number, but it was local. Hopefully, not another spam call.

"Hello?"

The twangy voice was familiar. "Jake Caldwell? It's Daisy. I need to talk to you. Now."

CHAPTER SEVENTEEN

Merle hoisted Jenny's body over the lip of the rusty barrel and lowered her gently to the bottom. Her broken neck twisted awkwardly against the side of the fifty-five-gallon drum. He bent over and tried to move it to a neutral position.

"She's dead, you moron," Charlene said, leaning against a wooden tool bench in the barn and wiping a trickle of blood from her forehead with the handkerchief she carried. "What the fuck are you worried about her neck for?"

Merle wrestled with the body to try to maneuver her into a seated position. "I don't want her neck sittin' that way for eternity. Don't talk to me like I'm an idiot."

Charlene crossed her arms, wearing the same crusty flannel shirt and overalls. "Of course I talk to you like you're an idiot. How else could you understand me?"

Merle dug his fingers into the lip of the barrel, the muscles in his jaw pulsing. He sucked in air through his nose and breathed slowly out his mouth, trying to tamp down his temper and remember Charlene as she used to be. Before their daughter died. Before every ounce of joy was sucked from her soul and replaced with venom.

She used to laugh. God, how he missed that laugh. It filled his soul. He went back to nights of fooling around on a blanket she'd laid out in the yard while they drank and gazed at the stars. Days where'd they'd walk through the woods hand in hand and talk. They didn't have much money, but they had each other and that'd been enough. After their daughter was born, it wasn't always rosy, and there were dark stretches, but they'd plugged the holes in the dam and kept going. There had still been love, but a different kind holding things together. Once Chloe died, the walls burst, the waters rushed over them and, after being beaten and battered against the rocks, they drowned.

"You going to bury it next to the other drum?" Charlene asked, rubbing the red crease on her forehead.

"That's the plan," Merle replied without looking at her. He rarely looked at her anymore. He didn't even want to listen to her anymore, but she made it impossible. "Wish you'd help me."

Charlene moved away. "It's your fuckin' mess, Merle. You clean it up. If the cops ever find that spot, you're a goner."

Merle waited until she left, her absence releasing the tension he held in his wide shoulders. He stood over the barrel opening, staring at Jenny's face. In death, she was like an image of Chloe photocopied over and over and over again. It resembled the original but was fuzzy. Still, it was close enough to squeeze his heart and cause the tears to press against the back of his eyes.

Before the drugs took over, Chloe was smarter than he and Charlene put together, which he knew wasn't an insurmountable peak, but still. She had potential. Maybe even college. Maybe something beyond the small-town life where options were limited. She was a kind and caring young woman, and those maybes could open the door to something great. That is, before the drugs slammed those doors shut forever.

Merle grabbed the drum lid and clamped it tight, unable to look at the dead girl any longer. He loaded the drum on a two-wheeled dolly, along with a shovel, and made the trek to the clearing behind the barn. He maneuvered the drum down the narrow dirt path as the branches scraped and scratched the metal sides, muttering useless apologies for the rough ride to the dead woman inside.

The dirt was still loose at the burial site, not yet fully compacted from the last drum he'd buried there months ago. The trees canopied over the site, fingers of light finding their way through the outstretched limbs. Despite the shade, the day was warm, and he wiped the sweat from his brow, taking in the bursts of color from the changing leaves and hoping they would lift the heaviness of his heart. They didn't. *Will the weight and emptiness Chloe left ever leave?* One of the two girls left would be the key. If one of them didn't do it, nothing would.

An hour later, his back muscles clenched tight from digging and chopping away at roots, but the hole was large enough for the drum. He pushed the dolly to the edge and rolled the metal-cased body into the hole. Once he filled and tamped down the hole, Merle stood at the edge, sweaty and grimy, his heart thumping from the effort.

Did he deserve to find happiness again with one of

the two remaining girls? Or did he belong in the hole with the dead? He considered getting his gun and letting a bullet take away the darkness. It would be that easy.

But hope flickered in the eyes of the new girl. Rebekka.

Can she beat back his emptiness and fill the hole Chloe left?

There was one way to find out. He lay the dirt-crusted shovel on his shoulder and set off for the cellar.

CHAPTER EIGHTEEN

Daisy waited for Jake at a corner park a few blocks from her house. A swing set with two black plastic seats attached to an aluminum A-frame sat behind a slide. Next to it was a tiny jungle gym atop a sparse spray of wood chips held in place by the surrounding railroad ties. She sat on a bench while a mother pushed a little boy on one of the rust-flecked swings, the corners of his mouth nearly touching his Dopey-sized ears as he kissed the sky with each upward motion. The mother was young and lean, dressed in jeans and a T-shirt, not unlike her own mom's favorite attire.

But Daisy couldn't remember her mom ever looking that clean. Maybe when Daisy was the boy's age, but that would've been a long time ago, and too much life happened since then. She was envious of the boy, his happiness and the thought that a simple back and forth motion like a swing could bring such joy. He'd never been beaten or locked in a closet under a rickety staircase that smelled like death. He'd never had to cook for himself even though he didn't know how, because nobody bothered to come home that night. He didn't have brothers he was separated from by an unknown canyon of distance and time. And he certainly hadn't been touched in ways she had, because if he had, he wouldn't be wearing that stupid innocent grin.

Daisy buried her face in her hands, face hot, ashamed of the overwhelming urge sweeping over her to stomp to the swing set and knock the boy to the ground. *Why should he get to be so fucking happy?* It wasn't fair.

"The fair comes into town once a year with a merry-go-round and this ain't it," she whispered. Something one of the many guys her mom brought home once said.

Was it worth it? The mental anguish over her mom? She raised her head and watched the mother lead the boy away from the park, his tiny hand wrapped in hers, slowing her longer stride to match his.

Yes, she decided. It was worth it. She longed for the chance to walk with her mom hand in hand again. The last time she'd seen Sharla, she'd been clear-eyed and clean and talked of a future together. *Things would be different this time.* Daisy heard the same promise before and didn't know how long the future her mom talked about would last, if it ever came to pass, but she wanted it more than anything in the world. She wanted to believe. She just couldn't let herself not.

A truck pulled to the curb at the park's edge. The driver climbed out and Jake Caldwell headed her way. He walked with purpose, like no other man she'd encountered. When he smiled at Daisy, it made her feel protected, a foreign feeling which rarely surfaced anymore. Nobody else ever smiled at her, and it was a nice change of pace.

———

Daisy's face lit up as Jake crossed the sidewalk into the park. Her thin lips didn't flash any teeth, but he had the feeling that was as close as she would get. She stayed seated and her eyes followed him as he sat by her on the bench in the otherwise empty park. He produced a Coke from his jacket pocket, popped the tab, and handed it to her. From his other pocket he pulled a pack of Hostess Cupcakes.

Daisy took a few drinks and set the can on the bench next to her. She ripped open the cellophane and scarfed one of the cupcakes, licking her fingers afterward. "Thanks, Jake. Mrs. Wilkinson never lets me eat junk food. I forgot how good it tastes."

"How are you?" Jake asked, leaning forward with his elbows on his knees, head cranked in her direction.

A gold chain wrapped around her clenched fingers. "Okay, I guess. Thanks for coming."

"Not a problem. You hired me. You call and I come running. That's how it works."

"Well, you didn't take my money."

Jake winked. "Doesn't mean I won't eventually take it. Consider me at your disposal. What's up?"

"You find out anything about my mom?"

Jake raked the ground with his boot. "I'm working on a few things. Speaking of which, you ever talk to the guy who lives in the tent behind your mom's house?"

"Mr. Oz?"

"Yeah, that's him."

She raised her bony shoulders toward her ears. "Once or twice. He's a nice man. Helped my mom with some yard stuff. Mom put out some food at the back fence sometimes for him."

"That was kind of her."

Daisy ran her fingers along the chain. "Yeah. She'd surprise me every once in a while."

"He ever come inside your house?"

She shook her head. "Mom invited him in a coupla times. He would smile and say no thank you, but he appreciated it. I kinda liked that about him for some reason. He knew the distance he should keep, and he kept it."

"Did it worry you having him so nearby?"

Her face crunched up. "You askin' if I got a bad vibe off him and if he creeped me out?"

"Something like that."

She chewed on the question for a moment. "No. I can tell a fucktard when I see one, and he wasn't like that."

Jake fixed a stare. "Language, Daisy Dawn."

"Sorry. I forgot and don't call me Daisy Dawn."

"Don't cuss and I won't. Deal?"

"Deal."

Jake patted her on the back. "Don't get me wrong, it's one of my favorite words, but not for you. Not yet." He noticed the chain she twisted in her small fists. "What do you have there?"

She unwrapped the chain and revealed a two-inch wide gold heart-shaped locket. She dangled the heart by the chain and passed it to Jake.

"It's nice," he said.

"It's cheap. You can tell by the weight of it."

Jake couldn't help but grin. This girl was wise beyond her years. "That a fact?"

"It is. But it's what's inside that made me call you."

Jake pried open the locket and studied the woman pictured inside. It wasn't Sharla, but the young woman's long hair and piercing green eyes looked familiar. On the opposite side of the heart was an older version with shorter hair and lines on her face. Jake flipped the locket over and ran his finger over the initials RJH engraved there.

"Am I supposed to know who this is?" he asked.

Daisy squinted. "Don't you watch the news?"

"Not if I can help it. Plus, I've been busy."

"It's that Rebekka Hammill, the girl who's been missing from Springfield."

Jake drew the picture closer. He'd heard the name over the radio but hadn't seen her picture yet. "You sure?"

She jerked her head up and down. "Positive. Saw it on the news a few minutes before I called you. I'm a thousand percent sure it's her."

Jake studied Daisy closely. "So how'd you get the locket?"

"Found it at the side of the road near my gramma's old house right next to the mile marker. I go to her house sometimes when I'm missin' her."

"When?"

Daisy shifted her weight on the bench, glancing away before answering. "Earlier this morning. I mighta skipped school."

"And where by your grandmother's house exactly? Can you describe it?"

Daisy detailed the location, and Jake knew he could

find his way to it. Jake wasn't going to chew on her for skipping school. He was her employee at the moment, not her dad. The language was the only thing he felt comfortable pushing her about.

"This is good, Daisy," Jake said. "This is a lead."

"What's it mean?" she asked.

"It means Rebekka Hammill at least passed through this area at some point, but how'd her locket end up on the side of the road?"

"Beats the hell outta me. That's why I called you. I'd show you the mile marker, but I'm kinda grounded for skipping school."

"Then what are you doing out here?"

She shot her eyes sideways. "I crawled out the window right after I called you and climbed down the wooden thingy attached to the side of the house."

"It's called a trellis."

"Why's it called that?"

"It's more formal sounding than 'wooden thingy'."

She sighed. "She probably doesn't even know I'm gone. I figured it might be tough to introduce Mrs. Wilkinson to my own private investigator."

"That's true. I'll check into this. It means we'll have to get the sheriff involved."

"Ah, shit," she said.

"Don't worry. Bear grows on you after a while. Daisy Dawn."

She smirked. "Guess I deserved that one."

CHAPTER NINETEEN

AFTER LEAVING DAISY, JAKE TOOK A DRIVE ALONG THE back road behind Sharla Babin's house, heading in the direction Oz said the mystery truck went. He passed Oz's tent but didn't see the man. The sun blasted through his windshield, and Jake cracked the window to let the Ozark air cool the cabin as he bounced along the rutted road. After a mile, the houses disappeared, and the road turned to the east before emptying out onto the highway. A bust.

Jake pulled into the Benton County Sheriff's Office a few minutes after two in the afternoon. Bear worked a grill set up in the parking lot while a handful of officers and staff stood near the double flagpoles outside the low-slung tan building. Jake parked his truck and walked toward the smoky aroma of cooking meat.

"Don't you have more important things to do besides grill out?" Jake asked as Bear flipped burgers and turned hot dogs.

"Employee retention. Trying to let the people I still

have know I appreciate them. Plus, Fuckin' Johnny left to go piss, and rather than tell someone to watch the grill for him, he abandoned it. I didn't spend all this money on meat to let it burn to briquettes."

Wendy Blackwell waved as she moved to a table next to the grill and arranged plates, buns, and condiments. "The troops are getting restless."

"If they want E. coli, I can serve 'em up now." Bear glanced to Jake. "What've you been up to?"

"I've had a productive day," Jake said, grabbing a can of Coke Zero from a nearby cooler. "Visited with Lonnie Kincaid, Sharla's neighbor, and Willie Dykes. Both saw a truck outside Sharla's house the day she disappeared. Older model, tan, white sticker of a cross in the back window. He said he gave the info on the truck to Wyatt, but from what I could see, the dipshit never put it in the report, even though he said he did."

"Who gave the info on the truck?"

Jake took a swig of the Coke, belched, and apologized to Wendy who waved off the offense with a grin. "Both Lonnie and Willie said the same thing. Did you know there's a guy living in a tent back there?" Jake asked. "He saw the truck, too, and a big man moving around that night."

"Why didn't he report it?"

"Didn't want to get involved. Said he wrote an anonymous letter and sent it to the sheriff's office."

"It's not in the file."

"I know. It's weird."

Johnny Mullins, one of Bear's deputies, emerged through the front door and returned to the grill.

Bear narrowed his eyes at him. "You know, Johnny?

You're just like a goddamn blister. You always show up when the work's done. You wash your hands this time?"

Johnny wiped his mitts on his shirt. "No need. Who doesn't like a little dry rub on their hot dogs?"

Wendy winced. "You're disgusting."

Bear grabbed a couple of hot dogs and buns, handing one to Jake. "Let's go inside."

"I wanted a burger," Jake said.

Bear tossed Johnny the spatula. "No, you don't. Dick hands over here made the patties."

Bear led the way down the hall toward his office as they ate their dogs. "We need to bring the tent guy in."

"You can, but I got a good vibe off him. Daisy said he was a good guy as well. He'd help out around the yard, and they gave him some food."

"Doesn't mean he didn't have something to do with Sharla."

"Maybe, but I doubt it."

"Your criminal radar didn't go off when you talked to him?"

"Not a ping. But Daisy gave me something I think we need to take a look at."

Jake told Bear about the locket, where she found it and showed him the picture inside.

Bear took the locket in his big hands and studied the picture. "That's Rebekka Hammill, alright. After you left, I received a bulletin from the Springfield PD on her and called Sheriff Gibson down there. I was afraid she might be around here."

"Why would you say that? What'd Gibson say?"

Bear sat behind his desk while Jake stood and chewed. "Gibson said the last person to talk to her was her AA sponsor who said Rebekka called him to say she was having a rough time with the temptations on her way to St. Louis. Sponsor told her to find a meeting, but Rebekka didn't say where she was. Family in St. Louis called because she never arrived, and her cell phone goes directly to voice mail. The last ping was here in town."

"Missing girl, dead phone. Not good after finding that body."

Bear wiped his hands on his pants. "Fuck me. That's a dead body and two more missing women. Let's take a drive out there and see where little Miss Daisy found the locket. You know where to look, or do we need to take her out there?"

"She's grounded for skipping school. She told me where and I'd rather not get her in anymore hot water with the Wilkinson lady than I have to."

"Want to go now?"

Jake checked his watch. Maggie. "Let me call home. I was supposed to meet up with Maggie before she headed to Nebraska."

Bear sang. "Thinkin' 'bout workin' up an appetite, lookin' for a little afternoon delight."

Jake winced. "Don't think there's going to be any skyrockets in flight today. And don't sing. There should be a city ordinance against you singing."

"Don't know what you're talking about. I have a beautiful voice. Let me go tell some folks to cover a few things. Meet me outside."

Jake punched up Maggie on his cell as he meandered to the entrance.

After he delivered the news, Maggie let a pregnant

pause hang conveying her disappointment. "That sucks, but I get it. Halle called and she has to close at the coffee shop tonight anyway. Thought I'd head up early in the morning and still be there in time for the football game."

"So I will see you tonight? Maybe pick up where we left off this morning?"

Maggie laughed. "If you can pry yourself away from your best friend long enough."

"If it means coming home to what I think it does, hell yes."

Twenty minutes later, Jake and Bear turned in the driveway of Daisy's grandmother's house. "Shame about the fire. That was pretty much the end for grandma. Once they put her in the nursing home, she went down fast."

He turned his truck west, and Jake pointed to the mile marker sign where Daisy said she found the locket. Bear turned on his flashers as he pulled to the side of the road. It didn't take long to spot the rust-colored stains on the weeds waving in the wind at the road's edge. Bear squatted down. It didn't take a forensic expert to see it was blood.

They combed the immediate area for any other clues, Bear bagging and labeling things which might be of interest, mostly along the tree line a good thirty feet from the road. They got a few false alerts with road trash. After ten minutes of carefully walking the area, Bear whistled to Jake and pointed to the ground at his feet.

Lying in the brush at the base of the tree line was a cheap, black cell phone with Consumer Cellular emblazoned in white.

Jake took a stick and flipped the phone over. The battery and SIM card were removed.

Bear let loose an exaggerated sigh. "We've got ourselves a crime scene."

CHAPTER TWENTY

MERLE CAST HIS EYES TOWARD HIS DINNER PLATE IN THE basement, not seeing the food in front of him but instead thinking of his daughter. He flicked his eyes to the empty chair where the dead girl he stuffed in a barrel once sat. His hands lay flat on the table, dark arcs of dirt caked under his nail beds despite scouring his hands after he buried her. The muddy lines embedded in his palms matched the blackness in his heart which felt as lifeless as the girl in the drum.

The two remaining young women sat in their seats at the table after devouring the Hamburger Helper and canned corn he'd prepared. The way they scarfed down the food wasn't surprising considering the morning's breakfast had been interrupted with a little neck breaking. They cleaned their plates and sat upright as if afraid to move and upset him. He stood and scraped his untouched dinner evenly between the two.

"Sorry, girls," he said as he sat back. "I don't have much of an appetite tonight. Don't let it go to waste."

The two girls shot a questioning look to each other

before they wolfed down what he'd placed in front of them. It helped knowing he'd done something to help them, to make their lives a little better in these trying circumstances. Lord knew he hadn't always done that for Chloe. Beautiful and vibrant Chloe, whose eyes had sparkled until the pills and the heroin sucked the life from them. It had broken his heart to stare into the abyss behind those dead eyes near the end.

He scratched the table with a grimy nail and turned to the woman to his left. "Listen, Chloe, I know I wasn't there for you when maybe I shoulda been. But you know I love you, don't you?"

Chloe 2, Rebekka's neighbor, responded with a flat and mechanical voice. "Yes, Daddy."

He glanced across the table to Rebekka. "You know I did everything I could to protect you from this evil world, don't you?"

Rebekka's mouth pressed into a line before she said, "Yes, Daddy."

"You know what I wuz thinkin' about last night? Your eighth birthday when we took you to Silver Dollar City." Merle ran a tongue over his crooked teeth as his eyes grew lost in a memory. "We didn't have much money, but we'd managed to scrape up enough to buy them overpriced tickets and get you in there. We stood in front of that giant rollercoaster...I don't recall its name...and you grinned at me like I was a king of the world for bringin' you there. I miss that smile."

"I'm sorry, Daddy," Chloe 2 said with the same amount of life as the plastic spoon on her plate.

Merle waved his hand. "Nothin' to be sorry about, baby. I was thinkin' how happy you were at that moment and how I was glad I had a hand in making you that way."

Tears stung the back of his eyes, and he drew a deep breath to fight them off. He could still feel those little arms clutching his leg with excitement as they moved through the line, getting closer and closer to the front and her giggles of glee as the coaster cars roared overhead, their passengers squealing.

"I wanna feel that way again, you know," he choked. "I want *you* to feel that way again."

He sat in silence as the image of the little girl in his mind's eye, his angel, morphed over time in an unwelcome montage. She turned from sweet and sassy to mean, hopeless, desperate, and thieving—a lost prisoner to the poison she stuck in her veins. He wondered if either of the two women could truly erase the image and transport him back to a time when he mattered to someone. *If they can't, what's the point of anything?*

Pulling the pistol from his waistband, he raised the barrel toward the ceiling, noting the widening eyes of the women at the table. Part of him was saddened in their fear. The dark part of him was thrilled. He batted the dark part away with a wave of the gun. He didn't want them to be afraid. He wanted them to understand.

"Why'd you let that poison kill you, Chloe?" he asked, his voice low and soft, his eyes fixed on the shiny barrel. "You chipped away at the souls of your mama and me a little bit every day until there was nothin' left. I don't even know if you knew that. We saw you slippin' away but didn't have any idea how to stop it, and I'm ashamed to admit we mighta stopped tryin' after a while. We gave up. God help me, we threw in the towel on you."

Merle turned the barrel toward himself, staring into the black circular maw of the gun's barrel, the faces of the dead running through his mind. "Can you forgive me for that, Chloe? Can we go back to bein' a happy family again?"

When no answer came, he swung the barrel of the gun in their direction, waving it between the two women like a metronome. His thick finger slipped over the trigger as his face hardened. His hands trembled as his finger pressed on the trigger.

"Because if you can't forgive me, what's the point of any of us living?"

CHAPTER TWENTY-ONE

REBEKKA'S BREATH CAUGHT IN HER THROAT WHEN THE man swung the barrel in her direction. She reached down and white-knuckled the seat of her chair when his finger slipped over the trigger and a hardened resignation dropped over his face.

She was going to die. He was going to shoot her in the face and that would be the end of it. For the first time in years, she wanted to see her family again. She'd wrecked everything in her path over the last couple of years and shredded all familial ties. Except for Aunt Trudy in St. Louis. That's where she'd been heading when she'd starting shaking, the black monster veil of the urge to use dropping down like a curtain at a theater.

She'd been good, following the program. Until the last hateful argument with her parents over money. They wouldn't let her live at the house. Not that she should blame them after all the shit she'd stolen and hocked. They wouldn't give her any money to find a place to live because they were afraid she'd drink it away or shoot it into her weakened veins. She shouldn't blame them for that either, though she did.

All this led her to the AA meeting in Warsaw and a fateful encounter with the man in front of her who'd locked her in a dungeon and forced her to stare down the black barrel of a .38 Special while he waxed philosophical about his dead daughter.

What was this murderer looking for exactly? Did he think her cell neighbor or herself were going to stand by his side and pick up where his junkie daughter left off? Did he really believe that or were they mirages in his sick and twisted mind, mirages that would, at least temporarily, fill a dark hole his daughter left?

As the man swung the barrel of the .38 toward Chloe 2, Rebekka followed its arc. Chloe 2's brows shot up, not from fear, but from hope. Rebekka's heart sunk when she realized Chloe 2 wanted him to pull the trigger, to end the nightmare she'd lived in for however long she'd been there. Chloe 2 closed her eyes, waiting for it, and Rebekka was terrified that before much longer, she'd be in the same psychological boat, welcoming the prospect of death.

But she wasn't there yet. It was time to stop fighting, embrace the situation, and play along with his twisted game until an opportunity to escape arose.

"I forgive you, Daddy," Rebekka said, her voice soft.

The man's eyes snapped to her and softened.

"You do?"

Rebekka nodded. "I can forgive you if you can forgive me for what I put you through. I'm so sorry and I wanna make things right, back to the way they used to be."

The man's bottom lip trembled. "Oh God, I wanna believe you, Chloe. I really do."

"You can."

The man stood and let the .38 dangle from his right hand. He wiped his running nose with his shirt sleeve. "Well, thank you. Best get you back to your rooms. I got a decision to make."

A few minutes later, she was secured by the ankle bracelet to her bedframe, the wires covering the opening to her cell humming once again. When his footsteps plodded up the stairs, and the sound of the door closing echoed through the basement, Rebekka slid to the wall by Chloe's cell.

"Hey, you there?" Rebekka asked.

Chloe's tone was sharp, accusatory. "Where else would I be? That was a nice performance out there. Academy Award winnin'."

"I was trying to buy us some time. Thought he was going to shoot us both."

Chloe chuckled, sad and raspy. "Personally, I was hopin' he was gonna blow his own fuckin' head off. He might've if you hadn't said anything. I was hopin' if he didn't off himself, he'd shoot me and end this."

Rebekka smacked the wall with her palm. "Don't say that. We're going to need each other to get through this. I can't do it alone."

Chloe barked a phlegmy cough and spit. "I think you're gonna have to do it alone, sweetheart. He said he's got a decision to make. If I was a bettin' woman, I'd say I'm gonna draw the short straw. With your little actin' job, you just signed my death warrant, and all I wanna say is thank you."

Rebekka turned and slumped against the wall, imagining her back pressed not against stone, but against Chloe's. If Chloe was right, Rebekka worried what it meant for her. What did it mean to be the replacement daughter of a homicidal, crazy madman?

CHAPTER TWENTY-TWO

JAKE AND BEAR STOOD IN THE CORNER OF THE conference room, thumbing through files and tossing empty soda cans across the room toward the trash can to break the monotony.

"That's three to one for me," Bear said, sitting and glancing to Jake before reading the open files in front of him. "I always was better at basketball than you."

"That's because you backed your fat ass in the lane until you planted right under the basket. A sumo wrestler would've had a hard time stopping that freight train."

"Hey, work with what the good Lord gave you. Springfield said Rebekka's AA sponsor told them she was having a rough time and searching for a meeting on her way to St. Louis to visit her aunt. We called the aunt and verified she never saw Rebekka or heard from her from the time she left Springfield."

Jake picked up the thread. "And somehow her locket ends up at the side of the road in bloody weeds. Did she make the AA meeting?"

"Have a call into Betsy Thompkins who heads up the Warsaw chapter, but she hasn't called me back yet. I'm still doing some follow-up on Bethany Sheets, the girl they found out by the dam. Klages tracked down her parents out in bumfuck Kansas somewhere. They're on their way to identify the body."

"Think she and Rebekka are connected?"

Bear popped the top on another can of Diet Coke. "No telling. Bethany ran around with some unseemly characters. Hell, for all we know, Shane Langston killed her himself."

Jake couldn't put Shane murdering Bethany Sheets out of the realm of possibility, though Gunner reminded him that burying her in the woods wasn't Shane's style. "Klages making any headway on other missing women and a possible AA connection?"

"She's looking, but nothing yet. She's also checking out the truck angle and seeing if we can get any local matches."

As if on cue, Klages entered the room writing on a notepad as she walked. She was short in stature, five foot three, slim waist and broad shoulders. Her long black hair was pulled back in a ponytail. She was a spitfire, and Jake liked her. Jake and Bear sat back in their chairs as she paused at the head of the table.

"I need help," she said.

"With what?" Bear asked.

"My limited brain has trouble focusing on two things at once. You want me to track down potential missing women or search for the truck? I can't do both."

"Have Howard help you."

"He's out sweeping the Headwaters Motel. Thank

you for not sending me out there, by the way. I can't wait until they tear that place down."

Jake passed Headwaters each day on his way home. It once was a cheap hotel, the kind where you paid a ten-dollar deposit on the remote control for the TV. Now, more dope passed through it than any other place in Warsaw. The low-slung, crumbling structure was scheduled for demolition. No telling where the cockroaches would scatter when it was.

"What the fuck are they doing at Headwaters?" Bear asked, deep lines etching his forehead. "They're supposed to be securing a crime scene out on MM. Have one of those morons call me."

Bear craned over his shoulder and called for Wendy. He downed the rest of his soda and hooked the can across the room. It banked off the wall and rattled to the bottom of the trash can.

"Nice shot," Klages said.

Bear held his shooting pose. "I'm kicking Jake's ass five to one."

"Four to one, you cheater," Jake replied. "And it's an unfair contest."

"Because you couldn't hit water if you fell out of a boat."

"Because I can't down a can of pop every sixty seconds. You should be drinking water."

Bear winced. "Yuck. Water sucks."

Wendy entered the room, a waft of her flowery perfume trailing behind. "You called, boss?"

"Klages is tracking some missing girls and our potential suspect's truck info and apparently can't generate the brain power to do both."

Klages narrowed her thin eyes. "Don't be an asshole, Bear. It's been a long day."

Bear grinned. "I'd like Klages to focus on the missing women and have you follow up on the truck. She has the potential hits. Check out the owners, registrations, etc. and see if anything pops up weird or if there's any of 'em we can eliminate."

"You want me to make calls to the owners?" Wendy asked.

"No, if it is our guy, we don't want to spook him. See if you can narrow the list down to something more manageable. Start with getting names and addresses, and we can see if there are any potential links locally."

Klages tore a page out of her notebook and handed it to Wendy. "What're you and Jake working on?"

Bear held up the locket. "Daisy Everleigh found this locket on the side of the road out by her grandma's place. The girl in the picture is Rebekka Hammill."

Wendy gasped, holding her hand to her mouth, the liver spots on the back of her hand looking like a roadmap of the Hawaiian Islands. "The missing girl on the news?"

"The very one. Found bloodstains in the weeds near the locket. We think Rebekka might have met with some foul play. This truck may be an important piece, so if you could jump on it right away, I'd appreciate it."

Wendy checked her watch. "It's five o'clock. Can I go home real quick and let the dog out and then come back? He'll pee all over my area rug if I don't."

"Sure. Thanks, Wendy." After Wendy left, Bear turned to Klages. "You have anything significant on your stuff?"

Klages thumbed through her notes. "There's a missing woman named Eve Maxwell who is also from Springfield. Last seen eighteen months ago at an AA meeting down there. Wait until you see her."

Klages handed over a piece of paper, and Bear studied it. Jake stood and read over his shoulder. It was a missing person's bulletin with a tiny reward and a phone number at the bottom. Young, pretty, long brown hair and green eyes.

The hairs on Jake's arms bristled. He nabbed the picture of Rebekka Hammill and placed it side by side with Eve Maxwell's. "Look at that."

Bear whistled a long, descending tone. "They could be sisters."

Klages smiled. "Thought you might like that. I'll take my 'atta girl' now."

"Atta girl," Bear said. "Keep digging. See if there's any others."

Klages left, and Jake dropped to a chair next to Bear. "We seem to have a theme now, don't we?"

Bear stroked his beard. "We certainly do, my friend."

Jake's cell rang. Daisy. Jake promised to swing by and talk to her and clicked off. "Daisy wants an update on the locket. And more junk food. Where's this Betsy Thompkins operate these AA meetings from?"

"Coach House Apartments on Jackson Street. Think there's one tonight we could hit up. Like 7ish?"

Jake stood and grabbed his keys. "Sounds good. I'll go talk to Daisy and meet you there."

"Hey, grab me another Diet Coke from the fridge, would you?"

"No human should drink this much soda."

"I drink it until my kidneys start hurting. They aren't hurting yet."

Jake hooked an eyebrow. "Don't look to me when you need a transplant someday."

CHAPTER TWENTY-THREE

AFTER A PHONE CALL FROM BEAR AND THE SOCIAL worker to vouch for his character, Mrs. Wilkinson allowed Jake to sit with Daisy on the front porch step and eat the bagful of food he picked up at Sonic while she eagle-eyed them from the front window.

"She's protective," Jake said. "That's a good thing."

Daisy sucked a mouthful of strawberry shake through a red straw. "If you say so. I think she's a royal pain in the—"

"Don't say it. Would you rather she let you wander off with a complete stranger?"

She chewed and swallowed a mouthful of fries. "I guess not. Beats the hell outta one of those group homes."

"You been to one?"

She studied the burger in her hands, pulling out a pickle and throwing it in the yard. "Once for a week. Worst week of my life."

"That bad?"

She took a bite and chewed. "The group home was

the worst. Some of the kids left you alone. Some were just scary. The people working there were nice enough, but there were so many kids and so many sad stories it couldn't be nothin' but depressing and sad. With the kids, it was like a contest on who had it worst. I was pretty sure some of them were full of it, but there was this one kid with an eyepatch because his daddy shoved a lit cigarette in his eye when the kid tried to stop him from beating his mom with a belt. How fucked up is that?"

"Daisy Dawn?"

"Sorry. I had some bad things happen to me, and I hope I forget them one day, but I'd rather be home alone not knowing if my mom was gonna come back than be back at the group home. And her being gone happened a lot."

Jake handed her a napkin. "How long would she be gone?"

"Usually a coupla days at most. Eventually, she'd sober up enough to realize she'd left me and come back with donuts and apologies."

"I'm sorry."

"Why? Ain't your fault. Besides, I love donuts. Chocolate covered cake donuts with sprinkles if you ever wanna surprise me."

Jake dropped his half-eaten burger in the bag between his feet. "I want to ask you something, and I don't want you to get mad. Promise?"

"I'll try."

Jake cleared his throat. "With the stuff that happened with your mom...the jail, the abandonment, the touchy guys she brought home, why do you want her back so bad?"

Daisy stared at the burger in her hands, her temple pulsing. "Because she's my mom and I love her, and I know there's someone worth saving in there. She was different this time when she came back. I could tell she was struggling, but her eyes were clear and her smile was back, even if she had to fake it sometimes. I saw in her eyes it was gonna stay that way. Is that a good enough reason?"

"Yeah, it is."

She plucked a couple of fries from her bag. "Do you love your mom?"

"I did. She died when I was younger than you from a heart attack."

"How about your dad?"

"He was a mean drunk. Broke my kneecap with a lead pipe when I was in high school to keep me from going to college."

Her eyes shot wide. "A lead pipe? No shi...I mean, no kidding?"

"That was a close one."

Daisy laughed. "Caught it just in time. What happened to him?"

The grin slipped away. "He died of cancer a few years back. That's why I asked the question about wanting her back. If Stony would've left or disappeared, we would've been better off. But that's me."

She sat in silence for a minute before looking at him. "You ever forgive him for what he did?"

Jake slowly bobbed his head up and down, remembering standing over Stony's grave and dropping his father's pain-causing ring into the grave. "I did. After he died, but I did forgive him."

"Did it help? Forgiving him?"

Jake nodded after a pregnant pause. "I think so."

"I'm sorry you had to go through that."

"We survive and move on. You have that spirit in you, and that's why I like you. That's why I'm helping you. You're a survivor and I think you're going to do great things in this world, Daisy. Don't let anyone tell you different."

She blushed and searched Jake's eyes as if looking for a sign he was kidding. He wasn't. He saw himself in her. The past leaves scars, but he knew she could overcome the events causing hers.

"Did my finding the locket help with that missing girl?"

"It did. It gave us a couple of leads Bear and I are tracking down. Fingers crossed."

"What about my mom?"

"Working on it. You have a whole crew in your corner, Daisy. We're going to find out what happened to your mom."

"Promise?" she asked, holding up her hand and crooking her pinky.

Jake looped his bent pinky around hers and winked. "Pinky swear promise. We'll find her."

He hoped he wasn't lying to her.

CHAPTER TWENTY-FOUR

MERLE SAT IN STUNNED SILENCE AT THE KITCHEN TABLE, dumbfounded by the news he'd been told. He thought he was being careful, covering his tracks and paying attention to detail. And yet despite all he'd done, they were closing in on him.

"How soon?" he asked.

His mother leaned against the kitchen sink, drying her hands on a dish towel. "I don't know. I tried to keep you protected and out of harm's way, Merle, but you seemed determined to march to the beat of your own drummer."

"I'm sorry, Momma."

His mother teared up, choking on her own words. "I begged you not to do these things. I told you they were dangerous and evil, but you did 'em anyway, God help you. I don't blame you for the girl out by the dam. She got what was comin' to her for what she did to Chloe. But they're digging into everything now, Son. Everything. How much trouble are you in?"

Merle dipped his chin to his chest. "Enough."

"This Hammill girl. Was that you? Did you take her?"

"You should see her, Momma. It's like Chloe reincarnated. The good Chloe."

His mother pushed off the sink and wrapped her arms around Merle's thick neck, kissing his temple. "We have one chance, Son. One. You have to clean up anything related to the Hammill girl and any of the other ones. Make it like they were never here."

Charlene slipped into the room, her overalls covered in dust. She sat in the chair opposite Merle. Her lip curled up in a sneer. "Hello, *Mom*. Hope I'm not interrupting the lovefest."

Merle's mother ignored Charlene per their usual arrangement.

"I can't get rid of her, Momma," Merle said, his vision shimmering. "She's the answer. I can't live without my Chloe anymore. I'm nothing without her."

"Nothing? Thanks a lot, dickless," Charlene said. "Good to know where I stand."

"Nothing is better than prison," his mother replied, squeezing tighter. "I can't lose you, Merle. You're all I have left."

"So what exactly do they got on him, *Mom*?" Charlene asked, leaning her dirty elbows on the kitchen table. "What's so damn important you would grace us with your presence."

Merle focused on the red line running from Charlene's scalp to the middle of her forehead. The dust muffled its appearance, like a faint birthmark, but he knew it was there. Her spirit was so ugly now, and it made him wonder how he ever loved her in the first place. His mother hated Charlene and long ago abandoned being civil, which was hard for her because his mother was a sweetheart to everyone. Merle had become the go-between over the last few years, like an ambassador between two warring countries.

"They got a general description of the truck," he said, twisting out of his mother's grasp. "A little girl found Rebekka's locket, Sharla's daughter, Daisy, of all people. Must've came off when I took her. Hell, maybe the little girl saw me take Rebekka. A guy in a tent behind Sharla's house definitely laid eyes on me."

"They know this place?" Charlene asked.

"I think we're safe here. Don't know many folks who could put me here."

His mother gathered her purse and jacket from the counter, draping them over her arm. "They'll figure it out eventually if we don't do something. We have to clean your trail."

Charlene narrowed her eyes. "The man in the tent?"

"I'll take care of tent man," Merle said. "I can't hurt the little girl. I don't have it in me."

Charlene snorted. "Never stopped your dumb ass before."

"I just can't," he said, rubbing his face with his grimy hands.

"Fine, that'll have to be my part, I guess."

An awkward silence ensued as the gravity of their plans settled in. Merle fingered the butt of the .38 in his waistband. How easy it would be to simply fire a few bullets and remove everyone involved in this mess, including himself. If they were dead, they wouldn't have to be around to survive the aftermath. But he needed to know. He had to know if this girl in the basement could be the one. She'd already forgiven him. Was it so beyond the realm of possibility that she'd be willing to leave this place with him and start over?

Merle stood and wrapped his arms around his mother.

She pulled back after a moment and held her son at arm's length, tears spilling down her pale cheeks. "I'm not gonna lose you, Merle. I'll do everything I can to protect you."

Merle grabbed the keys to his truck.

"Don't take the truck, you idiot," Charlene said. "Take the sedan."

Merle scowled at her, dropping the truck keys on the counter and lifting the keys to Chloe's old car from a hook by the door. He offered his elbow to his mom and escorted her out to her car.

She opened the door. "I love you, Son. We're gonna get through this."

"I love you too, Momma. Thank you."

With one final pat to his stubbled cheek, Wendy Blackwell climbed into the front seat and drove away.

Merle watched until she disappeared from sight before glancing over his shoulder to the house. Charlene was nowhere to be seen. She'd left the dirty work for him again. He plodded to the barn and grabbed a hunting knife from the workbench.

Pulling the dustcover off Chloe's old Honda Accord, he fired it up and set the knife in the passenger seat. The sun kissed the skyline as he pulled out of the barn. He turned south down Last Chance Road, heading for the man in the tent.

CHAPTER TWENTY-FIVE

AFTER LEAVING DAISY ON HER FRONT STEP AND WAVING farewell to a watching Mrs. Wilkinson, Jake pulled away from the curb, heading a block off Highway 7 to the Coach House Apartments on Jackson Street, to see if he could track down Betsy Thompkins. Five minutes later, he passed a row of twenty old-fashioned metal mailboxes and stopped in front of a gravel drive splitting two sets of white-sided buildings with nondescript doors and a handful of beater cars and trucks.

He dialed the number Bear gave him for Betsy, who answered on the second ring. After explaining the man Jake searched for, she told Jake it didn't ring a bell, but if he wanted to come by in the morning, they were having a meeting at ten o'clock, and he could check for himself.

Jake continued east toward downtown, the locket, Daisy, and the man with the tattooed bicep rolling through his mind as a thought occurred to him. He turned north and headed toward Sharla's house and the backroad behind it. If his new friend Oz had a drinking problem, maybe he'd attended the AA meeting in town. The AA meetings seemed to be a link. Maybe Oz had seen the man with the tattoo there as well.

Bouncing along the back road, Jake slowed the truck as Sharla's darkened house slid up on his left. He could barely make out Oz's tent by the moonlight. He stopped the truck and grabbed a flashlight from under the seat. Striding around the back of the truck bed, he called out to Oz and waited. He didn't want to spook the man but got no answer.

Jake pressed the button and the bright LED beam cut through the night, bouncing along the ground as he headed toward the tent, calling Oz's name several times. Twenty feet from the tent, his beam flashed over Oz's overturned lawn chair, and Jake's breath caught at a dark stain in the dirt—a dark red stain. He slipped his Sig Sauer from his waist. With the flashlight in his left hand, he propped his gun hand over the top, sweeping around the area in a circle. He had a feeling it wouldn't do any good to call for Oz again.

Splatters of blood covered the overturned chair, and a trail led from the puddle to the open flap of the tent. Oz lay inside, crumpled against the back like someone threw him in there. The flashlight beam caught the jagged cut opening the man's throat, and his dead eyes were locked on the tent's ceiling. No need to check for a pulse.

Jake's heart hammered as he shined the light through the tent. There was a bottle of Jack Daniels and a wallet by the sleeping bag Oz was thrown on. On the other side was a duffel bag with clothes popping out of the top and a battery-powered radio.

"Son of a bitch," Jake muttered. He tucked the flashlight into his pocket and called Bear.

Bear answered on the second ring. "What's up, amigo?"

"Oz is fuckin' dead."

"Who?"

"The tent guy living behind Sharla's place. Someone slit his throat. You could stick a whole deck of playing cards in the gap."

"What do you think? He get robbed?"

"This was a hit. All his stuff is in the tent with his dead body."

Bear yelled for Klages, and Jake waited while he barked instructions for her to get over there. "Don't touch anything, Jake."

"Don't worry, this ain't my first rodeo. You know, it's pretty peculiar that someone took him out right after I talked to him."

"Klages will be there in fifteen minutes. You think he went to town? Maybe talked to somebody there?"

"I don't know, maybe."

Bear clucked his tongue off the roof of his mouth. "Maybe someone around there saw you talking to him, Lonnie, or Willie?"

"Whoever did this was strong. They hacked the man's head halfway off. I wouldn't hand either of those two assholes a jar of pickles to open. But..."

"What?"

Jake stepped around the tree line, looking past Sharla's house to Lonnie's. The back porch bulb was lit. "Maybe they talked to the wrong person about the truck."

"You better go check. Think anyone will jack with the body?"

"Doubt it. There's nobody back here but him. I'll leave my truck here. Tell Klages the tent is twenty yards into the woods."

"Be careful, man."

CHAPTER TWENTY-SIX

DAISY SETTLED ON HER BED TO FINISH THE REST OF THE burger Jake brought her. She liked Jake. A lot. He was the first person she'd talked to in forever who understood her, the only one who seemed to be able to really see her. The therapists and social workers talked a good game and meant well, but it wasn't the same as talking to someone who'd experienced firsthand what she'd been through. Jake was the first person she'd allowed herself to trust since her gramma died. She didn't even mind when he called her Daisy Dawn when she cussed because she probably did too much anyway.

The doorbell rang and a minute later raised voices seeped through the floorboard. She dropped the burger on the wrapper, cocking her head. The voices moved from the living room and became fainter, probably into the kitchen. Daisy turned her ear toward the door and closed her eyes, trying to make out what Mrs. Wilkinson was yelling and who she was yelling at. Her tone didn't sound angry, it sounded desperate. Daisy jumped when a loud bang exploded below.

She froze as she sat atop the comforter. Her ears lied to her. It was a car backfiring on the street. She'd heard her gramma's car do that a time or two. That's what it was. Then the second bang, which was followed by Mr. Wilkinson's anguished screams. A third and fourth bang silenced them. Gunshots.

"Oh, Jesus," she whispered. "Shit. Shit. Shit."

Slipping her feet to the floor, she crept to her bedroom door. The floor groaned underneath her, and she stopped, heart pounding, waiting for the call for her from the Wilkinsons that didn't come. Instead, footsteps thumped the old front hallway floorboards and then on the tread on the stairs.

Hide. That's what her brain screamed. *Hide!* In the closet under the clothes. No, under the bed. The Wilkinsons were dead. The footsteps were coming for her. Maybe it was because of the locket she'd found. The footsteps coming for her by the man who killed Rebekka Hammill because he wanted the locket back.

"Shit, shit, shit," Daisy whispered, fumbling for a lock on the bedroom door and not finding one. The old dresser was too far away and too heavy for her to drag across the room in time.

Run, you idiot.

Daisy darted across the room, throwing on her coat, and opening the window, fearful tears shimmering her vision. She swung her legs over the ledge and pressed the tips of her tennis shoes into the diamond slats of the painted trellis, face scraping the vines covering it as she climbed down, fighting the panicked urge to jump. She imagined she heard those steps plodding up the stairs toward her room, could picture the gun swinging from a blood-spattered hand. Coming for her. A long dark arm clamping over the top of hers as she worked her way toward the ground.

Her right foot slipped, and gravity yanked her down. She held onto the trellis with her left hand, her body weight trying to pull her shoulder out of the socket and weakening her grip. Crashing the last ten feet to the ground, the air was knocked out of her as she gawked toward the open window trying to regain her breath. She was a sitting duck. A shadow appeared at the window, and she scrambled to her feet, running like her hair was on fire. She didn't look back. She didn't stop. She ran until her legs ached and lungs burned, the night air slicing against her face.

Daisy slipped into a backyard of a darkened house and pressed herself against the siding. Bending at the waist, hands pressed into her knees, sucking in the cool air as her heart thumped a drum solo in her chest and snot ran from her nose. She allowed herself to sink to the ground and sob, face buried in her folded arms and soaking the sleeve of her coat.

The tears subsided and she dropped her head back against the house.

"Think, Daisy, think," she muttered.

Whoever killed the Wilkinsons was there for her. She should call the police, but the only person she trusted was Jake Caldwell, and his card sat on the nightstand next to her bed. To make a phone call would require making herself visible to someone, and she didn't want to do that. Not when a man was out there trying to kill her. She needed to get somewhere safe and could think of one place that made her feel that way.

CHAPTER TWENTY-SEVEN

JAKE PICKED HIS WAY BACK TOWARD HIS TRUCK, MOVING past it into Sharla's backyard. He kept the Sig Sauer at the ready as he crept, his finger on the outside of the trigger guard. Stepping along the side of Sharla's house, he peered around the corner into Lonnie's garage. Lonnie sat upright on a stained double love seat with one cushion missing and the other spilling its stuffing from a rip in the side. The man held an empty beer bottle in his hand, his bristles of his beard pointed toward the lone bulb lighting the one car garage. Merle Haggard played from the Panasonic on the floor of the garage. For a moment, the thought flitted through Jake's head that he was dead too. Then Lonnie shifted to his left and a fart erupted, loud enough to cause his wiry frame to stir.

Jake tucked the Sig in his waist holster and hopped the fence between the two yards. He reached Lonnie in a half-dozen steps and tapped his outstretched feet with his boot.

Lonnie jumped and blinked away sleep. "Caldwell? What the hell do you want?"

"Where've you been all night?"

"Right here." He opened a small cooler at his side. "You want a beer?"

"No. You haven't gone anywhere?"

Lonnie picked up on Jake's agitated tone and sat upright. "No, been guardin' my stereo in case that klepto down the street sets his sights on it again. Why?"

"You didn't see or hear anything unusual?"

"Did I miss something?"

Jake kicked his foot again. "Just answer the question, Lonnie. You see or hear anything? Maybe a rumbling of that truck again?"

"Naw, nothin'. It's been quiet. What's goin' on?"

"You talk to anyone about the truck you mentioned to me?"

Lonnie reached into his cooler and popped the top on a beer can. "Ain't seen or talked to anyone since you left. Honest."

"You're going to see a whole mess of police lights behind your house. Don't leave this garage."

"Yes, sir. Got a twelve pack of reasons not to move," Lonnie said, raising his beer in a toast.

Jake stomped down the driveway heading toward Willie's. Five minutes later, Jake headed back to his truck, finding Willie in a similar state of ignorance. The only thing that made any sense was someone spotted Jake talking to Oz, but there was nobody back there to see them talking. The only house visible from the tent was Sharla's, and that was empty, wasn't it? Jake made a mental note to have Bear's guys sweep the house for any signs of life.

He crossed Sharla's backyard as Klages pulled up, lights flashing. Deputy Howard slid to a stop behind her. She exited her car and met Jake at the front of his truck. Jake gave her and Howard a run down and led them to the tent, explaining what was going on as his long strides carried him. Fifteen yards in, the hairs on the back of his neck stood up and he stopped cold.

What if someone knew I talked to Oz and killed him for it?

What if they'd been following me and knew who else I talked to?

Daisy.

Jake jabbed a finger in the direction of the tent and told Klages to go without him. Running back to his truck he called Bear. "I'm heading to the Wilkinsons'. If someone saw me talking to Oz, maybe they saw me talking to Daisy. I have a bad feeling."

"I'll call the Wilkinsons and meet you over there. I was heading that direction anyway."

"I hope I'm just being paranoid."

"I learned a long time ago to trust those bad feelings of yours."

Jake hopped in his truck and fired up the engine. "See you in a few."

Ten minutes later, he screeched to a halt in front of the Wilkinsons' as Bear pulled his truck at an angle from the opposite direction. They jogged side by side up the sidewalk toward the front door. The porch light was out, but a light from a living room lamp shined through the window. Bear checked the front window and gave a thumbs-up.

Jake took a deep breath and rang the doorbell. When nobody answered, he pounded it like a joystick button. Nothing. Bear flicked his head forward, giving Jake the go ahead. They drew their guns and Jake opened the unlocked front door. They raced inside the house, covering each other's angles, sweeping the front hall and the living room. Nothing. They continued down the hall into the kitchen, and that's where they found them. Jake's gun dropped to his side, and his hands hit his knees, his face flushed with anger.

Mrs. Wilkinson lay slumped against the kitchen sink, her chest a mess of crimson. An older man in khakis and a long sleeved button-down lay across her lap, a dark hole protruding through the shirt fabric.

Bear knelt and checked for pulses. He looked to Jake with empty eyes. They were gone.

Jake's eyes swept across the room, panic replacing the anger. He called out for Daisy and heard nothing. "I'll check upstairs, you check the basement."

Jake took the stairs two at a time, heart thumping as he swept through a teenaged boy's room and the master. The third bedroom at the end of the hall held a bed, a nightstand, and a pile of clothes Daisy's size under an open window, but no sign of Daisy or anyone else. He bound back down the stairs and met Bear who came up empty as well. They checked the garage and the backyard, the panic setting in when they found nothing.

Bear was on his phone while Jake turned in circles in the backyard.

"Goddamn it," Jake whispered, eyes darting around in the darkness before screaming, "Daisy!"

She was gone.

CHAPTER TWENTY-EIGHT

THE SWIRLING RED-AND-BLUE LIGHTS BOUNCED OFF THE houses and trees as police cars descended on the Wilkinson residence. Neighbors gathered on porches and the sidewalks, jackets and blankets wrapped tightly to ward off the night's chill and the faint drizzle that fell from a blackened sky. Their faces were curious and fearful as they stared at the Wilkinson house, likely able to pick up from the number of cars and flurry of activity this wasn't a medical emergency. This was something much worse.

Bear dispensed his few resources to start canvassing the neighbors, one cop to the right and another to the left. Jake searched between houses and in backyards for any sign of Daisy. In one backyard, he nearly had a heart attack when he discovered a crumpled form dressed in white lying at the bottom of a window well before he realized it was an empty bag of grass seed mixed in with fallen leaves.

He returned to the Wilkinsons', his brow covered in sweat and mist to find Bear on his cell in the front yard.

Bear raised his eyebrows in a question, and Jake shook his head. "Nothing."

Bear clicked off the call. "Placed an APB out on Daisy, and my crew's canvassing the neighborhood to see if anyone heard or saw anything."

"Anything interesting since I left?"

"Darla was shot in the chest and abdomen. Chester took one in the leg. Hit his femoral artery and he bled out. Found another bullet hole in the cabinet behind him."

Jake's brows pulled together. "Not exactly tight grouping on the shots."

"It's weird. Bad time for me to be short-staffed with three people dead at roughly the same time. You think whoever killed them took Daisy?"

Jake chewed on his bottom lip. "I'm hoping she fled the scene. Bedroom window was open. She told me at the park earlier today that she snuck out by climbing down the trellis. Maybe she did it again when she heard the shots fired."

"Maybe she didn't close it after this afternoon."

"Maybe, but it would've gotten pretty cold in the house. Someone would've noticed an open window."

Deputy Dawson jogged up the sidewalk with a notepad in hand. He was a slight, baby-faced man with owl eyes. "Bear, neighbors thought they heard some popping noise a few minutes after six."

"Thought?" Bear asked.

"They were in the kitchen making drinks and getting ready to watch one of those NCIS shows. At the time, they thought it was gunshots from the TV. Now they're not so sure."

"They didn't take a look out the window to investigate or anything?"

Dawson gave a couple of quick jerks of his head. "No, but it might give us a time everything went down."

"We don't need a time. We need someone who saw something."

Dawson looked to Jake and dropped his eyes. "Someone reported a suspicious guy sitting on the front porch with Daisy earlier. They pointed you out specifically, Jake. Sorry."

Jake waved the thought away. "Nothing to be sorry about, man. I was there eating a burger with the girl."

Bear pointed down the street. "Keep talking to the neighbors. I'll keep an eye on Mr. Suspicious here."

Dawson offered an apologetic, tight-lipped smile to Jake and walked away.

Jake breathed deep to combat the agitation at not knowing where Daisy was. Images of her lying dead in a ditch kept rolling through his head.

"You think this Oz guy and the Wilkinsons are related?" Bear asked.

"I do."

"Me too. But the MOs are polar opposites. Our tent guy with a knife that nearly decapitates him, and these two with haphazard gunshots. Doesn't make sense."

Jake studied the house, thinking through their entry. "No sign of a break in?"

"Nope. I double checked the front door. Back door was still locked too. Either the Wilkinsons left the front door open or they let in whoever ended up shooting them."

"Which might indicate they knew him."

Jake thought back to what Daisy had told him about the family. "Wait, didn't they have other kids?"

"A boy," Bear said. "Was staying with a friend down the street. Kid came running once he saw the sirens. The only one missing is little Miss Daisy. I hope to God whoever did this doesn't have her."

Jake's nails bit into his palms, lips crushed together in frustration, wanting to hit something. He hated feeling helpless. If someone took Daisy, there was nothing they could do until they figured out who. That would take time unless someone from the crowd or the neighborhood stepped forward. But, if his open window theory was correct, Daisy was on the run. Where would she go? Where would she feel safe? The proverbial lightbulb popped.

"I have an idea where she might be," Jake said.

Bear jerked his head. "Where?"

"If she's on the run from whatever happened here, the only place I can think of where she'd go is her grandmother's house."

"How would she get all the way over there? On foot?"

"Says she's done it before. I'm going to drive out there."

Deputy Dawson ran back before Jake left. "We might have a description on a car here earlier. Black sedan, last three digits she thinks were B26."

"She thinks?" Bear asked.

"Seemed pretty sure. Started babbling how she knew it because," Dawson paused to check his notes. "Because it was the number on the jukebox of a song when Aria and Ezra meet in the show *Pretty Little Liars* and that's her favorite show."

"Run it and see what you get back. Jake, go check the grandmother's house. You want anyone to go with you?"

"Seems like you have your hands full here. I'll be fine," Jake said.

"Jesus, I hope she's there and safe. I don't need another death cloud hanging over us tonight."

Jake turned toward his truck. "Nobody does. I'll call you."

CHAPTER TWENTY-NINE

Daisy crept along the gravel shoulder of the road leading to her gramma's house, head on a swivel scanning for approaching cars. Pulling her coat tight around herself to ward off the cold, she followed the curves, battling the occasional bout of tears and slapping herself to stop them. She wasn't going to be one of those stupid girls who seemed to dominate the movies and television shows, the ones who lost their shit and couldn't seem to put one foot in front of the other without falling down while crying hysterically.

The dark Ozark woods hugged the road on both sides, the night breeze rattling the dry leaves clinging to the branches. A branch snapped, and Daisy whipped around, walking backward, trying to see into the blackness as the clouds swallowed the moonlight. In the dark beyond the tree line, a shape moved, disappearing behind one tree before appearing in front of another. Tracking her. Watching her. She whimpered, her legs weakening as she waited for the shape to burst through the tree line and swallow her whole. Instead, she turned and ran. If that thing was going to get her, it would have to work for it.

Her legs wanted to give out, the muscles in her thighs screaming for relief, but she pushed on, leaving the thing in the woods in her wake. Headlights flooded the road ahead, and she dropped into the roadside ditch. The white light washed over her, and the car was gone. But her limbs were locked, afraid to move.

"They're gone, Daisy Dawn," her mom whispered, stroking her hair. "You're okay. We're okay, baby girl. He can't hurt you no more."

The swirling red-and-blue lights had faded from the wall of their Kansas City apartment, leaving echoed flashes of his hands touching her down there, the whiskey and cigarettes on his breath followed by the shouts and yells from Sharla, and the grunts and groans from the man as the handcuffs clicked in place. All that was left was her mom's soft kisses on her temple and her soothing voice telling her she was gonna be okay.

Raising her head out of the ditch, Daisy glanced over her shoulder, still feeling her mom's lips on the soft spot of her head. She didn't see the shape, and she let loose a breath of relief. She climbed to her feet, passing the sign where she found the locket and spotted her gramma's house in the distance. It was a black hulk against an even blacker skyline. If she didn't know it was there, she would've gone right past it. If she wasn't emotionally connected to the house and saw its foreboding look, she would've ran past it, because only stupid fucking girls walked into houses like that.

Daisy Dawn. Jake's voice echoed in her head, and she mentally drew a line through the curse word.

Exhausted, she plodded up the gravel drive,

watching the house and hoping she didn't see a light or fire or any other sign of life. This was the only place she could go. The tears of fear and uncertainty flowed down her frozen cheeks, and she wanted them to stop. She wanted to feel safe, but that wasn't happening anytime soon.

She slipped through the front door, listening for sounds of life, and heard nothing but the wind rattling through the jagged, open ceiling. Climbing the stairs, she made her way toward her old room and stared out the window into the night.

No shapes following.

No killer coming to finish her off.

Her gramma was gone.

Her mom was missing.

Her foster parents were dead.

She was truly alone in the world.

She watched the night out the window until self-pity tugged at her eyelids. Crossing the room, she shut the bedroom door and turned the deadbolt. She didn't know if it would hold if the killer came to break it down, but it was the only thing she could do. Her old bed sat against the center wall, the mattress speckled black with dirt and soot, but it was better than sleeping on the cold hardwood floor.

She lay on the bed, drawing the hood of the coat tight around her head and resting it on her outstretched arm. She tracked the slow-moving clouds and the moon peeking through them, thinking about God. She thought she'd given up on Him, because if He was there, why would He do this to her? He'd probably given up on her long ago as many times as she'd taken His name in vain.

If there was a God, and He was as just and forgiving as people said He was, she supposed it couldn't hurt to say something. She said a prayer for herself. She said a prayer for her mom. She said a prayer for the Wilkinsons. As the tears seeped from her eyes and sleep tugged at her brain, she said a prayer for Jake Caldwell to come and find her before the bad man did.

CHAPTER THIRTY

His truck engine roared as Jake cranked the wheel through the road's curves. When the truck's tires slipped off the asphalt's edge and the back end swerved uncontrolled, he forced his foot to back off the pedal. He couldn't do Daisy any good if he wound up in a ditch kissing a tree.

His strong hands wrung the steering wheel as permutations raced through his brain, making contingency plans if Daisy wasn't in her grandmother's house. There were literally thousands of places she could be hiding if the Wilkinsons' killer didn't have her, and even more places if he did.

An image of her terrified face and wide, tear-filled eyes flashed in his mind, her hands bound and duct tape across her mouth to prevent her from screaming as she lay huddled in a darkened trunk being taken to God knows where. He batted away the thought. Knowing Daisy, she'd be more likely to defiantly scream and curse at the bad guy and get herself in deeper trouble. Either way wasn't good, and he hit the gas harder, hurtling toward the grandmother's house. If Daisy wasn't there, he'd worry about the "what ifs."

The sign where Daisy found the locket blurred past on his left, and he jammed the brakes, eyes scanning the right side of the road for the house. A quarter mile ahead, he spotted it and turned, the headlights from his truck bouncing along the ruts of the graveled drive. The headlights blasted up the charred remains of the right side of the two-story house. A front porch awning teetered on the brink of collapse with half its shingles hanging on for dear life.

He swung the truck parallel to the house and shut off the engine, jumping to the gravel drive. Calling out Daisy's name, he waited to see if she'd come out or her face would appear in one of the few remaining windows. Nothing.

The smell of charred wood and decay lined his nose as he stepped up the wood-rotted front steps and through the front door. His flashlight beam sliced through the darkness as he moved through the lower floor. He found some trash, food debris, a couple of rats, and a handful of used needles, but no Daisy. He moved to the staircase, shining the light to the second floor. He called for her again but received no answer.

He tested the stairs with his weight, and they compressed like a sponge. Pressing his boots into the wood closest to the wall, he crept up, left hand holding the flashlight and right hand on the butt of his Sig Sauer. Sweat dotted his upper lip and his heartrate picked up. It was like he was in a horror movie, waiting for the monster to jump from the shadows.

Reaching the top, he checked two bedrooms and a bathroom which were empty save for some age-curled posters of cars and trucks and furniture that wouldn't pass muster at a flea market with a free sign tacked to them.

The wood floors groaned beneath his weight as he approached the last door. A closed door. His hand crept to the knob which turned. He tried to press the door open, but it wouldn't budge. The old wood gave a bit at the top, but not the middle. It wasn't stuck, it was dead-bolted. And if his memory of the house's layout was true, this would have been Daisy's room. The one looking out over the driveway.

Jake knocked softly. Behind the door bedsprings squeaked. "Daisy? Daisy, it's Jake. You in there?"

Footsteps approached the door, and metal scraped as the deadbolt slid back. The door opened, and Daisy's sleepy face eyed him, tracks of tears drawn in the dirt that had come to rest there.

"Hey, little girl," Jake whispered, squatting to her level. He reached out and gently rested his palm against the side of her head. "I've been tearing the town apart looking for you. You okay?"

"Shit no, I ain't okay," Daisy said before she burst into tears and threw herself into Jake's chest.

Jake held her tight and stroked the back of her head, whispering to her she was safe, and everything was going to be fine.

Daisy pulled back. "Sorry I cussed just then. It slipped out."

Jake smiled. "We'll let that one go. Deal?"

"Deal."

Jake scooped her up and she wrapped her arms around his neck, head resting on his shoulders. Now he needed to figure out what to do next.

CHAPTER THIRTY-ONE

JAKE ESCORTED DAISY OUT TO HIS TRUCK, FIRING UP THE engine and blasting the heaters. He called Bear. "I have her. She was at her grandma's house."

"Thank Christ," Bear breathed. "You going to bring her to the station?"

Daisy sat and shivered, holding her shaking hands up to the vents once the warm air blew. Jake scanned the darkness through the windshield as options rolled through his head. He considered taking her to the sheriff's office, but the timing of this stuck in his craw. Oz and the Wilkinsons at the same time, right as they were starting to make headway. There'd been all kinds of people around and lots of fingers in the pie as they worked the different angles of this case. People talked. Things leaked and things were lost. The last thing he wanted to do was to put Daisy in the middle of it and take her to a place she felt she couldn't call in the direst of situations.

"Not sure what I'm gonna do yet, but that isn't it," Jake said. "Somebody's talking to the wrong people from your shop. I'll call you when I figure it out. Until then, maybe call off the search but keep quiet about where she is."

"10-4. Call me back soon."

Jake clicked off and turned to Daisy. "You okay?"

"Glad I remembered my coat before I jumped out the window."

"You jumped?"

She offered a close-lipped smile. "I was scared enough to, but I climbed down. Once I hit the ground I just ran."

"You should've called me or Bear."

"I left your number on my nightstand and, in case you ain't noticed, I got trust issues."

Jake laughed despite himself, clamping his hand to his mouth. It was such adult sarcasm rolling from her mouth. Daisy's jaw dropped at his faux pas and grinned to let him know it was okay.

The smiles died away when Jake asked, "So what happened?"

Daisy locked her eyes on her lap as she recounted the doorbell, the screams, the gunshots, and the footsteps.

"I ain't gonna lie, Jake," she said. "I tried hard to be brave, but I was pretty damn scared. They're dead, aren't they? The Wilkinsons?"

Jake patted her on the back. "I'm sorry, yes. And I can't blame you. I would've been scared too. You didn't happen to see who fired the shots or any cars or trucks or anything that might give us a clue who killed the Wilkinsons?"

Daisy slowly shook her head back and forth.

"You ever hear the Wilkinsons discussing any arguments they might've had with anyone around work or friends or neighbors or anything like that?"

"Nothing. Sorry. They didn't talk about much of anything when I was around. What's gonna happen now?"

There was one place Jake could think of that made sense.

"Daisy, I know you don't trust much in this world," Jake said. "But do you trust me?"

She studied his face for a moment before dipping her chin down and up. "I do."

"Good. Let's get you somewhere warm and safe."

As they drove, Jake called Bear back. "I'm taking her to my house so Maggie can help keep an eye on her."

"You sure that's a good idea with this killer still roaming around?" Bear asked. "God help him if he came knockin' on your front door, but it's a risk."

"It's not a risk if nobody knows it. That's why you're not going to say a word to anyone. Nobody but you and me will know."

"Makes sense," Bear said. "While you were gone, the plate from our witness came back, and we got a local hit."

"Who?"

"Wendy."

Jake's brow furrowed. "Wendy Blackwell? That doesn't make any sense."

"I know Mrs. B," Daisy said. "She was at my house today."

"What? Hold on, Bear." Jake hit the speaker on his cell. "Daisy said Wendy was at her house today."

"Today?" Bear asked.

"She picked me up as I was walkin' home from my

gramma's house earlier today. She and my gramma were friends."

"What time was this?"

"Lunch time."

Bear whistled. "That's a relief. I'll follow up with Dawson on the time but that makes sense. I'm glad Jake found you, Daisy. I know you think I haven't been doing anything for your mom's case, but I want you to know there hasn't been a day that's gone by I haven't thought about her. I haven't given up hope yet."

Daisy peered at Jake's phone out of the corner of her eye. "Thanks, I guess."

Jake stifled a grin. She still didn't trust Bear, but as long as Daisy trusted Jake, he could work to bring her around.

"You're welcome. Call me later, Caldwell," Bear said.

Ten minutes later, Jake made the turn on Poor Boy Road. He glanced to Daisy and hoped Maggie would understand him bringing her home. He turned in the drive, the gravel crackling under his rolling tires as he passed under an overhang of trees. Their home was lit up, and he spotted Maggie in the kitchen through the front window, Connor attached to her hip.

"This your house?" Daisy asked, leaning forward to check it out.

"That work?"

She pumped her shoulders. "Beats the shi...heck out of a group home."

"Another close one."

"I think I'm getting the hang of it."

He shut the truck off. "I think you're going to like my wife. Be polite. No cussing."

She snapped off a salute. "Yes, sir."

Jake grinned as he hopped out of the truck, waiting for Daisy to come around the front. Jake laid his arm across Daisy's shoulders and guided her up the front steps. Maggie met them at the door, her eyes widening at Jake's guest.

Maggie's long, sandy hair was pulled back in a pony-tail and tossed over her shoulder. Connor gripped several strands of it in his chubby hands, chewing on the ends. "Well, I'm guessing you're Daisy. I'm Maggie. I'm so glad you're here."

"What's little man still doing awake?" Jake asked, plucking his son from her arms and kissing him on the forehead.

Maggie backed into the house and motioned for Daisy to follow. Daisy hesitated for a moment before taking several steps into the house. "He woke up screaming bloody murder a half hour ago. He's teething."

"My momma said she used to rub whiskey on my gums when I did that," Daisy offered as her eyes scanned the house. She caught Jake and Maggie's open mouths. "But I guess that probably ain't the best solution."

Connor made goo sounds and squeals. Jake squatted so his son was eye level with Daisy. "Daisy, meet Connor. Connor, this is Daisy."

Daisy reached out and grasped Connor's fat fist. "Nice to meet you, Connor."

Connor giggled and reached out to paw Daisy's face.

Daisy returned the giggle and let him jab her. "He's so cute."

"You hungry, Daisy?" Maggie asked. "I have some leftover pasta I could heat up."

Daisy scanned the house, checking things out. "No ma'am. Thank you, though. Can I use the bathroom?"

"Sure, let me show you the way."

In the living room, Jake played with Connor on the couch as Maggie returned, her voice low. "You want to explain?"

Jake laid out what happened at the Wilkinsons', with Oz, and finding Daisy huddled in the dark in the burned-out husk of her grandmother's house. "I'm the only one she seems to trust right now. The two of us and Bear are the only ones who know she's here. Until we figure out what's going on and who took Rebekka Hammill, I'd like to keep her here where she's safe."

Maggie threw a sad appraisal toward the bathroom. "That poor girl. It just breaks my heart. You're sure we're safe here?"

"Bear won't say anything to anyone, and I sure won't. You know what to do if anything gets weird."

"Retreat to the bedroom, get the gun out of the safe, and shoot center mass."

Jake winked. "Atta girl. This girl's been through hell and back. I'm going to get to the bottom of what happened to her mom and this Hammill girl. Until then, I want to keep her safe and give her some semblance of a normal existence. Oh, man."

"What?"

"Your girl's weekend. You were heading up to Lincoln in the morning."

Maggie rolled her eyes. "Well, that's a whole other story. Halle's coming home. The whole Mom's Weekend concept fell apart because nobody planned anything. She's leaving the sorority house for the weekend before she yells something at the exec committee she can't take back."

"Halle is going to love Daisy. You will too," Jake said, thankful he hadn't ruined her plans.

Maggie cocked her head as an eyebrow shot up. "Sounds like you already do, Mr. Caldwell."

Heat flushed Jake's cheeks. "Well, thank you for your help, Mrs. Caldwell. I don't deserve you."

Maggie leaned over and kissed him, whispering, "And don't you ever forget it."

CHAPTER THIRTY-TWO

THE GRANDFATHER CLOCK IN THE LIVING ROOM BONGED twelve perfectly spaced and mournful tones as Merle sat in the darkened kitchen at the table. In front of him were the knife with dried streaks of blood in the grooves, the .38 Special, and the hammer. Instruments of death. Not what he'd envisioned his life becoming, and he tried to think back to the moment where it unraveled. He knew it began when Chloe overdosed, but that had just been soul-crushing grief. It hadn't turned bloody.

He rubbed the scars across his wrist wondering, and not for the first time, if it would have been better if he'd bled out in the bathtub in the warm, pinkish water. If he would have slid the blade across his wrist a few minutes earlier or a little deeper, his mother wouldn't have arrived in time to save him and clean up the mess he'd made.

His gaze moved from his wrist to his hands, the blood coating them once again. Pressing to his feet,

Merle moved to the sink and turned the water on hot. He rubbed his hands together as the temperature warmed. The water ran clear, pink, then soapy red until he gritted his teeth as the water burned him. He fought the urge to pull away. He deserved to hurt for what he'd done. No matter how hard he scrubbed, the blood wasn't going to wash away.

Merle jerked his hands from the steaming water and slammed them on the edge of the sink, his chest rising and falling like a piston. He peered out the window into the midnight black, and ghostly white figures floated among the trees, edging toward the house. He knew their faces but not their names. Their eyes were hard and accusing. They were the main reason he hadn't tried to kill himself again, because he knew they'd be waiting for him on the other side. And Momma couldn't protect him from that.

He spun away from the window, simultaneously wishing Momma was here to hold him and chase away the ghosts of the women outside and hating her for always protecting him, even when she shouldn't have. His fingernails bit into his palms, carving bloody half-moon arcs as he remembered the isolation she forced him into. The utter loneliness crushing him after Chloe was gone was unbearable.

The anger at the bitch who'd given Chloe the fatal dose burned liked a furnace in his chest. He thought the heat would dissipate once he bashed Bethany's skull in with a rock after she'd admitted what she'd done to his baby girl. But, it didn't. It didn't fill the hole in his soul.

When Momma had brought the first girl to the ranch a week later, a runaway named Heather, Merle saw the possibilities. She'd looked the part but that was as far as it went. Charlene flew off the rails screaming at Momma. *You think you can just fucking replace her? You think you can replace my Chloe?* Merle had to hold his wife back, her arms flailing, nails scratching. Momma had smiled, climbed in her car, and left. Heather the Runaway didn't understand and wouldn't stay put. Merle had to turn the stalls in the cellar of the barn into the rooms and put Heather there. Eventually, she became one of those figures floating in the trees.

And that's how it went for years. Momma found them at first until she realized what Merle was doing to them. Charlene grew bitter and cold and mean when she realized these girls meant more to Merle than she did. Not every drop of the bloodshed was on Merle's hands. But most of it was.

He left the bloody knife, the gun, and the hammer on the table and stormed down the hall and out the side door. The night wind bit through his shirt as it moaned through the trees. Leaves swirled and rustled in mini tornadoes around his feet as he trudged toward the barn.

He knew what he needed to do.

Momma said the police were closing in on him. He needed to clean things up.

Merle paused at the barn door, hand on the handle. He checked over his shoulder, and the figures of the women who'd come and never left Last Chance Road were gathered in an accusatory arc. His judges, his jury, floating above the gravel drive as they watched his every move.

He knew what he needed to do. He needed to find

out if Rebekka was the one to fill the hole or if she needed to join her peers, his jury.

Merle slid the door open and headed toward the basement.

CHAPTER THIRTY-THREE

JAKE BLINKED THE NIGHT'S SLEEP AWAY A FEW MINUTES after nine the next morning. He normally didn't sleep late, but he supposed the chaos of the last forty-eight hours had taken its toll. Rolling away from a softly snoring Maggie, his feet hit the cool floor and slugged toward Halle's room where they let Daisy sleep. The sleepy haze fled his head and his heartrate picked up. She wasn't in the room.

He bolted from the room and ran down the short hallway toward the front of the house, seconds from screaming her name. A long breath of relief blew past his lips as he spotted her sitting at the kitchen table looking out the front window. A bowl of milk with a few Frosted Flakes floating on the surface sat in front of her.

She turned her sleep-mussed hair at his heavy footsteps and offered a quick wave.

Jake blew out the tension. "You scared the hell outta me when you weren't in your room. How long have you been awake?"

"An hour, I guess." She gestured to the bowl. "Hope

you don't mind. I was hungry."

"Eat whatever you want. Mi casa es su casa," Jake replied, moving across the kitchen to get the coffee started.

"I don't speak no Spanish."

"You don't speak *any* Spanish."

She cocked her head. "That's what I just said, didn't I?"

Jake decided to save the grammar lessons for another day. "It means my house is your house. Did you sleep?"

Daisy poured more sugar-coated flakes into the bowl and drowned them under the milk with her spoon. "I guess. I don't sleep great in new places. Keep waking up wonderin' where I am. It took me a whole week to sleep through the night at the Wilkinsons'. You sleep? You look like you didn't."

"I kept waking up and going to check on you. Hope I didn't wake you."

She blushed. "I saw you a couple of times. I didn't mind."

The coffee pot gurgled and spit forth its nectar. Jake caught a quarter cup of it in a mug, grabbed a bowl and the milk and sat next to Daisy. He poured a bowl full of Frosted Flakes, and they sat and crunched together.

"You like Frosted Flakes?" Jake asked.

"These are so much better than what we usually get. Mom or Gramma would get the generic brand 'cause they're cheaper. Think they call 'em Sugar Flakes. They're not bad but not as good as the real thing. The Wilkinsons had Raisin Bran or Shredded Wheat. And not the frosted kind."

"I'm sorry."

"There should be a checklist foster parents have to meet. One of them should be to not have gross cereal."

They ate in silence for a couple of minutes. Jake swirled his spoon in his now empty bowl, the food and the coffee clearing his brain. "You remember anything else from last night? Anything that might help us figure out what happened?"

Her face fell and Jake's demeanor followed suit. He didn't like to be the cause of that look, but he needed to know if anything came to her once the shock wore off.

She turned her head slowly from side to side. "Nothing. It's not like I don't remember because I saw something super bad like they do on TV. I really didn't see or hear anything other than Mrs. Wilkinson yelling and the gunshots."

"Nothing about the voice of whoever came over? What they sounded like?"

"Nothing. Can we talk about somethin' else? I just woke up and haven't had my coffee yet."

Jake sat back. "Coffee? You drink it?"

"It's what my gramma used to say when I threw a bunch of questions at her first thing in the morning."

"Fair enough," Jake said. "Listen, you're safe. Only Bear and I and Maggie know you're here."

"And Connor. Can he keep his mouth shut?"

Jake almost spit out his coffee. This girl was so beyond her years and seemed to follow his frequency. "I don't think Connor is going to spill the beans. My daughter, Halle, is coming home today from college and is going to keep an eye on you along with Maggie. And Connor."

"Where are you goin'?"

Jake stood and grabbed their empty bowls. "I'm

going to go do what I do. Chase the bad guys and figure out what's going on. See if I can find out something useful about your mom."

Dressed in one of Maggie's T-shirts hitting her above the knees, Daisy followed Jake to the sink. "You ever kill anyone before, Jake?"

Jake set the bowls in the sink. He lifted her under her armpits and sat her on the counter. She'd flinched initially at his move toward her but let him hoist her up. "Why would you ask me that?"

She shrugged. "I don't know. I heard things."

"From who?"

"Mrs. Wilkinson for one after you left. She was talking to Mr. Wilkinson how she was kinda glad you were there but also kinda scared you were there because of things she'd read in the news."

Jake pressed his lips together, unsure of how to answer her. Yes, he'd killed people. A lot of people. But they were bad people who deserved to die. Terrorists, drug dealers, murderers, mad bombers. There wasn't a notch on his proverbial belt he regretted carving. Still, it would be a heavy load to lay on a ten-year-old. That said, if he lied, he had a feeling she'd smell the bullshit.

"Yeah, Daisy. People have died at my hand before, but it's not something I take lightly, and there wasn't a one of them the world wasn't better off without. There also wasn't a one of them who didn't leave me a choice. Understand?"

Her eagle eyes darted between his, as if seeking a lie, and after a moment she nodded, apparently satisfied. "I hope when you find whoever shot the Wilkinsons and took my mom that they don't leave you a choice."

To her dark wish Jake had no reply.

CHAPTER THIRTY-FOUR

AN HOUR LATER, JAKE WAS ON THE ROAD HEADING TO town. He talked to Halle who'd left Lincoln the night before after work and stayed with a friend in Kansas City. She was due at the house in an hour. Jake gave her Daisy's general size information and asked her to pick up a few changes of clothes for her. Halle was full of questions, but Jake told her he would explain when she got here and to not talk to anyone about it.

On his way toward the Coach House Apartments, he called Bear to see if there were any updates on the Wilkinson shootings and Oz's tent death. They'd found some tire tracks on the back road but nothing that would match a truck. Deputies were scouring the houses up and down the back road and on the Wilkinsons' street. No pay dirt yet.

Turning into the gravel drive at the apartments, Jake pulled into the lot, parking between a pickup and a compact car that looked like someone beat it with a sledgehammer. He crossed the drive toward a group of people filing out of one of the rooms. All were drinking coffee from paper cups and most lit up cigarettes the second they hit the fresh air. Jake passed a couple asking if they knew Betsy Thompkins.

A weathered woman in her fifties with graying-black hair in stiff blue jeans and a paisley blouse raised her hand. "That's me. What can I do for you?"

Jake reached out a hand. "I'm Jake Caldwell, we spoke on the phone yesterday. Wondered if I could ask you a few questions about your meeting participants. I'm looking for someone in particular. Big guy, tattoo of a face on his bicep."

Betsy sipped from a Styrofoam cup. "It's Alcoholics *Anonymous*. I don't keep a roster or anything and don't generally give out information. People who come here like their privacy."

"Does the description ring a bell for you?"

"What if it did? Like I said, I don't give out names."

Jake cut his eyes to a nearby man who smoked and ogled the rolling clouds. The man either had one leg shorter than the other, causing him to lean in their direction, or he was eavesdropping. Jake jerked his head in the opposite direction, walking out of the man's range. Betsy followed.

"You know Sharla Babin?" Jake asked.

"'Course I do...did." Betsy shuffled her feet. "Jesus, I hope it's still present tense. I like Sharla. She was doing really good. Wish someone would find out what happened to her."

"That's what I'm doing. Her daughter hired me to find her mom."

A laugh burst through her lips. "Daisy? Daisy hired you? You must work cheap."

"Let's just say she plucked my heart strings."

The corner of Betsy's mouth curled up. "She either plucks 'em or cuts 'em. You either love that girl or you want to throttle her. Personally, I'm on the love side of the equation."

"Me too. That's why I'm trying to help her. The man I'm describing was seen behind Sharla's house the night she disappeared. Based on some other stuff I can't go into, we think he might have hit local AA meetings."

"We?"

"I'm working with Sheriff Parley on this."

"Bear, huh? Guess it means you're probably okay." Betsy popped a cigarette out of a pack and lit it with a Zippo. She snapped the lid of the lighter shut, her eyes darting around at the few people still milling around. "I think I've seen the guy, but he only came a couple of times and sat in the back. Asked him if he wanted to share his story and he just shook his head."

"When's the last time you saw him?"

She rolled her eyes to the sky, thinking. "Wednesday. Maybe two more times a few months ago, but I don't remember when exactly."

Jake did some mental math. "Couple of months ago? Maybe around the time Sharla Babin disappeared?"

Betsy's face paled. "Probably around then."

"Anyone else know who he might be?"

"I could ask around. There's another meeting tonight. Maybe make a coupla calls to some regulars who mighta been there when he was. Oh my God. You think he found these girls at my meetings?"

Jake handed her his card. "We don't know anything for sure. If you find anything out, please call me or Bear ASAP. And thank you."

Jake headed toward his truck across the gravel lot,

nostrils flaring as he picked up the scent of the man they were searching for. They had nothing concrete yet, but it felt good to at least take a few steps forward.

A voice sounded at his back. "I might have something for ya, big guy."

Jake turned to see the eavesdropper stepping across the lot toward him wearing dirty blue jeans atop scuffed boots and a denim jacket over a green flannel shirt. The man took a final drag from his smoke and flicked the butt across the lot. His face was gaunt, deep lines etched in a sun-beaten face. Gray-streaked black hair hung to his shoulders, the ends flipping up.

Jake folded his arms. "Who are you?"

"Dewayne Morgan. I know the guy you're lookin' for. Big with a face tattoo on his arm."

"I could tell you were listening."

The man spread his arms wide. "I hear everything. It's a gift."

"Tell me about the man, Dewayne. You know him?"

"Seen him, sat near him, talked to him."

"You catch his name?"

"Can you help me out on something if I tell ya?"

Jake rubbed the back of his neck as he inhaled deeply. Nobody did anything to simply help a fellow citizen. It always came with an agenda. Jake initially thought Dewayne looked like a slimeball when he spotted him eavesdropping but was trying to be a better person and not snap judge people based on appearance. He should learn to listen to his gut.

Jake set his jaw. "What is it you want, exactly?"

"You're friends with Bear, right?"

"Yeah."

"Maybe you could talk him inta droppin' certain

charges that may have fallen on me when I was in an inebriated state of mind a couple weeks ago. If you do that, it might jar my memory, and I could conjure up the name of the guy you're lookin' for."

"You trying to blackmail me into a favor for you?"

Dewayne flashed his palms. "No, no. I technically can't blackmail 'cause I don't have nothin' on you. I'm just sayin'—"

Jake took a step forward, clenching his fists, turning his aggression meter up a couple of notches. He didn't have time for this. "Maybe you should tell me now. There're more important things going on than your bullshit charges. I'll talk to Bear if you give me a name. No promises on the outcome."

Dewayne stepped back as Jake advanced. "Maybe to you they're bullshit, but I'd rather avoid some jail time. Charges dropped first, name second."

The vein in Jake's temple pulsed. This asshole could lead them to a killer, and he thought of nothing but himself. "Maybe I'll beat your ass into this gravel until you give me a name."

Dewayne continued backward until he slapped into the side of a parked truck, and Jake pressed into him. People tended to either fight or talk when their personal space was violated like this. Dewayne couldn't kick a tire down a hill.

Dewayne stared into Jake's chest. "Careful. You hit me too hard, and that name might fly outta my head and get lost in the breeze."

Footsteps shuffled behind Jake. He peeked over his shoulder and noticed a trio of people looking his way, one with a cell phone out and raised. Last thing he wanted was a video of him beating a man half his size landing on social media or Bear's doorstep. Not that Bear would do anything, but he had enough on his plate as it was.

Jake stepped back and grasped Dewayne around the shoulders, pasting on a plastic smile. "Don't fuck with me on this, Dewayne. You really have something on this guy?"

Dewayne met Jake's eyes. "Swear to God. Look, I've been clean since that deal with Bear, been to two AA meetings a day. I'm not tryin' to jerk you around, but I got a job I can't afford to lose and a kid I'm hangin' onto by the skin of my teeth. I can't go back to jail, man. You get Bear to drop the charges and I'll give this guy you're lookin' for on a silver platter."

Jake released Dewayne's shoulders. "If I get this done for you, you're not going to hit me up for something else like cash, are you?"

"No, sir. I mean, if you want to throw some my way, I'm not gonna turn it down. But the charges is all I'm lookin' at."

Jake heard bullshit before, and this didn't sound like it. Dewayne's eyes were clear and steady. "Where can I find you?"

Dewayne jerked his head over his shoulder. "Room 8. Gotta work at five, but I'll be here 'til then."

Jake spun and headed toward his truck. "I'll see what I can do."

Jake tried Bear on his cell but was kicked to voicemail.

Nothing was ever easy.

CHAPTER THIRTY-FIVE

REBEKKA LAY ON THE THIN MATTRESS IN HER CELL STARING at the ceiling. The iron bed, the dirt floor, her stone-walled cell guarded by electrical steel wires, wooden joists overhead. A sad laugh slipped through her lips over the eclectic construction materials of her prison cell. Swinging her feet to the floor, she groaned and rested her elbows on her knees, chin planted in her palms as she counted the cinderblocks in the opposite wall for the thousandth time. Ninety-six. And a half.

Is it possible to be bored to death and terrified at the same time?

Behind the ninety-six and a half blocks of concrete, Chloe rattled off a string of coughs followed by a groan. She didn't sound good at all. Incoherent ramblings drifted into Rebekka's cell in the middle of the night...or what she thought was nighttime. There was no way to tell in this hell hole. Chloe was also completely unresponsive to Rebekka's pleas to talk to her.

She edged off the bed to try again as the door thumped open at the end of the hall, and the man's footsteps thudded down the stairs. Any thoughts of being bored scattered like ashes in the wind. Rebekka shrank against the wall, drawing her knees to her chest. She pressed her eyes shut and prayed for a white knight to gallop to the cells and rescue them.

Instead, the light seeping through her eyelids dimmed. When she opened them, the man stood in front of the wires staring her down.

"You and I need to talk," he said. "I'll be with you in a minute."

Rebekka raked her top lip with her bottom teeth as the man moved to Chloe's door, trying to interpret his tone. Anytime anyone said—"We need to talk"—it didn't bode well for her. Not with her parents, her teachers, or myriad of boyfriends she'd had in her former life. But here, the man's tone had been robotic. Maybe a bit sad? Resigned? If so, what did that mean for her?

Chloe coughed again from beyond the wall, the phlegm rattling in her lungs. The deadbolt of Chloe's cell door echoed in the dungeon as it thumped back, and the man's shadow slipped from Rebekka's sight like a ghost. She wanted to run to the front of the cell and try to hear what was going on in there, but fear sapped the strength from her legs. If the man caught her, it would be bad.

Good girls don't listen in on other people's conversations, she imagined the man saying as he raised the fucking zapper again. If she escaped this place alive, she might go live on a desert island somewhere without electricity. It'd be worth it for the peace of mind of not being fried for the slightest transgression.

Chloe hacked up a lung again, and the man's deep voice bounced from the stone walls. His tone was low, soothing, though Rebekka couldn't make out a word of it. She heard Chloe crying softly, the man's voice again, some rustling and squeaks of the bedframe, and then silence.

A minute later, the man left Chloe's cell, crossed in front of hers, and opened the door. As it creaked open, the first thing she spotted was the zapper in his hand, and she pressed harder into the wall, the urge to pee pressing against her bladder. He sat on the edge of the bed, alternating glances between Rebekka and the hard dirt floor. Some unknown weight seemed to pull his giant frame down.

Is this it? Is this the end of my young life? My wasted life? Months ago she'd been on a razor's edge, literally, as she held a blade against her wrists. Her mental pros and cons list had been incredibly lopsided as her heart searched for one thing to prevent her from drawing her own blood. She imagined him telling her she'd failed him. She had no doubt his disappointment in her would be terminal. *We all die a Chloe.* All the things she still wanted to do in life raced through her mind. She'd never swim in the warm ocean waters, climb the Statue of Liberty, see a Broadway play in the Big Apple. She'd never get the chance to tell her abandoned parents and friends she loved them.

How will it happen? Will my end be as quick and terrifying as Chloe 1's? Will he simply reach across the bed and snap my neck? Perhaps he'd let her struggle, fighting as if she ever had a chance as he smothered her with the threadbare pillow on her bed.

"You're the one," the man said at last, eyes locked on the ground.

Rebekka's toes curled as her fingernails dug into her knees. *What does that mean? The one that is going to die?*

"The one *what*, Daddy?" she asked, cringing at using the parental term, but he seemed to like it, and if it kept him from choking the life out of her, she'd say it all day long.

Tears swam in the man's eyes as he lifted his chin toward the ceiling. "Today would've been my Chloe's birthday. Did you know that?"

"No, Daddy," she whispered, goosebumps erupting down her arms.

"Every year, Charlene would bake up a batch of cupcakes because Chloe loved cupcakes. Chocolate with chocolate icing. The more icing the better. She'd eat those things until she made herself sick." A sad smile passed over his face, and a tear slipped from the corner of his eye. "These last coupla years, we'd have a pile of 'em sittin' on the kitchen table, waiting for her to come home and eat 'em. But she never did. She couldn't, 'cause she was dead. But we still made 'em, and they'd sit untouched until they were hard as rocks and we throw 'em out."

The man dropped his chin and wiped the tears away with the palm of his hand.

Rebekka's eyes locked on the open door beyond the man. She longed to taste fresh air again, but there was not a chance she could get past him even if she wasn't still chained to the bed. She considered reaching out to stroke his arm and tell him it would be okay. Not because she wanted to touch him. She'd slit his throat if it meant getting out of here. But that wasn't the game to be played in the here and now. Not yet anyway.

"I didn't wanna believe she was gone." His rat eyes

locked onto Rebekka's. "Even when the cops came to the door to tell us what we'd feared. Even when we saw her body on the metal table in the morgue. Even when we brought her back here and buried her under the big oak tree. Even though I shoveled that last measure of dirt in the hole, I didn't wanna believe my Chloe wasn't coming back."

A spark of hope flared in Rebekka's chest as the vision of an oak tree sprang up. If she could get him to take her outside, she could run. She wasn't the fastest runner in the world, but she was pretty sure she could take the hulk in front of her.

The man reached into his pocket. "She's gone, but you're here now. You're the one. You'll be my Chloe." He pulled out a wrapped Hostess Cupcake and set it on the bed before standing. "Happy birthday, sweetheart."

Rebekka's eyes locked on the white swirls on top of the cupcake as relief filled her limbs. He wasn't going to kill her.

The man turned and headed toward the door. The relief turned to a bubbling panic. He was going to leave her in here for God knows how long again. If she was his new Chloe, did that mean being locked down here for the rest of her days?

"Wait," Rebekka said. The man turned toward her with one hand on the door. "Thank you for the cupcake, Daddy. If I'm going to be your Chloe, maybe it would help for me to talk to her under that oak tree. We could do it together. Make it official."

The man stood unmoving, assessing her. Rebekka held her own breath, wondering if she'd pushed him too far too fast.

"We could do that," he said at last. "Later. Daddy's

gotta take care of a coupla things first. Enjoy your cupcake."

The man left the cell and closed the door behind him. The lock thunked into place, and he plodded across the basement floor before disappearing up the stairs.

Rebekka stared at the cupcake with a thousand thoughts flying through her head. One thought covered her like a wet blanket. If she was the one, what did it mean for the Chloe next door?

With that little actin' job, you just signed my death warrant was what Chloe had said earlier. Had she?

Rebekka waited for the sound of the door closing upstairs to reach her before she slipped to the front of her cell, pressing up against the cold stone wall.

"Chloe? You there?"

No answer. No cough. No sound. The bile rose in Rebekka's throat. She closed her eyes, praying for a response.

"Chloe, talk to me, please."

Nothing.

Rebekka opened her eyes, and she noticed one important detail. Chloe's door stood open. The man hadn't bothered to close it. Her heart sunk. He hadn't bothered to close it, because he didn't need to worry about Chloe escaping anymore. Rebekka was the one and now she was truly alone.

CHAPTER THIRTY-SIX

BEAR ANSWERED ON JAKE'S THIRD TRY AND FED HIM THE address of a crime scene they were working at a house a few blocks away. Jake arrived within minutes and parked his truck behind Klages's cruiser. As he passed the cruiser, he spotted a twenty-something woman with crazy eyes and a blood-stained T-shirt in the backseat, hands cuffed behind her. Her sunken face made her appear fifty.

Klages stood on the front stoop of a single-story home with crooked gray siding, a broken front window covered with cardboard, and blood splatters trailing down the concrete stairs. "Hey, Caldwell. Never a dull day in paradise, is there?"

He stopped in front of her, staying in the grass. "If you're bored, you're not trying very hard."

Bear poked his head out the front door. "Gimme two minutes." He disappeared back inside.

Jake pointed at the blood splatters. "What the hell happened here?"

"You ever see the movie *Highlander*?"

Of course he'd seen it. It was a classic. "There can be only one, swinging swords and decapitated immortals. Wait, did that lady in your car—"

"No decapitations, though I give her a solid B+ for effort. She stabbed her boyfriend with a sword to set him free of the entities living inside him."

"What entities?"

She pumped her narrow shoulders. "Fuck if I know."

"He going to make it?"

"Wagon is on the way to transport him. You're going to be shocked. They both admitted to taking meth earlier in the day."

Jake dropped his jaw wide and pasted on an exaggerated look of surprise. "Meth makes you do crazy shit? Who would've guessed?"

"You think these people would eventually get the memo."

Bear emerged through the front door and stepped around the blood splatters on the concrete as he grumbled. "Morons." He snapped his chin toward Klages's cruiser as he slipped a tobacco pouch between his cheek and gums. "She say anything else?"

Klages rolled her eyes. "Just that she freed the demons, and they are now swirling around inside the house waiting to latch onto a new host."

"Great. That'd be my fuckin' luck. I get possessed. What's up, Caldwell?"

Jake laid out his meeting with Betsy. "I need you to drop the charges against Dewayne Morgan."

Bear drew his head back. "What for?"

"He says he knows who our mystery man with the arm tattoo is. Said the only way he'd give it to me is if my best friend," Jake flicked air quotes with his fingers, "dropped the 'bullshit charges' against him."

Bear spit into an empty water bottle. "I ain't droppin' anything against that guy."

"We need this info."

"Beat it out of him."

"I'm trying to be a better man."

Bear chewed on the whiskers of his upper lip. "Do you know what happened with that fucktard? I told Dewayne to move along after we shut down a house party on MM and, after he called me fat, he grabbed his crotch, then jabbed the crooked finger of his dick-grabbing hand in my chest. And if there's one thing you never do, you never, ever—"

Jake laid a hand on his best friend's chest. "Please don't say poke the bear."

Bear fixed a dangerous look. "Well, you don't. Especially after you've fondled yourself. Never, ever poke the bear."

Jake winced. "Jesus, that's corny as hell."

"It's not corny. It'll be my catchphrase."

"You're better than that."

Bear pumped his broad shoulders. "Not really. It's going to catch on."

"'Don't poke the bear' is not going to catch on unless Warsaw gets a fucking zoo."

"Just wait and see, my friend."

"Even if Dewayne did the unthinkable poking, do me a favor and drop the charge."

Bear pouted. "Come on, man. It's still assaulting an officer of the law."

"Drop it. For me. For Daisy."

Bear growled. "Fine but tell that sumbitch he better

not so much as glance at me sideways, or I'll run his skinny ass up a flagpole."

"You want to come with me? I have a feeling he'll want to hear it directly from you."

Bear turned to Klages. "You got this? Lipscomb and Tarley are still inside with the victim."

Klages sighed. "Can I please handle the booking and do all the paperwork, too, boss?"

"Thanks for volunteering." He ignored Klages's longest finger. "Where we doing this, Caldwell?"

"Back at the Coach House. I'll meet you there."

Jake and Bear headed toward their respective trucks on the street. Jake called out. "Hey, I appreciate you being the bigger man. At least Dewayne was right about that."

"You're such a dick."

CHAPTER THIRTY-SEVEN

JAKE THUMPED THE DOOR TO ROOM 8 AT THE COACH House Apartments, Bear's hot breath heating the back of Jake's neck.

Jake craned over his shoulder. "Could you take a step back? Your breath smells like coffee and Skoal."

"Sorry. I genuinely don't like this guy, and I'm a little amped up with everything goin' on. Plus, I don't like being strung over the barrel."

"Relax, man." Jake pounded on the door again. "Open up, Dewayne. It's Jake and Bear."

Dewayne's voiced sounded, "Gimme a second."

"You get sixty of them before I kick the door in." Jake leaned against the doorframe. "Where would someone get a sword, anyway?"

"Beats me. It was a nice lookin' one too. Had this shiny gold handle with red and green jewels. Blade was curved like one of those Samurai swords."

"Jewels weren't real though?"

"Hell no, they were all scratched up. I'm surprised

they didn't hock the sword for drugs. You should've seen the inside of that place. Don't know if I'll ever see a worse place as long as I live."

The door to Room 8 opened, and Dewayne stepped back to let them in. Jake and Bear crossed the threshold.

Bear's nose crinkled as he scanned the room. "I stand corrected."

Black trash bags covered the floor, some unsealed with half-eaten microwave meals and empty soda cans. Clothes were scattered over the bed and on chairs. Flies buzzed and Jake was pretty sure he spotted a mouse scampering toward the bathroom. No sign of booze at least. Underneath the haze of smoke was an acrid odor of urine.

"You have a cat?" Jake asked.

Dewayne backed through a narrow path between the bags. "Somewhere."

"Smells like it pissed on everything."

Bear pinched his nose. "Smells like it died under one of these bags."

Dewayne threw some trash bags out of the way and cleared a path toward a couple of chairs in the corner. "Sorry about the mess. My soon-to-be-ex threw all my stuff out on the lawn and this room isn't exactly spacious. I meant to clean up, but you got back here faster than I thought. You wanna sit?"

"Hell no," Bear said, backing toward the door. "If I stay in here another second, I'm gonna puke."

Jake followed him. "That might improve the smell. Outside, Dewayne."

Bear headed toward his truck and grabbed a Christmas tree air freshener from the rearview mirror and fanned it under his nose. He smacked his mouth. "Jesus Christ, I can still taste that room."

Dewayne joined them after pulling his door shut, tucking in the tail of his shirt into dirty blue jeans. "He talked to you, Bear? We have a deal?"

Bear stopped fanning the air freshener, eyes scanning up and down Dewayne's rail-thin figure. "We have a deal. If this pans out. Just know if you ever poke your dick-clutching fingers in my chest again, you're gonna draw back a stump. Give me the name and all shall be forgiven."

"Merle Wade. That's the name of the guy with the face tattoo on his arm I sat with at the meeting."

"You sure?"

"I remember Merle because I love Merle Haggard. And I remember Wade because of Wade Davis, the Royals pitcher. After the World Series win in 2015 when they spanked the Mets, I wanted to have another kid just so I could name him Wade."

"Merle Wade," Bear repeated. "Never heard of him. What did he have to say when you were chattin' him up?"

"He didn't say much of anything. Told me his name when we was introducin' ourselves. He had hands like dinner plates. Swallowed mine whole."

"You ever see him before this last meeting?"

"Maybe a coupla times drivin' around the backroads in this ratty old pickup."

"What color was the truck?" Jake asked.

Dewayne scratched his forehead as if the motion would bring the answer to the surface. "Light color. Maybe tan. But it was always in the boonies. I never seen him in town."

"Where in the boonies?" Bear asked.

"I don't know. Maybe down MM. Once off Poor Boy Road."

"Know where he lives?"

"Nope. That's all I know. You still good with droppin' the charges given my cooperation here?"

Bear squinted and closed the distance between them. "You sorry for pokin' me and being a general asshole?"

Dewayne licked his lips and jerked his head up and down. "I'm real sorry, sheriff. To tell you the truth, I don't even 'member doin' that to you. I'm tryin' to keep my nose clean and getting to see my boy every once in a while."

Jake jerked his chin toward the hotel room. "You take him in there?"

Dewayne blushed. "Not when it's that bad. My ex wouldn't like it."

"Nobody likes it like that," Bear said. "Have some self-respect. Stay clean and out of trouble. If I see you with your boy, I'm coming back to check this room. I see it like that again and I'll call Child Protective Service on you. We understand each other?"

"Yes, sir."

Jake and Bear tracked Dewayne as he plodded back toward his room.

"You heard of Merle Wade?" Bear asked.

"Nope."

"You believe this guy, or is he just trying to skirt the charge?"

Jake was an excellent reader of people. It had served him well in the past at the poker tables and dealing with people who were born liars and thieves. "I believe him. What do we do?"

Bear opened his truck door. "Meet me back at the station and let's see what we can find."

CHAPTER THIRTY-EIGHT

BACK AT THE STATION, JAKE AND BEAR HUDDLED AROUND Bear's desk. Bear slid the keyboard in front of him and pecked keys one at a time with his index finger.

Jake grimaced. "You never learned to type, did you?"

Bear's lip curled. "Shut up. I hate computers. Why would I want to be proficient in using them?"

"We took typing together in high school. Did you retain nothing from class?"

Bear continued pecking. "To retain something, you had to learn something. If you recall, I missed class a lot."

"Can I take over? This is painful. It's like watching a drunk toddler take his first steps, and you're terrified he's going to cave his skull in on the edge of the coffee table."

"I'll cave your skull in, you little shit. Alright, I'm in the system."

Bear entered Merle Wade's name, and after a moment the info popped up on the screen along with a mugshot. The man's face was square with a flat nose and bullish eyes. A mangy beard sprung from weighty cheeks.

"He ain't winning any beauty contests," Bear said. "Let's see...last known address in Clinton. Arrested in 2000 for a drunk and disorderly along with a DUI in 2004. Married to a Charlene Wade. Missing person report filed on her a couple of years ago in Clinton. That's it?"

"That's it."

"Wholly unhelpful."

"Let me call Benny Lawder. He's the Henry County Sheriff. Maybe he knows something."

Bear scrolled through his phone and punched a number. Bear put it on speaker and set the phone on his desk.

Lawder answered on the third ring. "I'm fishing. Why aren't you out here with me, you dumb son of a bitch?"

Bear rocked back. "Because you quit drinking. What's the point of fishing if you can't drink? Besides, you couldn't catch a fish with two sticks of dynamite."

"Feels like it today. What's up?"

"You know a guy named Merle Wade?"

Lawder was silent. "Unfortunately. Haven't seen him for a couple years, and it hasn't exactly left me with a case of the lonelies. What's he done this time?"

"We have a missing woman case from a few months back. Sharla Babin."

"I've heard of her. I've seen some fliers in town here. He a suspect?"

"Maybe. Found a witness who identified his truck and a man who has the same arm tattoo at her house the night she disappeared."

Lawson clucked his tongue. "You show him Merle's mugshot?"

"Can't. Someone slit his throat."

"Jesus."

Bear leaned back in his groaning chair. "Another witness saw him at an AA meeting here in town. Might be connected to another missing girl, Rebekka Hammill. We just found out his name and saw a reference to a missing person's report on his wife. It was filed with your office and thought you could shed a little light on things."

Lawson's breath rattled the speaker. "Ooh, boy. Let me see if I can recollect. He lived at the Four Square apartments on the outskirts of town when his daughter OD'd. Heroin spiked with fentanyl. Few months later, we respond to a domestic disturbance at the apartment with Merle and his ball-buster wife. Both were hammered, but we convinced him to leave for the night, and I never heard anything else until Charlene's family filed a missing person's report a month later."

"Interesting timing," Jake muttered.

"We followed up with Merle," Lawson continued. "He says she left him and was heading east to Chicago to stay with family. Couldn't take the loss of their daughter and couldn't stand being around Merle anymore. Now, I never liked Merle, but that Charlene was something else. Grade A bitch on wheels."

"She ever turn up?" Bear asked.

"Nope. We were looking hard at Merle as we tracked the wife's credit cards. Last used in a hole-in-the-wall gas station near St. Louis. No cameras there so it could've been anybody."

"Including Merle?"

"Nope. He was in our interrogation room when the card was used. We tore up the apartment, checked out friends and acquaintances, but found nothing to hold him with. The case is still open, but it's colder than a penguin's nuts in Antarctica."

Bear drummed his fingers on his desk. "He still live at those apartments?"

"They burned down last year. Don't know where the guy is now. Sorry, man. Wish I could help you more."

"One more question, Benny. Would you be surprised if he's involved with these missing girls? He strike you as that type?"

"I don't know, bud. As I said, I didn't like the guy, but I couldn't point to anything specific leading me to that feeling. There was somethin' wrong about him. Would it surprise me? I suppose not, but he was tore up somethin' fierce when his daughter died. That I remember."

After exchanging promises to get together and go fishing, Bear disconnected the call and folded his hands behind his head. Jake walked around the desk and dropped into a chair.

"What do you think?" Bear asked.

"I think we have shit to go on."

"Maybe we start showing his mug around town and see if anyone recognizes him or knows where he might be."

Jake ran his fingers through his cropped hair. "Maybe. But if he did do something to these girls, we could spook him and he'd run."

"Assuming he's still in the area. Dewayne said he saw his truck around MM and Poor Boy Road. We could start there."

Klages came in.

"You get Samurai Sarah squared away?" Bear asked.

Klages rolled her eyes. "Locked up. That woman is spouting some crazy shit. Feel like I need to take a shower with holy water after riding in the car with her. By the way, a neighbor of the Wilkinsons' came by while we were out." Her thin lips disappeared for a moment. "We have a plate hit on a deer cam he set up on his street."

"A deer cam on his street?" Jake asked.

"Kids kept taking a bat to his mailbox, and he was trying to catch them in the act. Howard ran the plate when we got back."

Klages handed Bear a piece of paper, holding it out with her eyes locked on the floor like a kid handing his parents a bad report card.

Bear read the page and shot upright in his chair, his thick eyebrows shooting to the ceiling. "When did the neighbor capture this footage?"

"It's in the window of when the Wilkinsons were murdered."

"Who does the plate belong to?" Jake asked.

Bear's eyes widened at Klages. "Where is she now?"

"Not here. I tried to call her at home but there was no answer. Kuhlmann was a few blocks away, so I had him swing by the house. Waiting on his call back. Thought I should bring it to you."

Jake flicked his eyes between the two of them. "Whose license plate is it?"

Bear read the paper again like he couldn't believe what it said. "Wendy Blackwell."

CHAPTER THIRTY-NINE

"Wendy?" Jake asked.

"Howard verified the footage that Wendy was at the Wilkinsons' earlier in the day dropping off Daisy," Klages said. "But she was also there around the time of the murders, or at least her car was."

Klages's cell vibrated, she answered, listened, and said thanks. "That was Kuhlmann. Wendy's not home and neither is her car. He checked around the house and in the windows. Didn't see anything suspicious."

"There's gotta be an explanation why she was there," Bear said. "No way she could've been tied up with this."

"Be nice to find her so we can ask."

"She wouldn't do something stupid like trying to track down those truck leads in person, would she?" Bear asked.

"God, I hope not," Klages said. "The list is still sitting on her desk and doesn't look like she's touched it. Maybe she went to the Wilkinsons', saw the bodies, and freaked out."

"Don't you think she would've called it in if she saw

something like dead bodies?" Jake asked. "Maybe she was there to check on Daisy. Daisy said Wendy and her grandmother were friends. Maybe Daisy left something in her car, and she was returning it. Maybe she knows the Wilkinsons."

Crimson creeped up Bear's neck. "And maybe she's hurt. Maybe whoever shot the Wilkinsons killed her too and took her car."

"And the possibility exists that maybe she's tied up in this somehow." Jake gave Bear a hard stare. "Dude, we gotta look at her."

Bear shifted in his seat. "Just because—"

"She hasn't done anything with the truck report. Oz's witness statement isn't in Sharla's file, no letter from Oz that he said he mailed here, and Wendy has access to everything. And now she's AWOL? Something doesn't smell right. I know you've worked with her forever, but we need to look at her."

Bear growled as he pulled out his cell. "I hate it when you make sense."

Wendy answered on the fourth ring. "Hello?"

"Wendy, it's Bear. Sorry to call you on your day off. I tried to reach you at home. What are you up to?"

Wendy paused. "I was running some errands around town, and I have to go get my medicine. I'm not feeling terribly well. What's going on?"

"I'm surprised you haven't called in with all the commotion going on?"

"Commotion? I haven't seen or heard anything. What's happening?"

Bear's mouth pushed to one side at her statement as his eyebrow raised in a slant. "You haven't heard what happened at the Wilkinsons' last night?"

"Umm...no. Oh dear, did something happen to poor Daisy?"

"No, no. She's fine. Listen, someone gave a description of a car and a plate number at the Wilkinsons' house, and it came back to you."

"Well, that's strange," she said. "Oh wait. Yesterday morning. I dropped Daisy off. I found her walking back from her grandmother's house and gave her a ride home."

Bear glanced at Jake and Klages, his face crunched in uneasy puzzlement. "And have you been by there since you dropped Daisy off?"

"Why are you asking me this, Bear?"

"No reason. Just filling in holes. Can you come in the office, Wendy?" When she didn't respond, Bear's voice softened. "Please? We're a little slammed at the moment with everything going on and could use your masterful touch. I'll pay you time and a half."

"Like I said, I have to go get my medicine but will come in right after. Does that work?"

"That's fine," Bear said. "The sooner the better, though. Thanks."

Bear eased the phone on the cradle. "Well, that's weird as shit."

"Why didn't you tell her about the Wilkinsons?" Klages asked.

"Because she's lying," Jake said. "Bear knew it. You could hear it in her voice."

Bear drummed his fingers on his desk. "And she said she was in town and didn't know what the commotion was about? I guarantee everybody within ten square miles knows what happened to the Wilkinsons by now."

"Worse, she didn't ask Bear to elaborate," Jake said.

"He leaves it open-ended that something happened there but doesn't say what. She doesn't ask because maybe she already knows."

"So why is she lying?" Klages asked.

"That's what we have to figure out," Bear said. "Put out an alert on her car to our crew. See if anyone spots her. If they do, have them call me."

Klages left the office.

"How long have you known Wendy?" Jake asked.

"I don't know, five years give or take."

"And you trust her?"

"As much as I trust anybody. I'm having trouble connecting the dots on why Wendy would've been at the Wilkinsons' in our kill window."

Jake rubbed a hand across his head. "Maybe she wasn't there but somebody drove her car."

"It would seem more plausible. We'll ask when she gets here. But wouldn't she offer it up?"

"Probably. She have any family in town?"

"Not that I know of. She has a son somewhere. Think his name was Dean or Dawson. Some D word, but she won't talk about him. They had a sort of falling out years ago, and I quit asking her."

"Husband?"

"Died years ago. Are we grasping at imaginary straws?"

Jake stood and paced. "I don't know, man. We both had the same read on her. It was like it was a genuine surprise to her we placed her at the Wilkinsons' before she realized what it could be."

"It's like when Audrey tells me I promised to do something, and I have no idea what she's talking about, and I'm thinking she's lost her mind," Bear said. "Then it slowly seeps in she's right, and I've gotta cover for my screw up."

"That happen a lot?"

"A helluva lot more than it probably should. Don't tell her I said that. Lemme pull Wendy's personnel file and see if there's anything in there."

Jake slipped his cell phone from his pocket to call a hacker he had on a kind of retainer. "I'll call Cat and have him run a background on her. That guy digs up the goods if they are there to be found."

Bear slid his chair to a file cabinet and rooted through folders. "Must be nice having your own personal hacker at your beck and call."

"If he comes up with anything, I'll bill you for his services."

"Jesus. I'm going to have to take a second job."

CHAPTER FORTY

MERLE SAT ON THE EDGE OF THE LIVING ROOM COUCH, eyes locked on the hammer on the coffee table in front of him as Charlene paced the hardwood floors. She moved so fast and furious Merle worried she would start a fire. His heart thumped in his throat, acid churned in his gut, and hands clinched so tightly they ached. He couldn't take much more of this.

"This is your fault," she spat. "You let this happen. You wanted this to happen. You and your bitch mother."

"Stop it, Charlene," Merle whispered.

His teeth ground so hard together he thought they might shatter.

"Who did you do this for? All this blood spilled and for who? It sure wasn't for me. It sure as hell wasn't for Chloe, you dumb hick son of a bitch."

Merle risked a peek to his wife. Her eyes were filled with white-hot hate, her mane of strawberry hair sticking out at all angles, and her face as pale as the moon. There was no love in those eyes. Any love for him left the station when Chloe died. He'd lost both his women that day.

Charlene drew in close, her breath rotten. "You got somethin' to say to me, Merle? Or are you just gonna sit on your cowardly yella ass and cry?"

Red dots spotted Merle's vision, furry glowing crimson orbs as the pressure in his head built. He squeezed his eyes shut and clasped his trembling hands against his ears, digging his fingers into the side of his head. But it didn't drown out her grating voice. God, he wanted her to stop.

"You knew what she was goin' through, and you did nothing," Charlene growled. "Did you want her to die, Merle? Did you?"

"Jesus, no," Merle said.

"Why didn't you stop her that night from leaving? You knew where she was gonna go."

"I didn't...we didn't know."

"Yeah, you did. I told you not to let her leave, and you just let her roll away."

Merle rocked on the couch, nails digging into his palms, breaths coming in gulps.

"Admit it, Merle. This is your fault."

"No! It's not."

"It's your fault. She died because of you."

Merle's eyes flew open.

He snatched the hammer from the table, feeling the wood handle bite into his palm.

You did this.

Spinning toward Charlene, he raised it to the ceiling, every muscle in his body tensed.

This is your fault.

He jerked his arm toward her skull, bringing the

metal down in an arc, aiming for the red line dripping down her face.

The hammer head swung through her skull, striking nothing but air, and his momentum carried his stumbling body across the room. He crashed into the wall on the far side and crumpled to the ground, dropping the hammer to the floor.

You can't kill me twice, Merle.

He swept his eyes over the empty living room, her voice echoing in his head. Picking up the hammer, he pushed himself to his feet and lumbered out the back door toward the barn. The late-morning sun slipped behind a bank of rain-soaked clouds, and the breeze kicked in as he shuffled across the driveway. The damp earth smell of impending rain soaked the air.

Entering the barn, he shuffled toward the double doors, throwing them wide open. He plodded down the eighteen stairs to the cellar, counting each one off in his head. At the bottom, he flipped on the light switch, and bare bulbs flooded the dungeon with light.

He dragged his boots along the concrete floor to the corner where the coloration in the stone was darker. Out of the corner of his eye, he saw Rebekka huddling in the darkness of her cell, gasping when she spotted the hammer swinging at Merle's side. He continued on until he reached the stool and sat.

This is your fault.

He opened his hand and the hammer fell to the floor.

You can't kill me twice.

He buried his face in his hands and cried.

CHAPTER FORTY-ONE

CAT CALLED JAKE BACK AN HOUR LATER, AN UNUSUALLY quick turnaround for the hacker, but Jake applied an unusual amount of pressure. Cat bent over like a cheap hooker if a hint of violence to his person was uttered. Jake had laid his hands on Cat once when Jake was a collector for mob boss Jason Keats. Cat remembered the outcome and didn't want to go through it again. The hacker didn't mind getting under Bear's skin, though.

Jake raised his ringing phone. "It's Cat. Be nice."

Bear threw on an angelic grin. "Now, when am I not nice?"

"Whenever you talk to him."

"It's not my fault he's an asshole."

"What do you have, Cat?" Jake asked, putting the man on speaker phone in Bear's office.

Cat crunched his signature Cheetos over the speaker. "Is Bear with you?"

"Right here."

"Good to know," Cat said. "I'll make sure not to call you a fat bastard behind your back, ya fat bastard."

Bear's lip curled as he towered over the phone. "I'll break those orange-stained fingers one at a time, you little piece—"

"Children, children," Jake said. "Let's play nice in the sandbox."

Klages entered the office as Cat laughed over the speaker. Bear's clenched fists shook as he bit his tongue.

"You wanted this fast, so I only hit the basics. Old lady Wendy is clean as a whistle. No criminal record. Worst I could find was a speeding ticket from eight years ago for going sixty-eight in a sixty-five. The cop must've been bored that day. Lives in Warsaw in a house she and her husband bought fifteen years ago after moving from Kansas City where she spent most of her life. House is paid for. Had two children. Byron, who apparently died a long time ago, and Dawson."

"Didn't know she had one that died," Bear said.

"That's it?" Jake asked. "Not exactly helpful."

"Well, there wasn't much to find. Only other thing I was able to track down was through a property records search. She has another property in Benton County she and her husband bought ten years before moving there. It's called the Last Chance Ranch on the innovatively named Last Chance Road. Maybe a little over a hundred acres."

"I think I know the place," Bear said. "East of town. Duran Creek runs along the border of the property."

"I'll keep digging," Cat said. "Jake, I'll send you my bill after applying my friends and family discount."

"Bear's paying for this one," Jake said.

"In that case, I'm doubling my fee."

The call ended before Bear could jump through the phone.

"I fuckin' hate that guy," Bear growled. "I know he's great at getting you intel, but I'd love to find his basement lair in his mom's house so I could pay him a painful visit."

"That's why I don't tell you these things. You know where this place is?"

Klages stepped up. "I do. My old man worked there for a year or so back when I was in high school, because he couldn't find a job anywhere else around town. Judging from his appearance when he came home, it was the worst year of his life. He said it's called Last Chance because if you worked there, you were down to your last chance. I don't think it's been a working ranch for a long time."

"You remember anything?"

"Not much. He didn't like to talk about it. Came home smelling like cow shit. My mom and I took him lunch there one time. I remember a house and a barn and that's it. Pull it up on Google Earth."

Bear squinted. "Google what?"

Klages sighed. "Earth. Good Lord, Bear. Let me at your computer."

As she clicked away on the keyboard, Bear craned to Jake and whispered, "I know Google. You know what Google Earth is?"

"It's like a virtual globe using satellite images. You can type in an address and get a real picture of the area you can zoom in on. I use it on occasion to scout a place and get a lay of the land. It's not live. I think the average date of the images is like three years."

Klages pulled up the website, typed in Warsaw, and the Earth image zoomed into their town. "If you zoom in enough, it'll tell you the date of the image in the lower left corner."

Bear leaned in. "Whoa. That's cool as hell."

Klages scrolled to the east, using the wheel on the mouse to blow up the image a bit. After some back and forth, and fighting Bear's guidance on where to look, she eventually found what she searched for.

"Here you go," she said. "This long access road is the one way in or out. There's the house and a barn. You ever been out there, Bear?"

"Nope. Heard of it but never been there. No vehicles showing. How old is this image?"

Klages pointed to the bottom of the screen. "May of last year. Pretty recent actually."

"Amazing. You learn somethin' new every day." Bear stepped back from the computer. "Wendy ever show up?"

"Not yet and she's not answering her home phone or cell," Klages said.

"I'm worried," Bear said. "Something doesn't smell right. Klages, take a drive out to her house. Jake and I will drive out to Last Chance and see if she's there."

"I'm on it," Klages replied, hopping up from her seat.

Bear grabbed his jacket and led the way out of the office. They exited the building to a darkening afternoon sky as deep purple storm clouds rolled in from the south. Thunder rumbled in the distance.

"Mother Nature's gonna piss all over us in a little while," Bear said as he climbed into his truck.

Jake settled in the passenger seat. "I just hope she doesn't poke the bear."

Bear cringed. "Jesus, you're right. That does sound corny."

CHAPTER FORTY-TWO

Rebekka pressed against the cinderblock wall of her cell, peering at the man sitting in the corner. His shoulders shook as he buried his face in his hands. She noticed the discoloration of the floor, like newly poured concrete and wondered what was buried there. Maybe he was like John Wick and buried the tools of his trade he didn't think he'd need anymore. The hammer he'd been carrying around for the last few hours definitely worried her. She waited for him to advance and bury it in her skull.

One thing she knew for sure, she was anxious to get out of this cell. If she made it out of this nightmare alive, she'd never do anything with even the most remote possibility of landing her in a legitimate prison. She couldn't take it. She'd go insane. If she escaped out of here, she would get her act together. *If* she escaped.

Her mother used to tell her good things came to those who wait. This psychopath had even said the same thing to her at one point. *Fuck that.* Death came to those who wait. She'd been calling to Chloe in the next cell, praying for an answer but it wasn't coming. She'd waited and look where it landed her. It was time to go on offense, because she wasn't going to get away sitting behind cinderblocks and electrified wire barriers. She clenched her stomach and breathed out slowly, taking the nerves out of her voice.

"Daddy?" she asked, trying to sound sweet and innocent. "Are you okay?"

Calling this asshole "Daddy" made her want to vomit, but it had the intended effect.

The man wiped his eyes and twisted on the stool. He offered a tight-lipped smile. "I'm fine, baby doll."

Baby doll. Rebekka's skin crawled. "What's wrong?"

The man groaned to his feet and walked to the wires, the hammer swinging at his side. Rebekka willed herself not to look at it. She focused on the man's defeated face.

"Everything's wrong," he said. "And I don't know if there's any way to fix it anymore."

Rebekka stood, blinking away the dots as the blood rushed to her head. She swayed for a minute, touching the wall for balance. She needed food. *No way to fix it anymore.* If the man gave up, he could leave her here to rot or do something with the hammer to get rid of the loose ends. She shivered at the thought. She needed to keep him on the line, give him hope.

"How about you?" the man asked.

She acted shy and demure. "Just hungry, Daddy. I think my blood sugar's a little low. Think we could get something to eat? I'm a good cook. I could make you something."

She cringed inside, hoping she didn't overplay her hand. She was starving and weak, but she'd run with every last ounce of energy in her body to get away from him, and the only way she could run was to get out of this dungeon cell.

The man studied her before flashing his jagged teeth. "I know you're a good cook. How 'bout a batch of biscuits and gravy like your momma made."

Rebekka didn't have a freaking clue how to make either of those, but she'd promise she could disprove Einstein's theory of relativity if it meant getting out of there.

The man slid the handle of the hammer in the waistband of his jeans and moved to the door. The lock grated back, and Rebekka stepped back as he entered. The man produced the key to her ankle shackle and bent over to unlock it. For the first time, he didn't have the electric remote in his hand. It was progress. Rebekka eyed the dull metal of the hammer head, picturing herself nabbing it from his pants and crushing his demented skull with it. She even twitched her hand in its direction, but the angle was wrong. She'd never get to it in time.

The man stood and grasped her shoulders, peering into her eyes with uncomfortable intensity, almost pride. She considered kneeing him in the balls and running past him, but he'd probably fall back into the open door and block her escape. *Damn it.*

"You are beautiful," he whispered. "Just like your momma."

"Thank you, Daddy."

"Lemme see your hands." The man produced zip tie cuffs from his back pocket and bound her wrists together. Hope snuffed out like a candle. He must have seen the desperation in her eyes. "Baby steps, Chloe. You trust me, don't you?"

"Yes, Daddy."

"Come on, then."

He gently took her by the elbow and guided her out the door of the cell. Rebekka bit her lip to keep from screaming as she cut her eyes to Chloe's open cell door. The woman lay on the bed, one foot over the edge and flat on the ground, arms splayed to the side, and a swollen tongue protruding from her mouth. Her head lolled to the side, her dead eyes aimed in Rebekka's direction. Heat flushed Rebekka's body. He didn't even have the decency to close her fucking eyes.

The man guided her to the stairs. Welcome daylight shined through the opening at the top of the steps like a warm, heavenly glow. Potential freedom. As the man stalked behind her up the steps, she searched for ways to get away from him. No matter how things went down, she made up her mind she wasn't going back into that dungeon alive.

CHAPTER FORTY-THREE

JAKE BOUNCED WITH THE RUTS OF THE ROAD FROM THE passenger seat of Bear's truck as they headed toward the Last Chance Ranch. The navigation system in Bear's truck went haywire and kept changing, telling them to backtrack multiple times. Bear turned it off in frustration and had made a couple of wrong turns along the way but seemed to be heading in a general easterly direction. Maybe. It was hard to tell at that point.

Jake swung his head around at the barren farmland surrounding them. "Where in the hell are we? You have me so turned around with your wrong turns."

Bear wheeled right down a two-lane, north-south road. "It's not my fault the navigation system is a piece of shit."

"I thought you'd been to this place before."

"Klages has been to it before."

"Maybe you should've brought her instead of me."

Bear shot Jake a sideways glare. "Good Lord Almighty. You gonna bitch and moan the whole way?"

"I'm bitching because you're jerkin' your truck all over Benton County, and it's making me car sick."

Bear swerved to avoid a pothole hard enough to spill Jake against the passenger door of the truck. "Can I get you a Dramamine pill, pumpkin? Think we're on the right road now. How's Daisy doing?"

Jake straightened himself in the seat. "Seems to be good. We had breakfast together this morning. Seemed in pretty good spirits."

"She say anything else about the shooting at her house?"

"She hoped I killed whoever killed the Wilkinsons and took her mother."

"Jesus, that's her in pretty good spirits? That's dark."

"Maggie and Connor both took to her quick. Halle should be back from Lincoln by now. She's in good hands."

Bear chewed the bristles of his beard. "I hope Wendy's at this ranch place. If she's not, I'm gonna start to worry. Something isn't adding up right. Why would she lie about being at the Wilkinsons' around the time they were shot and then not even ask what happened to them?"

"Because she had something to do with it?"

Bear's face crunched. "See, that makes sense from someone who doesn't know her. If I were you, I'd think the same thing. But I've worked with this woman every day for the last five years. I can't get there."

Jake only talked to Wendy the one time. She seemed like a nice older lady, but facts were facts. "When you have eliminated all which is impossible, then whatever remains, however improbable, must be the truth."

Bear huffed. "You're quoting *Star Trek* now?"

"*Star Trek*? That's Sherlock Holmes."

"Bullshit. It's Spock. He said it in the remake they did with that Zachary Quinto guy. Just watched it the other night."

Jake pressed a thumb to his forehead. "Is it possible Spock was quoting Arthur Conan Doyle?"

"Who's that?"

Jake sighed. "Never mind. And great...here's another dead end."

The road ended a hundred yards ahead with a couple of molding hay bales stacked across the road. To their right was a shell of a barn and a rotting fence along the roadway. Jake did what he should've done in the first place and pulled up Google Earth on his phone. He zoomed in on their area and showed Bear.

"Crap," Bear said, studying the map. "I should've turned right instead of left at the last junction. I was close."

"Close only counts in horseshoes and hand grenades."

They reached the junction and continued straight in the direction they should have gone in the first place. After two hundred yards, they turned back east down a narrow, dusty road with patches of weeds growing in a stripe down the middle.

Jake peered through the thinning trees and spotted a house in the distance. He hoped this panned into something. If it didn't, he wasn't sure what they were going to do.

"How do you know Sherlock Holmes said that quote?" Bear asked.

"Because I read the book. We had to in Mr. Holcomb's English class our senior year, remember?

You did a whole presentation on it in front of the whole class."

Bear blinked. "I did? I didn't realize I was that learned in literature."

Jake laughed. "That's learn-*ed*. Not learned."

"See? This is why nobody likes hanging around with you."

CHAPTER FORTY-FOUR

DESPITE THE FACT HER HANDS WERE BOUND BY PLASTIC ZIP ties and a murderous maniac had her by the elbow, once the afternoon sun kissed Rebekka's face, she felt free. She stopped, her eyes pinched against the glare, tilted her head back and gulped in a cool lungful of the Ozark air. It never smelled sweeter. The sunshine was brief before it disappeared behind a bank of dark clouds.

Her eyes took in her surroundings. The barn they'd just walked out of was tall, with peeling red paint accentuated by white trim and a hint of gasoline and oil. A white-sided ranch home sat across a wide, graveled drive where a dark sedan parked. In front of the house, a sprawling expanse of grass led downhill toward a line of trees. The sweetness of the air dissipated as she realized they were out in the middle of nowhere. She could probably detonate a stick of dynamite, and nobody would hear. If she escaped, it would be a lot of running. A lot.

"Come on," Merle said. "I want to show you something before we eat."

He wrapped his fingers around her elbow and gently guided her down the gravel drive. Her eyes followed the road as it disappeared into the trees. Patches of the road were visible through the foliage as it turned on the other side and followed the tree line.

Can I wrench my arm away and make a run for it before he clocks me with the hammer?

How far is it to a house, a main road, town?

If she ran, she'd be running for a long time, and she hadn't run more than a hundred yards in one stretch since high school. If she didn't make it, he'd kill her. She'd seen how he'd snapped Chloe 1's neck like a twig when he was angry. Fighting back the urge to take off, she decided to wait and see how this played out.

Thirty yards down the drive, a stone bench sat in front of a lone, massive oak tree. Their feet waded through the long grass, and she shivered as the fall breeze cut through her. She opened her senses, looking, listening, and smelling for any signs of life other than this place. Nothing but the scurry of animals in the leaves and the earthy tones of the Ozarks.

The man stopped in front of the bench and guided her gently to the seat. His misty eyes locked on the base of the tree. Rebekka had a hint of why they were there but waited for the man to talk.

"We buried you here on a Saturday," he said. "Your mom put you in that green dress you hated that she loved." He stared Rebekka in the eyes. "I asked her why she'd put you in something for eternity you hated, but she told me to do it and shut up about it. I felt bad."

"I don't mind it, Daddy," Rebekka said. "I appreciate you stickin' up for me."

"That's what daddies do," the man replied, patting her on the hand. "I'm sorry about the fight that night and the things I said, but you gotta know how scared we were for you, Chloe."

Rebekka drew in a breath. *Keep playing the part.* "It's okay, Daddy. I gave you reason to be scared."

Merle sniffed and cast his eyes on the ground. "You stormed out with the money you took from my wallet and tore out of this driveway so fast. Did you even know I ran after you?"

"No, I didn't."

"I chased your car down this driveway and stopped right at this here tree and watched your taillights disappear 'round the corner. I bet I stood here for an hour, waiting for you to come back. Prayin' you'd come back."

The man released Rebekka's hand, and she fought off an audible sigh of relief. When he touched her, she wanted to scream. She wanted to dig her claws into this murderer's face, to grab the hammer and bash his skull with it. She didn't want to be Chloe. She'd rather be dead in that cell next to the other girl. But, if she wanted another chance at life, to live it this time, to see her family and friends again, she'd have to play along.

"I stood here like an idiot and watched you leave. Next time I saw you, you were layin' on the rocks out by the dam with the needle still stuck in your arm and the strangest smile on your face. It was like you was at peace, finally."

Rebekka looked down the hill, and in the distance, she noticed a plume of dust.

A moving plume.

A couple hundred yards away and moving in this direction.

Her heart pounded. *Should I make a run for it?* She bet she could beat him to whatever vehicle headed down the road toward them. Her legs tensed to go for it, but she stopped. *What if it was one of his accomplices?* She'd won his confidence and that would blow it. *Goddamn it. What should I do? Buy time.*

"And so you brought me here, back home?" she asked.

The man raised his gaze to the overhead branches. "You loved this tree. You used to sit here and read and—"

The man stopped and leaped to his feet, his eyes tracking the plume heading their way. His beady eyes darted from the plume back to the house, his hand white-knuckling the hammer. Rebekka tensed. He obviously wasn't expecting anyone. If she was going to make a run for it, now would be the time.

Lines creased the man's brow. "Who is that?"

Rebekka edged away, sliding along the stone bench. Her heart raced and palms grew slick as she counted down. Three. Two. One.

Jumping to her feet she ran, her clasped hands bound in front of her. Stumbling over a root of the tree, she crossed the driveway, hope burning in her chest. She imagined meeting the car as it cruised down the road toward them, trying to figure out what she'd say to impart the danger of the situation, wondering if she'd be able to get out anything intelligible at all.

"Chloe," the man yelled.

His feet slammed into the gravel behind her. She willed her legs to pump faster, but his steps grew close.

Tears blurred her vision and she stumbled and screamed and ran, begging for help from anyone. His hand thudded against her back. The gravel bit first into her palms and then her face as it slammed into the ground. Then blackness and silence.

CHAPTER FORTY-FIVE

BEAR SLAMMED ON THE BRAKES AND YELLED OUT A strange mashup of curse words as the deer leaped from the tree line and darted across the road. The truck slid along the dirt and slammed into the animal's body, sending it flying ahead into a ditch along the side of the road.

Jake unbuckled his seatbelt and opened his door, the hinges uttering a high-pitched screech. He met Bear at the front of the truck as they examined the damage. The front quarter panel of the truck was bashed in, along with a broken headlight.

"Stupid deer. Thank God for my cat-like reflexes," Bear said.

"Or what? You would've hit it?"

"Or it might've ended up in your lap. Let's go check it and make sure it's dead."

As they walked, Jake scoped the road and peered through the line of trees toward the Last Chance Ranch. He stopped and squinted, moving his head back and forth as he thought he saw flashes of white moving in the distance. He took a few steps further down the road but saw nothing else.

Bear stood at the side of the road, looking down into the ditch. The dead doe lay in a shallow puddle of water, neck twisted unnaturally, and a bloody track down its face. "Why'd you have to go and do somethin' stupid like run in front of my truck?"

"We spooked her. They get confused on which way to run when they're scared."

Bear slowly craned his neck toward Jake. "No shit, Sherlock. It was a rhetorical question to the deer."

"That's two Sherlock Holmes references in less than twenty minutes. That has to be some kind of record."

"At least my reference made sense in the context of the situation."

Bear's cell rang and he slipped it from his pocket. He listened for a minute, said thanks, and clicked off.

"Klages," he said as he turned back toward the truck. "No sign of Wendy or her car at her house. Still not answering her cell either."

"The more I hear, the more I think she's involved in this," Jake said.

"I hope there's an explanation, but I gotta agree with you, partner."

Jake glanced back toward the tree line across the road. Patches of the house and barn flickered between the trees. He saw something, didn't he? Could've been another deer, but it didn't feel that way. His hand dropped to his waist and the comforting grip of his Sig Sauer against his hand.

Bear noted Jake's hand on his gun, and he mimicked the motion. "What? What do you see?"

Jake scanned the tree line one more time and let his hand drop. "Nothin'. Let's get to the house."

They hopped back in Bear's truck and a minute later made the turn onto Last Chance Road.

CHAPTER FORTY-SIX

MERLE LUMBERED UP THE DRIVEWAY WITH AN unconscious Rebekka over his shoulder. Despite her petite size, his heart pounded and legs burned from the effort. The years and mileage were beginning to take a toll on his body. He risked a peek over his shoulder and didn't see the plume of dust. His brain registered the heavy thump and the skid of tires on dirt right before he'd clocked the girl between the shoulder blades. Whatever happened bought him the precious minutes he needed to get her back to the barn.

The barn door bounced in his vision as he ran toward it, and cold drops of rain began to fall. An icy fist had closed over his heart the second she ran from the bench. It was all an act. His face flushed with rage and shame. Shame she'd duped him and rage she would dare to play with his love for Chloe to save herself. Oh, she would pay for that deception as soon as he got rid of whoever headed their way.

The house loomed to his left as gravel popped behind him. He shot a glance over his shoulder and spotted a black truck making the turn around the tree line. *Damn.* He wouldn't make it to the barn without being seen. He scampered around the sedan to the side of the house, throwing open the door with his free hand, struggling with the dead weight in his arms, bouncing off the wood-paneled walls of the dim, narrow hallway.

"Momma!" he yelled.

By the time he reached the living room, Wendy stood by her chair, one hand on the back and the other covering her horrified mouth as she realized what Merle carried over his shoulder.

"Oh, Merle," she choked, tears welling up in her eyes. "Not again. What have you done this time?"

"We don't have time for this, Momma. Someone's here. They're pulling up the driveway now."

Wendy moved to the bay window, jerking the cord for the blinds and closing them. "It's the sheriff. Oh God help us, it's Bear. Who is she and why'd you bring her here?"

"You know damn well who it is," Merle said, shifting Rebekka. Now wasn't the time for her to pull her selective memory act. "I didn't have time to get back to the barn before your boss showed up. What do I do? Oh Lord have mercy. Maybe this is it. Maybe I should give up."

Wendy took two steps toward him and slapped Merle across the cheek. It had been a while since she'd struck him like that. "No. I can't lose you. I can't. You've been keeping her in the barn?"

Merle nodded.

Wendy's face went ashen. "I thought we were done with this foolishness."

Wendy had brought several girls to Merle over the years. But, after Charlene and one other girl, Wendy pledged to stop, to help save him that one last time and get rid of the evidence. She'd taken Charlene's credit card and ran up charges on the way to St. Louis to create a feasible trail when the police were questioning Merle. She'd helped him bury the first one and protect him from any evidence that might point in his direction.

"I thought she was the last one, I swear," he said. "We need to move, Momma."

Her bottom lip trembled. "Damn it, Merle. Are there others in the cellar?"

Before he could answer, the sound of Bear's truck pulled up. Merle's heart stopped, and their eyes shot wide. Wendy pulled the blinds back a hair and peered to the front before returning to her son.

"Quick," she said, shoving him back the way he came. "That Caldwell guy is with Bear. Get to the barn without them seeing you. Stay there until I get rid of them."

"Thank you, Momma. I don't know what I'd do without you."

"Momma will take care of everything. Now scoot."

Wendy waited until the back door squeaked open and clicked shut. She dried her sweaty palms on her denim shirt, pasted on a smile, and waited for the doorbell.

CHAPTER FORTY-SEVEN

JAKE AND BEAR TURNED UP A RUTTED INCLINE TOWARD the Last Chance Ranch and a barn. They passed a massive oak tree with a bench in front of it in a clearing. Rain dotted the windshield as they rolled closer to the house. Straight ahead, in between the ranch and a good-sized red barn sat a black Ford Taurus.

"There's Wendy's car," Bear said. "Thank God. I was getting worried."

They pulled in front of the house and climbed out. Bear headed around the front of the truck and walked up a set of steps leading to the porch. Jake stopped, nostrils flaring as his eyes scanned the area.

"What're you doing?" Bear asked.

Jake did a slow full circle turn. "Something doesn't smell right. My Spidey sense is tingling."

"You get bit by a radioactive spider and not tell me?"

"You know what I mean. Something's off, man. I have a weird feeling."

"Maybe it's because you're standing there getting

wet. At least step up on the covered porch while you sort through your sensations."

Jake followed Bear onto the porch, and they stood on either side of a white front door. Bear reached out and pressed the doorbell. Jake's eyes swept over the landscape. The barn was hidden by the house from their vantage point, so he saw nothing but trees and grass that needed cutting.

Bear's eyes settled on Jake. "I think you're bein' paranoid, but I learned a long time ago to listen to that sixth sense of yours. I'll keep my eyes peeled." Bear rang the bell again. "Assuming she answers the freaking door."

Thirty seconds later, Wendy Blackwell opened the door, eyes wide with surprise. "Bear? Jake? What on earth brings you out here?"

"Everybody and their dog has been trying to get ahold of you," Bear said. "You didn't come back to work yesterday. No answer at your house or on your cell."

"Well, I get terrible cell service out here. Been trying to find a better provider."

They stood in awkward silence staring at each other for a moment.

Bear pointed to the interior of the house. "Can we come in for a minute?"

Crimson crawled up the folds of Wendy's neck. "Oh goodness, where are my manners? Of course, come in."

Bear entered and Jake crossed the threshold as his cell vibrated. He checked the ID—Klages. Jake held up the phone and a finger to Bear and Wendy and stepped back onto the porch.

"What's up, Klages?"

"You with Bear?" she asked.

"We just got to the Last Chance Ranch. Place seems aptly named. Wendy's here."

"Well, that's one mystery solved. You remember the physical similarities between this Rebekka Hammill and the Eve Maxwell girl that's missing from Springfield?"

"We said they could be sisters. Why?"

"So I pulled the missing person's reports from the surrounding counties and checked girls who looked similar to those two."

"And?"

"I found a third girl who looks eerily like the others. Harley Reese, twenty-two years old from Hermitage."

Hermitage was a town of six hundred people in Hickory County to the south of Benton County near Pomme de Terre Lake. Jake traveled through there last year chasing after a bail jumper. "I know the area. When did she go missing?"

"Six months ago. I made a call to the Hickory County Sheriff's Office, and they called me back a few minutes ago. Take a guess where Harley was last seen?"

Jake's arm hair tingled. "An AA meeting."

"Bingo. That alone should land me on the medal's podium."

Jake could tell she had something else. Her excitement radiated through the phone and Klages didn't get excited much. "You going for the gold?"

"I got it locked. I reached out to the head of the Pomme de Terre AA chapter down there and he remembers a big guy with a face tattoo on his arm. He didn't remember the guy's name, but he remembered the man at the meeting. Said he creeped everyone out, like someone took a ball-peen hammer to his teeth."

Jake allowed himself a fist pump. They were closing in on Merle Wade. Now he just needed a breadcrumb on where the guy was. "Good work, Ronda. You get anywhere on tracking down the truck?"

"Wendy was doing that. I just walked by her desk and the list I gave her is still sitting there. Ask her while you're there. I gotta fly. A 911 call came in about a fight at the Roadhouse, but I'll dig into the truck when I get back."

"Little early in the day for a Roadhouse fight, don't you think?"

"It's a Saturday afternoon. Some of these guys started drinking when they hit the lake before sunup."

"Be careful. I'll let you know if we find out anything here."

Jake clicked off. As he shoved his phone in his pocket, it occurred to him that his cell phone reception was just fine. Wendy said she got terrible service, which was why she didn't answer Bear's calls. Maybe they had different carriers, but as he headed inside the house, the feeling that something was off about this place not only hadn't left, it grew stronger.

CHAPTER FORTY-EIGHT

JAKE ENTERED THE HOUSE AND FOUND BEAR SITTING ON A floral couch from the seventies, sipping coffee while Wendy served him cookies off a chipped white platter. The living room walls were striped with vertical wood panels and decorated with old paintings of country scenery, complete with snow-crusted fields, mountain streams, and deer grazing under a rising sun. A muted television with some soap opera played near a gas fireplace with fake logs surrounded by bookshelves with paperback novels and a handful of pictures.

If Wendy owned a house in town, why was she here, and why did the place look so lived in? Jake scanned the décor, and it didn't match what he envisioned Wendy's home to be. It was dated, almost masculine.

"Would you like some coffee, Jake?" she asked.

Jake waved her off. "No thank you."

"It's no bother," Wendy said. "I'll go get you a cup. Be right back."

"No, really I—"

"Don't bother," Bear said, his voice low. "I said the

same thing, but she got it for me anyway."

"How're the cookies?"

Bear see-sawed his hand. Jake decided to pass on the calories.

"Who was on the phone?"

"Klages," Jake said. "She said she found—"

He cut himself off as Wendy reentered with a steaming mug which said *I drink coffee for your protection* on the side. Wendy sat in a La-Z-Boy by the window. Jake crossed the room and stood by the fireplace. He took a sip of the coffee, resisted spitting out the burnt-tasting liquid, and set the mug on a coaster on the bookshelf.

Wendy brushed phantom wrinkles from her legs. "What brings you boys out here today?"

"I was worried," Bear said, wiping cookie crumbs from his fingers. "You never came in the office, and nobody could get hold of you. You didn't follow up on tracking the trucks like I asked, which isn't like you. Thought it was worth a visit to check on you."

Her upper lip twitched. "Well, isn't that sweet of you. How'd you find me? I don't think I ever mentioned this place."

They couldn't very well come out and say they'd done a property search on her, because she seemed like she might be up to something shady.

Bear shot a glance to Jake. "I don't know. You must've said something at some point. Otherwise, I wouldn't have known to come out here. Everything's fine?"

Her lips disappeared for a beat. "Well, to tell you the truth, I told you I wasn't feeling well after I checked in on my dog. I ran out of my medicine at home, and I keep extra here. I decided to stay and sleep here."

That was definitely a lie. Good thing Wendy didn't play poker. But why was she lying? Jake's eyes drifted over the bookshelves. A lot of Louis L'Amour westerns, some Christian books, and photos in gold frames.

"How long you had this place?" Bear asked. "I'm surprised you never talk about it. Didn't picture you for a rancher."

"My husband and I bought this place years ago. Harold wanted land for the longest time, but we couldn't afford it. We came into a little money once his father passed. Harold knew the man who was selling this place. He was in dire financial straits, and my husband negotiated a good deal. We never worked it as a ranch. Just liked the property and the setting."

Jake's eyes settled on a picture of Wendy and an older man with a face lined with deep cracks dressed in a flannel shirt, blue jeans, and a cowboy hat. The picture was taken in front of the house. Neither Wendy nor her husband looked like they wanted to be in the photo.

"Is this Harold?" Jake asked.

"Not a good picture of us, I'm afraid." Her eyes flicked to the bookshelf on the other side of the fireplace and darted back to the coffee table.

Bear shifted to the edge of the sofa and set his coffee on the table in front of him. "Listen, Wendy. You said you dropped Daisy Everleigh at the Wilkinsons' yesterday morning, correct?"

"I did. Around noon," she said, her fingers tapping the side of her cup. "I'd stopped by Tanya Blanton's house to say hello and drop off some homemade soup. Poor thing isn't feeling well. On my way back, I saw little Daisy walking down the road by herself. Her grandmother and I were such dear friends, so I offered Daisy a ride back to the Wilkinsons'. Why?"

"And that was the only time you were at the Wilkinsons' yesterday?"

"Umm...yes. After I dropped her off, I came into work and was with you all day."

"What about after work? You said you had to go check on your dog before you could come back in and run down possible leads on the truck the guy in the tent spotted."

Wendy's eyes shot to the ceiling, a tell that she searched for an answer. "Let's see. I let Muffin outside for a few minutes and made a sandwich."

"Even though you weren't feeling well?" Jake asked.

Her voice was flat as the plains. "I thought a little food might settle my stomach."

"Before you came back out here for your medicine."

"That's right."

Bear piped in. "But you didn't come back to the office to run the trucks."

The sweet grandmotherly visage disappeared for a heartbeat before Wendy forced a smile. "I have a computer at home. I thought I'd do the checks there rather than drive all the way into the office."

Jake bit his lip. Klages said the list sat on Wendy's desk. He supposed she could've made a copy of it, but he doubted it. She lied through her teeth, but he didn't know why. Something bubbled below the surface of her demeanor, maybe the real Wendy waiting to come out. He was tempted to jump in and ask her about it, but Bear was good at this. Best to let him continue the line of questioning.

Jake slid over toward the bookcase on the opposite

side of the fireplace to check another framed photograph. It was another picture of Wendy and her husband on a beach somewhere with red drinks in long glasses with umbrellas sticking out of the top. They looked marginally happier in this picture than the one in front of the house.

"And you didn't go back to the Wilkinsons'?" Bear asked.

Wendy's face reddened. "I told you I didn't. Why are you asking me these questions? I feel like I'm being interrogated."

"I'm asking you because the Wilkinsons are dead, Wendy. Someone went into their house and shot them last night."

Wendy threw a hand over her mouth. "Oh no. That's terrible. I saw Darla Wilkinson when I dropped off Daisy. She was such a nice woman. Who could've done such a thing?"

"That's what we're trying to figure out," Bear said. "The thing is someone spotted your car a house down from the Wilkinsons' around the time they were shot. Can you explain that? Anyone else have access to your car?"

"Just me. There has to be some sort of mistake. I never went back there." She sat for a moment before her mouth dropped open and fire flared in her eyes. "Wait just one minute, Sheriff James Parley. You don't think I—"

"I'm askin' the questions that have to be asked. You know how this works."

"Your witness must be mistaken."

Jake set the beach photo back on the bookshelf. As he did, the dim light shining through the blinds revealed a bare spot in a thin layer of dust. The dragged lines in the dust swept toward the stack of books on the shelf. The bare spot was the approximate size of a photo frame.

"He had the license plate number and everything, Wendy," Bear said. "I'm trying to figure out how your car ended up outside of a murder scene."

Wendy opened her mouth before slamming it shut again.

Jake poked through the books and found a silver framed photograph jammed in between some hardbacks. It was a family shot. Wendy stood in front of the large oak tree out front, but the husband wasn't there. She appeared a little older, a little wider than the shot on the other side of the room. Next to her was a red-haired woman with her arm around a girl in her late teens, chunky with straight auburn hair and a frown on her round face. *Why put the picture frame in with the books?*

"Well, I don't know how it got there," Wendy said at Jake's back. "But I swear I didn't go back to the Wilkinsons'."

Next to the redhead and the scowling girl in the picture was a man. A big man with a widow's peak and bad teeth. Jake's breath caught.

The bare spot in the dust on the shelf.

The photo hastily jammed between books where nobody would see it.

Now Jake knew why.

Plastered on the man's arm in the photo was a tattoo.

A tattoo of a face on his bicep.

CHAPTER FORTY-NINE

Rebekka tried to blink away the fog shrouding her brain. Pain radiated from between her shoulder blades as she bounced while being carried. Cold rain pelted her face. The light seeping through her eyelids dimmed, and the scent of coffee swirled around her as the bouncing stopped. Muffled voices...a female and the man.

She faded out and was thrust back to her old room in her parents' house, leaning against the wall next to the door as their muffled shouts permeated the floorboards. The argument was about her. It was always her. Not about her perfect older brother who she would never match up to. Her skin itching, her soul gnawing as she held the dripping needle in her left hand and spread the toes of her bare foot with her right. The only thing that made the world bearable was inside the syringe. She pierced her skin with the needle as shouts from below reached their crescendo.

Moving again. Her eyes opened to slits, exposing dirt, gravel, weeds, and moving legs clad in denim. A black car slipped by on her right. She tried to move her head to track it before nausea bubbled up, and she slammed her eyes closed again.

She was being carried. Arms were locked around the back of her legs, bounding her tight. A bulbous shoulder pressing into her stomach as her mind raced to recall how she'd gotten here. It flashed like pictures revealed in a strobe light—the man, the tire iron, the dungeon, Chloe's dead stare, the oak tree, and the plume of dust. The plume of dust. Someone coming. That's why she'd run.

Forcing her eyes open, she raised her head and spotted the pickup in front of the house. A truck she'd never seen before, dust coating the sides. She'd been unsure if the dust plume had been friend or foe. That's right. That's when she ran, and that's when the man chased her.

She still didn't know if the truck was from a friend or not, but her brain registered where she was being carried. The barn. The dungeon. Chloe 1's snapped neck echoed. Chloe 2's pale dead face and purple, swollen tongue appeared. Only this time, Rebekka saw her own reflection lying dead in the cell.

There'd been many a time over the last several months before the kidnapping when she wasn't sure if she wanted to live anymore. She'd stood on the edges of bridges and high rooftops, a breath away from jumping into the abyss before she'd chickened out. Another time with a gun in her mouth at her own hand before worries surfaced about blowing half her face off and living through it. And that last night when she woke with cum-stained thighs in an alley she had no recollection of going to, eyeballing the broken bottle neck on the ground next to the dumpster, within reach. A way out—it was "get her shit together or slit her throat with the broken glass."

But now the will to live boiled inside her. A scream worked its way up her throat as she was jostled across the driveway toward the barn. It stuck in her throat and wouldn't come. She willed her leaden arms to move, to fight. The man quickened his pace at her movement. Around his waist, she watched the red of the barn drawing close, mere feet away, and she knew if he secured her inside, she was dead.

The image of her lying dead in her cell played in front of her eyes, purple rings around her throat from where the man strangled the life from her. Rebekka saw her own face raise up and stare at her, mouthing the word *scream*. *Scream*. *Scream*.

And before the man closed the barn door, that's what she did.

CHAPTER FIFTY

As rain tapped the front bay window, Jake picked up the family photograph and drew it close. Besides the man with the face tattoo on his arm, the young woman in the picture appeared familiar, though he was sure he hadn't seen her before in his life. But she had a certain look. It took a moment for him to realize where he'd seen that look before. He'd seen it in Rebekka Hammill, and he'd seen it in Sharla Babin. The same with Eve Maxwell from Springfield and, according to Klages, Harley Reese from Hermitage. They could be sisters. If the tattoo man was Merle, Jake had a good guess who the other two were.

"Hey Wendy," Jake said, stepping toward her and showing her the picture. "Who is this with you and your husband?"

Wendy's face drooped. "That's my son, Merle, his wife Charlene, and my granddaughter. Chloe."

A heat came over Jake's face as his mouth went dry.

Merle. Merle Wade is her freaking son? If the gauge needle of suspicion wavered when he and Bear pulled up Last Chance Road, it was pegged to the right now with smoke emanating from the instrumentation panel. Merle Wade was the man Dewayne said frequented the AA meeting where Rebekka Hammill was last seen and drove a light-colored truck that happened to be spotted outside Sharla Babin's house the night she disappeared. Jake wanted to go into a full-court press, but he wanted to alert Bear, make sure they were on the same track.

Jake walked the picture to Bear and pressed his finger against the glass on Merle's tattooed arm. "Looks like a guy we went to high school with, doesn't it?"

Bear's hard eyes met Jake's. "Yeah. It does."

"They live around here?" Jake asked.

"St. Louis originally where I grew up," Wendy said, her voice trembling a hair. "Merle's dad ran off when Merle was six and I married Harold a couple of years later. We tried to get Merle to take the Blackwell name, but he didn't want to do it."

Jake wasn't interested in her life story and tried to jump in and cut her off, but Wendy kept on rolling.

"The Wade name carried a lot of baggage in the area where Merle grew up," she continued. "He married Charlene against my advice, and they moved to Clinton. Things were good for them for a spell until Chloe hit high school. Then everything went bad."

Bear slid to the edge of the couch. "I thought your son's name was Dawson."

"Dawson Merle Wade. We called him Merle after his grandfather." Her lip curled a twitch. "As time passed, Merle and his grandfather had a parting of the ways. My boy grew to hate the name and went by Dawson. But *she* didn't like it because she had a bad relationship a long time ago with a boy named Dawson. So, he switched back to Merle."

"She?"

"Charlene. His wife...ex-wife, whatever you want to call her."

The sweet cotton candy of her demeanor changed to barbed wire when she talked about Charlene. The curled upper lip, the pulsing temple, the clenched fists —there was zero love lost between the two. Jake and Bear knew Charlene had disappeared, and their daughter Chloe had overdosed, but Wendy didn't know they knew it, so they played it cool.

"Ex-wife? When did they divorce?" Jake asked.

Wendy wrang her hands, beads of sweat dotting her brow. "Chloe got into drugs. Her favorite was heroin. She overdosed a couple of years ago and it wrecked Merle. Absolutely devastated him. Charlene blamed him for some reason and the fighting grew worse. She forbid him from talking to me. From his own mother, if you can imagine. Then she said she couldn't take it anymore and ran off. Just disappeared and nobody has seen her since. I guess they technically didn't get divorced, but they might as well be."

"And she never contacted Merle again?"

Wendy's shoulders rose and fell, a hangdog look on her face. "I wouldn't know. I haven't talked to him in a long time. After Charlene left, he stopped returning my calls. Like I said, it wrecked him. She and I didn't along. She did everything she could to try and split me and my boy apart. I guess she succeeded because I don't even know where he is."

Jake watched her features, her body language. If she lied about this, she did a better job covering it up than her previous statements. But how could she not know where her son was when he apparently lived in the area? Warsaw wasn't that big. Jake could buy she hadn't talked to him, but to not know his whereabouts seemed unbelievable. But again, how could they broach the subject without giving away Merle was the one and only suspect in the disappearance of these women?

Jake thought of his brother. Nicky with his dimpled smile dead on the dock of their pond with the heroin needle still jabbed in his vein. The image still haunted Jake. "I'm sorry for what happened to your granddaughter. I lost my brother the same way."

She bit her trembling lip. "It's devastating. Was your brother recent?"

"It's been a number of years. That kind of pain doesn't ever go away, but it gets better."

"It hasn't yet for me."

Bear shot a knowing look to Jake before reaching across and laying his hand on hers. "I didn't know any of this, Wendy. I feel awful you've kept it to yourself."

"I didn't want to burden anyone with it. Can we talk later? I'm not feeling well again and would like to lay down."

"Sure thing," Bear said.

Wendy stood and smoothed the wrinkles from her shirt. "Thank you."

Jake glared over Wendy's shoulder to Bear. *Is he going to let this slide until later?*

"One more thing, Wendy," Bear said. "Would you happen to have a number for your son?"

Lines popped on her brow. "What do you need to call him for?"

"Well, we still have the issue of your car being

outside the Wilkinsons' house around the time of their murder. Since you obviously weren't there, someone with access to your car must've taken it. One obvious person would be Merle."

Jake let loose the breath he'd been holding. He should've known Bear wasn't going to let her walk away. Not with the knowledge in their possession.

"But we don't even talk anymore. He doesn't have keys to my house or my car. It couldn't have been him."

Bear patted her on the shoulder. "Probably not. We just need to talk to him and verify his whereabouts at the time of the shooting to check the box."

Wendy's face hardened and her eyes flickered between Jake, Bear, and the photograph of Merle. "You think he did all this, don't you?"

"We need to talk to him," Bear said. "Only talk."

"Merle wouldn't have anything to do with this. He's a good boy. A grieving father."

"Then let us talk to him. We can check the box and move on."

Wendy's hard eyes bore holes in the two of them. "I think I have it in a drawer over here. Though I'm not sure what good it will do. He hasn't answered it in forever. At least when *I've* called."

She stomped across the room to the bookshelves and rooted around the embedded drawers.

Jake blocked her view of Bear with his back and whispered, "This is the fucking guy. I don't buy for a second she doesn't know where he is."

"Neither do I," Bear whispered back. "We just have to—"

A scream split the air. A woman's scream, coming

from the driveway. Merle. Merle had someone here. It felt right.

Jake spun around to run toward the door, his hand on his holstered Sig Sauer.

Wendy faced them with a gun in her hands, arms extended and pointed in their direction. "Oh dear. Now I'm afraid we have a mess. Don't move."

CHAPTER FIFTY-ONE

BEAR TOOK A STEP AWAY FROM JAKE TO PROVIDE separation. "Wendy, what the hell are you doing?"

Wendy jabbed the Glock in his direction, her finger on the trigger. "You're not taking my boy away from me."

Bear raised his hands. "Who said anything about taking him from you? Besides, you said you hadn't talked to him in years."

"I lied. What else could I do? You can't have him. He's all I have left." Wendy's bottom lip shook. "Don't make me kill you both. I don't want to, but I'll do it if I have to."

Jake rested his hand on the Sig in his waist holster. *Can I pull it out before Wendy's dancing finger puts sufficient pressure on the trigger of the Glock?* He didn't want to put holes in a grandmother, but if it came down to her, or him and Bear, he'd do it in a heartbeat. *Will the ballistics report from the Wilkinson shootings match the gun in Wendy's hands?*

"Stay calm, Wendy," Bear said. "Tell me why we'd take your boy."

She swung the gun between Jake and Bear, causing Jake's nerve endings to fire, adrenaline dumping through his body. Her finger sat on the trigger, but the gun barrel wavered. Fully loaded, the Glock 19 only weighed thirty ounces, but Wendy was old and weak, and the gun was too large for her hands. The longer she tried to hold it up, the more the gun would start to drag her arms down.

"You know why."

Bear showed his palms, his face pained. "We've been friends for a long time, Wendy. Put the gun down and let's talk this through."

She shook her head. "It's not his fault. You can't take him because it's not his fault."

"What's not his fault?"

Her eyes watered, she was losing it. "Charlene. You weren't around. You didn't know her. She was an evil woman. She had it coming with her constant badgering. Nobody could take that mouth of hers forever, and my Merle was a saint for putting up with it as long as he did."

Wendy took a half step forward. The way she handled the gun told Jake she didn't have much experience with one. But, even if she couldn't hit the broadside of a barn if she tried, at this range she could still easily blow a hole in either one of them.

"What happened to Charlene?" Bear asked, his eyes widening as he connected the dots.

"Do you know how hard it is to wash blood from your hands?" Wendy asked, her eyes traveling to her trembling hands. "Do you?"

"I do," Jake said, edging forward an inch at a time. The haunted look on her face as she stared at her hands told him she'd done more than cover for her son. She'd gotten dirty. "You wash and scrub. Then wash and scrub some more until the skin's so raw it hurts to be under the water."

"But it's still there," she whispered.

"Whose blood do you have on your hands, Wendy?" Bear asked.

Tears welled in her eyes. "Darla and Chester Wilkinson."

"You shot them?"

"God help me."

Jake took another half step forward and slipped the Sig from his waist, aiming the barrel at the floor. He was still too far away to make a move. "That blood will always be there, Wendy. Their deaths, whatever part you played in the rest of this, it won't go away. But it doesn't mean you have to add to it. We can fix this. Give us the gun and let's talk."

Her nostrils flared as she jabbed the gun toward Jake's chest. "Get back. Both of you stay away until I figure out what to do."

Jake slid back. As distraught as she was, she could pull the trigger without even realizing it.

"Who was screaming, Wendy?" Bear asked. "What's Merle got himself mixed up with?"

"You know who it is," she said. "I told him to stop. The bitch who gave my little Chloe the poison that killed her deserved to die."

Bear's lips disappeared. "Bethany Sheets. She's the one who supplied Chloe."

Wendy's head jerked up and down. "Merle told me he took care of it, but he wouldn't ever say how. When you found the body Thursday night, I knew it was

Merle that did it. I guess I knew what happened deep down, and I was okay with it. She deserved it. The others didn't."

Jake's breath stopped. "What others?"

Teardrops snaked down her cracked face, a hysterical pitch creeping in her voice. "I told him to stop. That it wasn't going to bring her back. But he wouldn't listen."

Jake thought back to the missing pieces—Oz's tent, the anonymous letter, and the information about the truck. "You scrubbed the information in Sharla's file."

Her shoulders trembled as she fought off sobs. "I didn't want to believe it was Merle, but I wasn't sure, so I shredded those parts of the report. He told me he'd stopped, but I didn't want to take the chance. Oh, dear Jesus, please help me."

"We're trying to help you. You can't fix what you've done, Wendy," Bear said, his voice smooth and soothing. "But you can fix what's going to happen now. Who was screaming?"

She turned toward Bear and the gun barrel spit fire. The gunshot sound hung in the air, split by Bear's grunting as he dropped to the couch, clutching his leg. A blossoming crimson stain spread over his khaki pants.

The gun dropped to her side. "Oh Lord, what have I done? Bear, are you okay? I'm so sorry. I didn't mean to."

"Give me the gun," Jake said, his Sig aimed at her heart, ready to shoot if she twitched another muscle.

Bear gritted his teeth. "Give Jake the gun, Wendy, before anything else happens."

"This is my fault," she sobbed. "I raised a monster. I'm a miserable disgrace of a mother."

"Give me the gun, Wendy," Jake said, edging

forward, his hand extended. "Come on. You'll make it through this."

"I can't take losing another child. I'll be all alone," she cried. "I'll have nothing."

Jake slid his finger over the trigger and took another half step forward. Almost within reach. "Just give me the gun. You'll be okay."

"I'll be okay?" Wendy asked, her eyes wide. "You really believe that?"

"I do."

Her plump shoulders rose and fell. "Well, I don't."

The hair on the back of Jake's neck stood. "Wendy, don't—"

"I'm sorry, Bear," she said, a sad smile creeping on her face. She jerked the Glock to her temple and pulled the trigger, splattering the bookshelf with gore before crashing to the floor.

CHAPTER FIFTY-TWO

MERLE WASTED SIXTY SECONDS FROZEN BY INDECISION. Sixty seconds he couldn't spare, flicking his attention between the truck and the door to the cellar. He could throw the girl in the truck and make a run for it. But how far would he get? Or he could lock her in her cell again, which would free him to deal with the two interlopers. *Maybe they didn't hear her scream. Maybe they'd ask a few questions and leave.* If they didn't leave, it would be two against one, and he had home field advantage.

A minute later, Merle slammed the door on Rebekka's cell, not bothering to hook her to the ankle bracelet. With the wires activated, she wouldn't be able to get out of the cell, anyway. After she screamed, he'd slammed her to the ground of the barn and knocked her unconscious.

He checked the panel and made sure the current ran through the wires covering her cell and scanned the empty cells along the wall of the cellar. How did things get this screwed up? Before Chloe died, he'd been a good man. Not a saint, but a hard worker who wasn't afraid to roll up his sleeves. Dedicated to his family even when Charlene made it nearly impossible to do so. Charlene did everything in her power to drive a wedge between him and his momma to the point where the two women in his life couldn't even be in the same room together.

The truth was he blamed Charlene for driving their daughter to the needle. Charlene wrecked Chloe's self-image. She badgered her about her lowlife friends, hounded her about her weight, nitpicked everything Chloe did. Things had to be Charlene's way or no way. He watched Chloe slipping away and he did nothing. Tears welled up in his eyes as the truth dawned on him, he was responsible too. His baby girl had reached out a hand for help, and he'd slapped it away because he was too afraid of his wife to do anything else.

But he could make things right with Rebekka. *Chloe.* She could be his new Chloe. Despite her trying to get away, she could still be his. It would just take more time. He'd have his daughter again without Charlene's meddling. All he needed was Momma making the men go away, and he could escape with the girl.

His head jerked toward the muffled sound of the gunshot.

"Momma?" he whispered.

His brain raced through scenarios, and none of them bode well for him and his plan. Dropping to his knees in front of the workbench along the wall, he fumbled with the padlock combination. He snapped it open as the second shot rang out and his stomach dropped. That couldn't be good. Momma told him people were going to come for him.

Two shots.

Maybe Momma killed the two men to protect him.

He batted the thought away. She killed the Wilkinsons for him, but they were just an ordinary older couple. There was no way she took out two professionals.

That left one alternative.

Rage replaced dread. Red specks dotted his vision as his pulse raced. The big bad sheriff and his lackey came for him and killed his mother. The only woman who'd stood by his side.

Merle threw open the lid to the workbench and grabbed the AR-15. Slapping in the magazine, he racked in the round and took the stairs two at a time. At the top of the stairs he stopped, staring at his truck.

Charlene sat on the hood. "You should run, you idiot. Forget the girl. Forget your bitch of a mother and run."

His chest heaved from the climb. "They'd catch me."

She laughed, ticking her chin toward the gun. "They'll kill you if you come at 'em with that."

"They'll kill me anyway. After everything I've done, I'm dead either way."

Her grin disappeared. "Then what the fuck are you doin', Merle? Why don't you throw the gun on the ground, drop your drawers and back your bare ass up and let them—"

Merle swung the barrel up and drew a bead on Charlene's head. "Shut up!"

She spread her hands wide. "Make a decision, Merle. The right one for once."

Merle turned his head toward the open barn door. Nothing coming from the house. Charlene said run. He checked the truck again, thankful Charlene was no longer sitting on the hood. *How far can I get in that old thing? Not very goddamn far.* He wouldn't make it to the county line before they caught up to him, and that would leave Rebekka to the wolves. If he didn't have her, what had he done all this for?

He could wait for them to come to him and pick off the two men as they came out of the house. Shit. The whole place could be swarming with cops before that happened. He could make a stand. He stocked enough ammo downstairs to make them pay dearly for coming after him. But what was the point of that? He just wanted his daughter back.

He needed to get to them first before they sounded the alarm with the local cops. His only chance was to strike first. He could disappear with the girl and start a new life if they didn't have the chance to raise an alarm.

Maybe it was too late. Only one way to find out.

Merle raised the buttstock to his shoulder and stepped out into the drizzling rain.

CHAPTER FIFTY-THREE

WENDY CRUMPLED TO THE FLOOR, AND BLOOD POOLED ON the hardwood beneath her snow-topped head.

Jake kicked the gun away from her hand, even though there was zero chance she would use it.

"Damn it." Jake dropped to the couch next to Bear and yanked out his phone. "I'm calling 911."

"I'll call the ambulance. Go get the girl," Bear said through gritted teeth, slipping his belt from his pants. "This is the third time I've been shot around you. Do I have a sign hangin' around my neck that says 'shoot me first'?"

"I'm just lucky."

"Or I'm fatter and a bigger target."

Jake grabbed a towel and wooden spoon from the kitchen. He dropped the towel on the wound and handed Bear the spoon. "Use the spoon to make a tourniq—"

"I know how to fuckin' do it. We went through training a coupla months ago."

Jake helped him cinch the belt around his thigh, a few inches above the bullet hole.

Bear fished his cell from his pocket. "I'm good. Go get the girl. I'll call in reinforcements."

"Keep pressure on it. I'll be right back. I hope."

Jake turned and ran down the hall, peeking out the side door toward the barn. Everything was too quiet. It meant Merle would be waiting for him. He hoped the screaming girl was still alive. He slipped his Sig from its holster and crept out the door.

Rain spit down from the steely afternoon sky, and thunder rolled in the distance. The barn was thirty yards across a gravel drive, the view partially blocked by Wendy's car. Was Merle on the run or was he waiting for them?

Jake darted out the side door and ran to the cover of the Taurus. He stationed himself behind the front wheel and the engine block. Wet gravel chewed into his knees as he sucked in a few deep breaths, steeling himself for the move. Edging forward, he peeked around the front of the Taurus toward the barn.

The barn stood thirty feet tall and maybe a hundred feet deep, covered in traditional red paint peeling away in strips. A few hay bales and a grimy diesel tank sat toward the back. A large roll-up door was closed in the middle of the structure, and a regular door stood open toward the south end closest to the driveway. No windows on this side from above. Jake squinted against the rain toward either end of the barn. Nothing.

Keeping low, he held the gun in front of him, sprinting toward the open door. His heart pounded in his chest with his vulnerability.

Something moved in the doorway of the barn before

stopping. A face broke through the shadows. Merle. Merle with a rifle against his shoulder. Jake broke left as a muzzle spit five or six times, one of the bullets whizzing by his head close enough to part his hair.

He slammed himself to the side of the barn, chest heaving, and gun locked in on the door opening. That sounded like an AR-15. Jake trained his sights on the opening.

"Come on, motherfucker," he whispered. "Show me your head again."

Nothing.

After several breaths, he had this image of Bear lumbering out of the door, and Jake yanked his cell out of his pocket.

"Holy shit," Bear breathed. "You okay?"

Jake kept his voice low. "I think Merle has an AR-15. Missed me, though. Didn't want you running out and getting shot again."

"I got a bullet in my leg. I ain't runnin' anywhere. Where is he?"

"Barn. Was sitting in the darkened door waiting for me. Good thing I run like a cheetah."

"That's not the animal I was thinking of," Bear said. "I called in the cavalry. They'll be here in fifteen minutes. Sit tight and don't do anything stupid."

"Whoever screamed is in there somewhere. We got Merle backed into a corner. He could kill her any second."

"Caldwell—"

"Don't worry, I'll be careful. I'm gonna find another way into the barn. If I sit here any longer, he could shoot me through the wood."

"You dumb son of a—"

Jake hit the end button and checked to ensure the phone was silent. Last thing he needed was for Bear to give away his position with a call back. He pressed to his feet, thankful for the barn's overhang giving him a brief respite from the steady downpour.

Keeping the gun trained on the doorway, Jake stepped backward until he reached the rear of the barn. He swung the barrel around the corner and swept his field of vision. Nothing but a line of trees fifty feet back and a boneyard of rusty farming implements tossed haphazardly in a pile. The barn stretched another seventy-five feet across with a door at the end closest to him.

Jake picked his way through the debris, careful not to step on anything that would give away his location. He reached a window next to the door and risked a quick peek, hoping not to see Merle's face and the black barrel of the AR. Instead, he took in a narrow, dark room flanked by old wooden workbenches and an open door leading to the interior of the barn.

Ducking under the window, he slid to the door and tried the knob. It turned and Jake eased the door open, wincing at the rusty groan from the hinges. He paused, listening for the sound of footsteps. Nothing. He wished he knew what lay ahead of him and where the girl was. Only one way to find out.

Sucking in a lungful of rain-tinged Ozark air, he slipped through the opening into the darkness.

CHAPTER FIFTY-FOUR

DIM, CLOUD-COVERED DAYLIGHT PUSHED INTO THE narrow storage area from the window at his back. Jake listened hard for any sounds where Merle might be lurking. He slipped past hand tools and mason jars full of bolts and screws covering the workbenches on either wall. A dust-laden pinup calendar of John Deere tractors from 1994 hung by a nail hook.

Jake edged through the open door into the barn, slashes of light slicing through holes and gaps in the siding and roof. Dust motes floated in the air. He could make out a big vehicle under a dark tarp ahead. Creeping along with his gun sweeping the path in front of him, he made his way toward the shape. He could tell by the way the tarp hung it was a pickup, and he had a pretty good idea what exact truck was hidden underneath. Moving to the back end, he slipped up the tarp on the right side. Even in the dim light, he could tell the truck was a light color and the taillight was broken. And he knew without checking there was a white cross in the driver's side window.

Something metal tinked up ahead and to his left, and Jake dropped to one knee, holding his breath, his pistol trained at where the sound came from, finger tight on the trigger. A mangy cat ran past the front of the truck and disappeared into the darkened corner of the barn. At least he hoped it was a cat. Could have been a giant ass rat. The thought sent a shiver down his spine. He hated rats.

Jake's eyes swept the darkness beyond the truck. He spotted a lawn mower and an ATV with a snowplow attachment sitting in front of a dusty, dark-colored Chevy Blazer. No more sounds, no movement. He rose from his knee, keeping his body below the body line of the truck, ears straining for any sound that might give away Merle's location. Jake scanned overhead to see if there was any way Merle could hit him from a hay loft or something, but he saw nothing but old wooden beams spanning the roof.

He stopped.

It was too quiet. *Did Merle go after Bear?* Bear was in no condition to fight off a maniac with an AR. No, if Merle did that, Jake would've heard the gunfire by now. *Did he run? Does he have another vehicle stashed somewhere?* Maybe he was getting away while Jake dicked around in the dark overthinking the situation.

Jake's heart thumped in his throat, a mix of adrenaline and fear coursing through his veins. He wasn't ashamed to admit to himself he was afraid. Any man who didn't experience some measure of fear while creeping around in the dark with an armed lunatic hunting him was either a liar or a dumbass. *The only thing we have to fear is fear itself.* Bullshit. He was no historian, but Jake didn't think Franklin Roosevelt ever faced the working end of an AR.

In the old days, Jake would move hard and fast, taking the risk of catching his prey by surprise. But that was before Halle, Connor, and Maggie. He had a family now and a lot more to lose. The fact that Merle hadn't hit him with the AR while he was out in the open was a miracle. Jake would've needed a single squeeze of the trigger to drop someone from that distance. Merle had spit out five or six. Maybe Merle was as good a shot as his mother.

"Help me! Somebody help me!"

A woman's voice, muffled by distance and dirt. Somewhere to his left and below.

Screaming meant Merle wasn't with her, which meant he was probably up here with Jake. *If he is here.* In the long run, sitting there would do no one any good. If he didn't find Merle and take him out before the sirens of the coming cavalry sounded, Merle could grab the girl and kill her, or they'd have a hostage situation. If Jake found Merle first, the girl would be safe and the threat eliminated before any of Bear's crew hit the scene. That was his only play.

He peeked around the front end of the truck. The door leading to the outside where Merle took the shots at him sat thirty feet away. Light flooded in from the doorway, shining on a set of wooden double doors set at an angle along the wall. A cellar.

"Please! Somebody!" the woman's voice cried again.

She was definitely through those doors. Locked in the cellar.

He'd been sitting still long enough he would've heard Merle if he tried to flank him.

Jake pictured the barn and its layout. The door where Merle shot from was twenty feet from the end of the barn. That meant there was another room on the other side of the wall holding the cellar doors. If Merle was still here, that would be where he waited. Time to see if he'd bite and reveal himself.

Grabbing a rock the size of a golf ball from the floor, Jake hurled it to the darkened corner where the cat scurried, away from the door. The stone bounced off something metal and glass shattered. Jake trained his gun barrel on the doorway, waiting for Merle to stick his head out.

"Come on, you son of a bitch," Jake muttered.

Nothing.

Screw it. Jake left the safe cover of the truck and crept toward the cellar door, slow and steady, his boots soundless as he carefully placed them on the dirt-covered floor. He breathed in through his nose and silently released the air through his mouth, willing his heartrate to slow.

Fifteen steps in the open until he reached the wall. The smell of oil and diesel mixed with the musty smell of age and dirt.

His finger rested on the trigger guard, ready to slide down in a microsecond if Merle showed his face.

Ten steps.

He risked a quick glance behind him to ensure Merle wasn't creeping up. Nothing but the rain beating on the roof. Water dripped on the back of his neck from one of the many holes in the barn roof. Back to the doorway.

Six steps.

The two cellar doors were made of vertical slats of

plywood with a rusty metal handle on each side. Nothing holding them shut but gravity.

Three steps.

"Somebody, please," the girl sobbed, the desperation in her voice growing.

Where the hell is Merle? It occurred to Jake that maybe Merle wasn't around the corner. Maybe he was sitting at the bottom of the cellar stairs waiting for someone to fling open those doors. It would be a great place to make a stand. Likely limited entry points, probably only the one.

He checked back toward the door leading outside. He should clear the room behind the wall first. Sliding along the wood, he reached the corner. Crouching, he drew in a breath and swung around the corner, finger tight on the trigger. If Merle waited for him, he'd likely aim for the chest which would give Jake the split second he needed to drop him. He let his breath out when nothing but empty space and a cobweb-covered diesel tank took up residence.

Thinking about the cellar, he poked around a tool bench set along the wall and found a palm-sized flashlight in a drawer. He thumbed the button, and a weak beam spit out. Batteries on their last legs, but it was better than nothing.

He crept back to the cellar doors, reaching out for the closest handle. If Merle was still on-site, he'd be down there waiting. But why? He was no expert, but in his experience, most cellars didn't have multiple points of entry. Either Merle was an idiot, or he didn't mean to leave the space alive.

If he's down there. If he is, I'm walking into a kill box.

If he's not down there, I could be trapping myself.

"Shut up," Jake whispered to himself.

If Merle didn't mean to leave the space alive, maybe he meant to take Rebekka with him before he went.

He grabbed the cellar door handle and flung the door open.

CHAPTER FIFTY-FIVE

AFTER FLINGING OPEN THE DOOR, JAKE DUCKED BACK OUT of range, waiting for a burst of gunfire. When nothing came, he counted to ten and took a couple of quick peeks. No bullets and no revelations of what lay in the darkness at the bottom of a set of stairs leading into the cellar.

Setting the gun over the flashlight, he flicked on the weak beam, shining it down the steps. The light pushed back the darkness well enough for him to see nobody was waiting at the bottom of the stairs. But it didn't mean Merle wasn't hunkered down somewhere in the cellar.

"Who's there?" the woman yelled.

If Merle was there, Jake's presence would no longer be a secret. "Sharla? Rebekka?"

"Jesus Christ, yes! It's Rebekka," she cried. "Help me, please."

Jake kept the barrel of the Sig trained on the bottom of the stairs. "Are you alone down there?"

"Yes! Get me out of here."

"Hold tight. I'm coming."

If it was Rebekka down there alone, where was Sharla? Was she ever here at all? Or was she buried in the woods somewhere like Bethany Sheets?

Jake swung away from the mouth of the stairwell and yanked his cell from his pocket. He hit the speed dial for Bear.

"What the hell is going on?" Bear asked.

"How far out are reinforcements?"

Bear groaned. "Maybe five minutes. I dragged myself in the corner away from the windows, so make sure you announce your ass when you come in the house."

"I'm hitting a root cellar in the barn. Rebekka Hammill is down there. Says she's alone, but I haven't gone down yet."

"Where's Merle?"

Jake scanned the area again. "I don't know. She says he's not there. I'm starting to think he hightailed it out of here on foot. Maybe he has a car stashed somewhere. Either way, tell your crew to keep their eyes peeled. Maybe Klages can spin up her drone and scour the area."

"Will do. Be careful."

"Always."

Merle on the run made the most sense. Jake slid around to the cellar entrance. If he was still here, he would have taken another round of shots at Jake by now. Still, no reason not to be cautious.

Rebekka screamed. "Get me the fuck out of here!"

"Hold tight," Jake yelled, shining the beam down the stairs and setting his boots on the first step. "I'm coming."

He carefully set his boot heels on each step as he

descended, eyes locked on the bottom of the staircase. What lay beyond widening into view with each step.

"Please," Rebekka sobbed. "Please help me."

Jake took another couple of steps, bending at the waist to try to get a more expansive view of what waited for him. "I'm almost—"

Merle jumped from a cutout in the stairwell. Jake turned, too late to stop the rifle butt from striking him in the head. Jake's arms pinwheeled as he fell back. Gravity kicked in hard as he bounced and tumbled down the rest of the stairwell, cracking his head against the floor. He tried to blink away the stars, seeing nothing but flashes.

He flexed his hands, realizing they were empty. No telling where his gun landed. Thoughts were coming slow, the world fading in and out. He tasted blood. The stench of death engulfed him as he lay in the dirt.

CHAPTER FIFTY-SIX

MERLE'S FOOTSTEPS PLODDED DOWN THE WOOD STEPS, and between long blinks, Jake spotted the barrel of the gun pointed in his direction. An AR-15. For once, Jake was less than thrilled to be right. Jake tried to roll away, but his body wasn't cooperating, and a sharp pain radiated from his lower back. Head thumping, he pressed his eyes closed and tried to slow his breathing, swallowing the rising panic. He wanted to conjure visions of Maggie, but his thoughts were hazy.

The footsteps reached the cellar floor. They stopped, and light flooded through his eyelids. The sound of something—or someone—scuffling along the dirt came from behind him. Jake cracked his eyes open and stared up at Merle. He expected to see a triumphant grin of a madman who had conquered his foe. Instead, Merle's eyes were sad, his features drooping like a wilted flower.

"Merle," Jake groaned. "Don't do it."

"I don't wanna do it. Believe you me, I don't wanna. But I ain't got a choice."

Jake propped himself on his elbows, the foggy haze

clearing a bit. "You always have a choice, man. Cops are on the way and will be here any minute. Put the gun down and I promise you'll make it out of this."

Merle pasted on a tight-lipped smile. "You can't promise any such thing. 'Less you can bring back my Chloe. But you can't, can you?"

"I can't. But that doesn't mean—"

Merle's face turned into a snarl. "Shut up. Just shut up. I had a plan and you two ruined it. Now you gotta pay for screwing it up."

Merle pressed the butt of the AR against his shoulder and his finger slipped to the trigger. Faces now rolled through Jake's mind—Maggie, Halle, Connor, Daisy. The only people in the world who were counting on him, and he failed them. His senses were returning, but they wouldn't be back in time to stop the bullet about to split his skull.

"Daddy?" Rebekka's voice floated across the cellar. "Don't do it, Daddy."

Merle paused, his vision floating over Jake's prone body.

"Don't shoot him, Daddy. Please. For me?"

Daddy? Jake's eyes blinked away the rest of the fog. His brain calculated the distance between him and Merle. Trying to figure out a way to get out of the gun sights and make a move to take the big man down. But Merle was now a good six feet away. There was no chance he could do it.

"It's too late," Merle whispered.

"It's not. Put him in a cell. Lock him in and I'll go with you. I'll be with you and take care of you, Daddy."

Merle's voice hitched. "You'll run the first chance you get."

"You let that man live." Rebekka choked back a sob. "And I promise you'll have me by your side. There's been too much killin' already."

The barrel of the AR dipped. "You mean it, Chloe? You really mean it?"

Jake blinked. *Chloe? What the hell?*

"I do," she said.

Merle steeled the AR against his shoulder again and fixed his wide eyes on Jake. "There's a cell door ten feet behind you, to your right. Start movin'."

Jake tried to push himself to his feet, and Merle stepped forward and kicked Jake's feet. He fell onto his back, tasting the mustiness of the cellar air.

"No, sir," Merle said. "No need for you to get up. Crawl. You try anythin' and I'll have to break my promise to my little girl. Like she said, there's been enough killin' already."

My little girl. Some of the puzzle pieces fell into place. The overdosed daughter. The missing girls. The cells. He slid his injured body along the cellar floor, leaving a trail in the dust like a snail, staying on his back. Razors cut into his neck as he craned over his shoulder to see his destination. A thick open door and ropes of wire crossing a six-foot opening next to it. He spotted several other doors farther down and a dirty face peeking out from between the wires two cells down. It was Rebekka Hammill, eyes wide and teary.

He dug his elbows into the hard dirt floor. Jake was bewildered. Why hadn't Merle shot him? Maybe he was telling the truth—there had been enough killing. If he wanted to, he could snuff Jake's torch at any time. The cops were on the way and would free Jake soon enough. But, if Jake slinked into the cell like an obedient little puppy, it would put Rebekka and Bear at risk. From the look in her eyes, she'd had enough. Plus, it increased the chances Merle would get away before the cops arrived.

Merle kicked the bottom of Jake's boot. "Move it. I won't ask again."

"There's a way out of this, Merle. You're right. There's been enough killin'. Don't do something to add yourself or anybody else to the body count."

"Shut up and move," Merle growled. His finger slid from the guard to the trigger.

Jake craned over his shoulder at the cell. No fucking way he was getting in there. Too much could go wrong if he did. Instead, he gave an exaggerated wince and rocked his elbows back a few inches, grunting as if he was in too much pain to move any faster.

Merle took a half step closer.

The slower Jake moved, the greater the distance Merle closed—his impatience growing and making him careless.

Jake groaned as he slid back a few more inches.

Merle stepped closer. "Faster, damn you."

The barrel of the AR was still pointed at Jake's head. Merle's feet grew close enough for Jake to make a move. The question was if he could do it and surprise Merle before the man squeezed the trigger and blew his head apart. Jake needed a distraction.

Merle jabbed the gun forward in a half-lunge. "You got two seconds before I—"

Rebekka's voice floated, sad and mournful. "Daddy?"

Merle glanced up, and that was the diversion Jake needed.

CHAPTER FIFTY-SEVEN

WITH MERLE'S ATTENTION LOCKED ON REBEKKA, JAKE jammed his left instep against the front of Merle's ankle. At the same time, he hooked his right foot behind Merle's knee, yanking it forward and pulling the man off balance. Merle cried out as his leg buckled, the AR spraying a stream of bullets into the ceiling. Deafening gunfire echoed off the walls of the cellar.

Merle collapsed on top of Jake, two hundred thirty pounds of him knocking the air from Jake's lungs. The rifle clattered to the floor nearby, and Jake tried to roll to get the man off him, but it was like trying to move an elephant.

Jake threw weak jabs into Merle's side, but he couldn't generate any power behind them. Merle lay nose to nose with Jake, fire burning in his crazed eyes, and spittle dotting his cracked lips.

Merle's hands worked their way to Jake's throat and clamped around it, squeezing. Jake banged at Merle's arms, but it was like slapping a slab of granite. Those crazed, bloodshot eyes locked on Jake's—black dots speckling Jake's vision.

As Jake struggled, he forced his racing mind to focus. If he continued this futile resistance, he would be unconscious in fifteen seconds, and God only knew what would happen to him then. Jake tried to yell, but no air came. Merle's jagged teeth faded in and out.

He tried to work his arms up under Merle's so he could attack Merle's face or break his straight arms at the elbows, but Merle's arms were like tree trunks held close to his body.

Rebekka screamed in the background for Merle to stop. "Daddy!"

Jake thought he heard sirens in the distance, but it could have been wishful thinking. It wouldn't matter if they were whipping up the driveway. He'd be dead before any backup figured out where they were.

Panic creeped into his brain. He saw an image of him lying in a coffin with giant purple rings around his neck as Maggie and Halle sobbed over his dead body. No. That was not gonna happen. Jake needed to create an opening, and he needed to do it fast.

Sliding his feet under his knees, he threw his hips up. Merle bucked a few inches, but somehow tightened his grip around Jake's neck. The black dots covered most of his vision as the last molecules of oxygen were cut off from his brain.

He bucked up again with every ounce of strength left in his body. As Merle tossed forward, Jake managed to work his arms between Merle's, pushing his face toward the ceiling. The move lessened Merle's grip around Jake's neck, and Jake threw an elbow into the inside of Merle's, knocking Merle's left hand away as glorious oxygen flooded Jake's lungs.

Before Merle could recover, Jake jabbed two fingers into Merle's trachea, and the giant gurgled and rolled off, grabbing his throat.

Jake rolled away from him, feeling with his hands along the floor, trying to find the AR among the clearing black dots spotting his vision. It lay on the floor three feet away, but he was half blind. Gasping for air, Jake crawled toward the gun, his fingers grazing the stock before Merle grabbed his foot and jerked him away like a ragdoll.

Jake kicked Merle in the face, and the man's head rocked back. He dove for the gun, hands wrapping around the stock. Jake rolled to his back and squeezed the trigger as Merle lunged. Nothing happened. The gun was out of bullets.

Jake gritted his teeth. "Shit."

Merle dove, and Jake managed to swing the butt of the AR with enough force to knock Merle to the side.

Sirens drew closer outside as the two men climbed to their feet, staggering and out of breath.

Jake held the gun in front of him, ready to use it however he needed to survive. He tasted copper in his mouth and his chest heaved. "It's over, Merle. Give it up, man."

"You ruined everything," Merle said, his face red and full of fury.

"Not the first time I've heard that," Jake replied. "Cops will be swarming down here any second now. You don't have to die."

Merle's bearded lip curled. "But you do."

He charged and Jake swung the rifle, catching the

giant on the shoulder. It knocked Merle off his trajectory, but not before he grabbed Jake and slammed him into the thick cell door next to Rebekka's.

Jake grunted as his head knocked into the solid wood. He blocked Merle's roundhouse and threw a jab into his face, feeling the man's nose crunch as his head rocked back. Merle waded in, arms close to his body, throwing jabs at Jake's head. Some missed, some didn't.

As Jake spun away, his vision swept across an open cell door and the body of a woman in a blue dress, her mouth ajar and dead eyes locked on the ceiling.

Jake caught Merle with an uppercut to the chin, and Merle countered with a left hook nailing Jake in the head. Blood trickled into Jake's right eye, his ears ringing over Rebekka's screams. He managed to land a kick to the side of Merle's knee, buckling it long enough for Jake to land a jab, sending the giant careening back into the wires covering Rebekka's cell. Merle's face locked in a scream as if he were being shocked. Those wires were live.

Merle peeled himself off and staggered forward. He and Jake exchanged blows as they moved into the center of the cellar. Jake felt the energy sapping away, like it was leaking through his shoes. On any normal day, he could've taken Merle. But the fall down the stairs and almost being strangled to death had taken their toll.

Merle caught Jake with a roundhouse, and Jake stumbled back, crashing into a wooden table in the middle of the room. The table collapsed. Jake fell to the floor, plastic bowls filled with food remnants tumbling on top of him.

Merle grabbed a wooden chair and with a grunt brought it down like an executioner's ax at Jake's head.

Jake rolled to the side, and the chair exploded into shrapnel.

Merle's heavy feet slid in the dirt behind Jake, and Jake grabbed a broken chair leg. He pushed himself to his knees, and with every last ounce of energy, he swung the jagged end toward the approaching giant and sunk it into Merle's belly.

The air wheezed from Merle's surprised face, his mouth gaping like a fish out of water. Jake climbed to his feet, keeping hold of the broken chair leg, and pushed it harder into the soft flesh. Hot blood flowed over Jake's hands and pattered on the dirt floor. Merle grasped the wood jammed in his stomach as he stumbled back against the stone wall between cells.

Rebekka's cries behind Jake turned to whimpers. Footsteps pounded the floor overhead.

Merle slid down the wall, the surprise turning into fear. Tears trickled from the cracked corners of his eyes, crimson leaking from his mouth. Jake followed him down, his hands locked on the wooden stake.

"What happened to my momma?" Merle wheezed.

"She shot herself in the living room."

Merle's eyes moistened as he gulped for air. "All I wanted was my daughter back."

"Where are the others, Merle?"

"She was all I had. I didn't wanna hurt nobody. I just wanted her back."

Jake released the stake and dropped to his knees next to Merle. Everything hurt. Even his eyelids. "What did you do with the other girls?"

Merle coughed. Blood bubbles covering his lips. "Will I be forgiven?"

"You have a chance. Their families have to know what happened to them. Where are they?"

Merle's voice garbled. "In the clearing behind the barn. Maybe fifty yards."

The light was fading in Merle's eyes, like a candle about to be snuffed.

"How many?" Jake asked.

Merle's hooded eyes locked on Jake's one last time. "I don't know. Too many. Am I forgiven now?"

Jake stood. "Ask the devil when you see him."

The candlelight in Merle's eyes flickered out. He slumped to the ground, dead eyes staring at the blood-soaked dirt.

CHAPTER FIFTY-EIGHT

REBEKKA CRIED AS JAKE STUMBLED TO HER CELL, TEARS carving tracks down her dirt-streaked face. Her blue dress was torn and stained, hanging limply on her bony shoulders.

"Are you okay?" he asked.

She sniffed, wiping her eyes with the back of her hand. "I think so. Get me out of here before he wakes up."

"He's not waking up. You're safe now."

Emotion cracked her voice. "I don't think I'll ever feel safe again."

Jake tried the door, but it was locked.

"He kept the key in his pocket," she said. "Don't touch the wires."

Jake drew back and ran his eyes along the wires covering the cell. "Jesus."

"Jesus hasn't been down here for a long time," she whimpered.

Jake moved across the cellar floor, wincing as sharp needles of pain jabbed his side. Merle must have cracked a rib. With the adrenaline leaving his body, the aches and pains from the fight were unmasking. Digging in the dead man's pockets, Jake found the key. He stood as footsteps pounded down the cellar staircase.

"It's all good," Jake yelled before they made their way into the room. "It's Jake. The bad guy is down."

Deputy Klages led the way with her weapon drawn. A couple additional cops followed—Kuhlmann and Smajda. Their faces crunched in confusion at the image before them.

Klages holstered her gun as she approached Jake, eyes cutting to Merle's body before sweeping around the cell doors. She held out a white handkerchief and motioned toward Jake's face. "You okay? You look like shit."

Jake winced as he pressed the cloth against the split in the skin above his eye. "Shit would be three steps above how I feel."

"What in God's name happened here?"

Jake moved past her toward Rebekka's cell. "Long story."

The deadbolt scraped back, and the door swung open. Rebekka sat on her knees, eyes wide at the opening.

Jake squatted next to her, a groan escaping his lips as pain knifed through his knees. He rested his arms on his thighs, the bloody handkerchief in his hand. He kept his movements slow. With everything she'd been through, he didn't want to scare her any more than she already was. "Hey, I'm Jake. You're safe now, Rebekka. It's over. He can't hurt you anymore."

Her eyes found his, tears brimming then spilling

over. She reached out, and Jake helped her to her feet before she locked her tawny arms around his waist. The emotions released like a dam gate, and she sobbed in his arms.

Jake glanced over his shoulder and spotted Klages and the two deputies moving around the cellar, checking Merle's body and the other cells. When Rebekka's cries subsided, Jake motioned Kuhlmann over.

"Rebekka, this officer is going to take you out of here. We'll talk more in a bit."

Rebekka shuffled off with Kuhlmann. Jake hobbled out of the cell and stood next to Klages, who had entered the adjacent cell and shined her flashlight on the face of the dead woman.

"It's Sharla Babin, isn't it?" Jake asked.

Klages placed her hands on her hips and sighed. "Yeah. Goddamn it. I always held out hope."

Daisy's face popped into his mind. The movie played out where he had to tell her that her mother was dead. She was ten. He'd spare her the gory details.

"I promised Daisy I'd find her mom," Jake said.

Klages patted him on the shoulder. "You did."

"But not alive."

"You're good, but you can't win 'em all, Caldwell."

Jake clenched his fists. "I wanted to win this one. For Daisy. Did you see Bear?"

Klages turned and Jake followed her out of the cell. "For ten seconds next to Wendy Blackwell's body before he ordered us down here. Think he's going to be okay. What happened to Wendy?"

Jake nodded toward Merle. "She was covering for her son. Shot herself."

"And did Bear get fucking shot again? How is that possible?"

Jake allowed a grin to slip up. "He's lucky I guess. I'm never going to hear the end of it now."

Klages dragged her eyes around the contents of the cellar. "What in the world was going on down here?"

"Rebekka knows. But I'm not sure how bad I want to find out or how much she wants to tell right now."

Jake labored up the stairs, pulling himself up by the handrail, his internal battery light blinking low. In addition to a cracked rib or three, his bad knee ached, and his head throbbed like a drum. Flashing lights enveloped him as an ambulance made its way up the rutted driveway. The rain had stopped, the Ozark air fresh. Clean.

Passing Wendy's car, Jake trudged into the house and found Bear in the living room with a couple of cops on either side of him and an EMT tending to his leg.

Bear's eyes shot up as Jake entered the room. "Did you get him?"

"Yeah, I got him. He's dead and Rebekka's alive."

"Good. Looks like he didn't go down without a fight."

"They never do. You gonna make it?"

Bear grinned. "I'm tougher than I look."

Jake winked. "And dumber."

"Asshole."

"Did you call Audrey?"

"I will in a minute," Bear said. "Wanted to make sure you were okay before I broke the bad news to her. At least I won't show up looking like my face was caught in a meat grinder."

Jake pressed the handkerchief against his eye. "At least I didn't get shot. Again."

Bear bit back a grin. "And so it starts."

"I'm not scared to poke the bear."

CHAPTER FIFTY-NINE

AS THE MEDICAL PERSONNEL TENDED TO BEAR AND loaded him on a stretcher, despite his protests, Jake found the bathroom and washed away the blood and dirt from his hands and face. The cut over his eye was going to require stitches. The rest of the bumps and bruises would heal over time like they always did. He rubbed at the caked blood on his hands as the hot water washed it away, lamenting how many times in his life he'd gone through this very exercise, pondering what he told Wendy.

After Bear was loaded in the ambulance, Jake told Klages what he knew about Merle and the bodies in the clearing behind the barn. As he talked, he spotted Rebekka sitting in the back of Klages's car with a blanket wrapped around her.

"It's going to be a long night," Klages said. "I'll start making some calls after we get her to the hospital. What are you going to do?"

"I'm going to go home and break the news to Daisy."

"The girl is tough as nails. She'll be okay, eventually."

"I sure hope so."

Jake limped to Rebekka and squatted, wincing from the effort. "You going to make it?"

She held his gaze for a few moments before nodding. "I think so, all things considered."

"I'm sorry you had to go through this. I can't imagine how you feel."

Rebekka held out a grimy hand. "Thank you. Thank you for saving me."

"We saved each other. Remember that. If you hadn't spoken up, Merle would've blown my brains out, and who knows where we'd be right now. Thank you for doing that."

The corner of her mouth ticked up a little. "Guess I didn't think about it that way."

"Listen, when things settle down, and after you answer the same questions over and over until you want to scream, you're going to have to deal with a bunch of emotions. It might be days, weeks, or even months down the road, but eventually, they're going to demand their time in the sun. You have someone you can talk to?"

"Not really. I burned a lot of bridges."

"Haven't we all? Bridges can be rebuilt. But, in the meantime, here's someone I recommend." Jake fished a battered business card of Dr. Danielle Tate from his wallet. Dr. Tate was Jake's court ordered therapist after he tried to strangle a mass murderer who wanted to blow up the country a few months ago. As much as he hated to admit it, the sessions had been helpful.

Rebekka's eyes narrowed as she read the text on the card.

"I know you don't know me from Adam," Jake said, empathizing with her reluctance. "If you're anything like me, you probably think psychotherapy is a bunch of mumbo jumbo. But, this woman is different. She helped me. She can help you too."

Rebekka turned the card over in her hands. "Thanks."

Jake slowly worked his way to his feet, fighting the stabbing pains hitting every muscle and joint in his body. "Someone told me once that the worst thing is never the last thing. You were a strong woman to get through this ordeal, and you have what it takes to get past it. I can see it in your eyes."

Rebekka pressed her lips together in a line, the tears brimming again. "Thank you again."

Five minutes later, Jake was on the road heading home in Bear's truck. He'd cleaned up his face the best he could at the ranch, but it still looked like he'd been hit by a freight train. Maggie and Halle were going to most likely freak out. But it was Daisy who worried him. *How is she going to take the news about her mother?* Deep down, she had to have known her mother's death was the most likely outcome. That said, she was still a child. A child who cared enough to try to hire someone to find out what happened to her mother with every cent she had.

He pulled up the driveway to his home off Poor Boy Road. Lights burned through the kitchen and living room windows, his wife and daughter darting past as they spotted his headlights. Jake eased himself from the truck, his arms pressed against his ribs, knowing he was going to get crushed.

Halle made it out first, bounding down the front porch steps.

He held out his hands. "Take it easy on me."

She wrapped her arms gently around his waist. Jake kissed the top of her head and caught Maggie's smile, only to watch it fade as she took in the damage on his face.

Halle released him, and she took in the carnage, her face pinched. "Jesus, Dad."

"You should see the other guy. I'm fine, sweetheart. I'm glad you're here."

Halle made way for Maggie.

"Hey, gorgeous," he said, kissing her.

She drew back, deep lines furrowing her brow. "Wish I could say the same about you, sweetheart. We should get you to the hospital. What happened?"

"The usual. Bad guys lost."

"You mean—"

He nodded. "We got him. Long story."

"And Sharla?"

Jake peered over her shoulder and spotted Daisy standing in the hallway, Connor on her hip gnawing on the head of a G.I. Joe action figure. Her eyes were wide and waiting, full of hope. A cannonball formed in Jake's gut knowing he was going to wipe that hope away.

Maggie read his face and whispered, "Oh no. You sure?"

Jake placed his palm on her face and muttered, "Saw the body myself."

They made their way into the living room. Jake plucked Connor from Daisy and kissed his son on his chubby cheeks. His ribs screamed in pain, but it was worth it. His boy gurgled and smacked Jake on the head with the G.I. Joe. Jake planted one more kiss and passed the boy to Halle, asking her to take Connor into the bedroom for a minute.

He and Maggie sat on the couch, and Jake patted the cushion for Daisy to sit between them. Daisy crossed her thin arms, lips pressed in a line, feet locked in place. It was as if she thought if she didn't move, Jake couldn't deliver the news she knew was coming. Jake motioned her over again, and she relented, dragging her feet across the hardwood and settling on the couch.

Her wide eyes shot up. "She's dead, ain't she?"

Jake rested his palm on her back. "I'm so sorry, Daisy. We found her today."

Silent tears leaked down her face. "Did she suffer?"

Jake could see Sharla's emaciated body, the dead eyes, the swollen tongue, the purple rings around her throat. He couldn't even imagine the amount of suffering that woman went through in her last weeks and moments on this earth.

"She didn't suffer, honey," Jake lied.

Maggie's arm circled Daisy's trembling shoulders. Her fists were clenched so tight her knuckles blanched white, her arms tensed as she fought the grief. As Maggie's soft voice soothed her and pulled her close, Daisy let go and she let loose the cries she'd been holding back for months, the ones she probably never let anyone see.

After several minutes, Daisy straightened. Jake handed her some Kleenex from the coffee table and a glass of water from the kitchen.

Daisy drained half the glass before peering at Jake,

the familiar fire creeping back into her eyes. "Did you get the sumbitch who killed my mom?"

Jake patted her hands. "Yeah. I got him. He's burning in hell as we speak. You don't have to worry about him anymore."

Daisy dipped her head toward her lap. "What happens to me now? I don't know where to go."

Jake glanced at Maggie who threw on a knowing smile. "You can hang with us for a while if you'd like to."

Daisy alternated looks between Jake and Maggie. "I like it here. I like playing with Connor."

"And he likes you," Maggie said. "You're welcome to stay with us while we figure everything out."

"I promise I won't even curse no more around him."

Jake gripped Daisy's hand. "I'm sorry I couldn't save your mom, Daisy. I tried. I really tried."

Daisy stood and wrapped her arms around Jake's neck. "I know you did, Jake. I'm glad I trusted you."

She squeezed him tight for a moment, released him, and disappeared into the back bedroom.

Jake collapsed on the couch and groaned from the physical pain and the emotions he now fought back. Maggie slid close, gently stroking the bruises on his face.

"You okay, baby?" she asked.

"I will be."

"I want to know everything that happened. You want me to fix you a drink, first?"

"God, yes."

Maggie stood and as she turned to leave, Jake grabbed her hand. "And you might want to call Audrey. Bear's going to be perfectly fine, but he got shot."

Maggie's eyes bulged. "Again?"

CHAPTER SIXTY

A FEW DAYS LATER, JAKE AND HIS FAMILY GATHERED around Bear, who was recuperating in his lounge chair in his living room. His leg was wrapped with nearly enough bandages to stop another bullet. He had a bottle of pain killers and a glass of whiskey on the coffee table next to him. He appeared comfortable leaning back with the television remote in his big paw.

Bear muted the television as Jake and Maggie sat. Daisy took Connor and bounced him on her knee in a chair by the fireplace, and Halle joined her. Jake wasn't sure if Connor's feet had touched the floor since Daisy came to stay with them, and Connor didn't seem to mind one bit. *Daisy* might be his first word.

Audrey brought in a tray of iced tea in tall glasses. "Thank God you all are here. If I have to watch one more episode of *Gunsmoke*, I'm going to smother him with a pillow."

"We're only on season three, honey," Bear said. "There's seventeen more after this."

"Seventeen?" Audrey poked Jake in the shoulder. "Why did you buy him the boxed set?"

Jake shrugged. "I thought it'd give him something to think about besides his leg."

"Take him to your house then."

Bear pursed his lips, and Audrey bent over and kissed them. "Thank you, sweetheart. I love you."

"I love you too, you old coot," she said. "You girls want to help me fix some sandwiches?"

Halle plucked Connor from Daisy's arms, and they followed Audrey into the kitchen.

"How you feelin' there, partner?" Jake asked.

"I've got painkillers and whiskey. I'm fucking fantastic."

"You're not supposed to mix those, you know."

"Bah. What do doctors know? Besides, it's not like I'm going to drive anytime soon. I'll just lay here and get fatter and make myself a bigger target. Must be nice to be bulletproof like you."

"The way Wendy was slinging that gun around, I'd say it was a fifty-fifty chance which one of us caught the bullet."

Bear dropped the remote on the coffee table and grabbed his drink. "I'm surprised she could hit anything." He swirled the amber liquid, the ice cubes clinking off the sides of the glass. "Can't believe she shot herself. What a waste."

Jake let Bear have his moment, taking a glass of tea for himself. "What's the latest on the aftermath at Last Chance Road?"

"Sharla Babin was strangled in her cell in the basement of the barn, but you saw her. They found the bodies of Eve Maxwell, a girl who was abducted from

Springfield eighteen months ago, and Jenny King, the girl from Clinton, in barrels in the clearing right where Merle told you. Found three other bodies wrapped in tarps that we haven't identified yet. Glad I wasn't there to see it. Klages said it was awful."

"We were right on the AA angle."

Bear sipped his whiskey and wiped his beard. "Dead right. No pun intended. Looks like Merle met most of them at AA meetings. Same with Rebekka Hammill. Wonder how she's doing?"

"Talked to her a couple of days ago for a few minutes," Jake said. "She's having nightmares about the cellar and Merle. She has an appointment with the shrink I was forced to talk to during the Anarchy Road debacle. She's staying with her older sister in Kansas City for a while. She was happy to finally get her Blazer back from Merle's barn."

"What about the Harley Reese girl from Hermitage who went missing six months ago?"

"Haven't heard anything. Hell, there might be bodies buried all over the property," Bear said. "We have cadaver dogs sniffing around, but the Harley girl could be like Bethany Sheets we found out by the dam. Merle's bodies could be everywhere. We showed her picture to Rebekka, but she didn't recognize her. The only two she saw down there were Sharla and Jenny King."

Jake took a sip of the tea and set the glass on the coffee table. "So that's seven we know, maybe more."

"Eight for sure. You remember the discolored concrete in the cellar? Merle's wife Charlene. Merle bashed in her skull with a hammer."

They discussed how the pieces were falling into

place based on what they'd discovered and from interviews with Rebekka and those at the local AA chapter. Everything started when Chloe overdosed from junk given to her by Bethany Sheets, who she met at the AA meeting that sent Merle over the edge.

Bear scratched the worn leather on the arm of his recliner. "Man, I've seen people do some crazy shit in the name of grief, but this takes the cake. All those girls killed just to try and replace what can't be replaced."

"At least we stopped him before there were anymore and we saved Rebekka."

Bear jabbed a finger at his best friend. "You saved her. We wouldn't have stopped him if you hadn't stuck your nose in the middle of it."

"I wouldn't have done it if a little girl didn't try to hire me to find her missing mother," Jake said, looking toward the kitchen where Daisy was. "Sad it had to come to that. Not blaming you, dude. I know the limitations you're operating under."

Bear drained his whiskey. "Bah. Limitations and constraints make for an easy excuse. Maybe I should consider hanging up the sheriff hat. Besides, who's gonna elect a fat bastard like me who's now gotten shot three times?"

"You'd really quit?"

"Not quit, maybe let my term expire and not run for reelection. With these bodies on my watch, I'd have a hard time winning anyway. Hell, Klages would do a great job. You and I would make a good team working together, you know?"

Jake nodded. "We would. Hell, we do already. Lord knows I'm tired of turning down leads. Wouldn't mind spending some more time with my family."

"Speaking of family," Bear said, craning over his shoulder to make sure the girls were out of earshot. "How's your little Miss Daisy?"

Jake beamed. "She's great. Really responding to Maggie, and she loves Connor to death. I know the trauma is going to catch up with her at some point, but we like having her around. However long that's going to last."

"You have that look in your eye, Caldwell. What are you gonna do?"

Jake held up crossed fingers. "Got a few irons in the fire. I don't want to jinx anything."

Bear's lips disappeared. "Be careful, Jake. Never underestimate the system's ability to crush the best laid plans of mice and men. Oh shit, did I just nail a Sherlock Holmes reference?"

"It was Steinbeck, but I'll let you have it."

CHAPTER SIXTY-ONE

PURPLE STORM CLOUDS DRIFTED OVERHEAD TO THE WEST as a cool breeze rattled through the fingers of the cemetery trees. The gathering of people around Sharla Babin's grave was no more than a handful, mostly Bear and his family, a few people from the local AA chapter, and Jake's clan.

Daisy was clad in a new dress and overcoat she and Maggie bought in Sedalia. Her hair was pulled back in a somber ponytail, tears perpetually brimming in her eyes but not reaching the point where they'd tumble down her pale cheeks. As they stood by the casket, she held Jake and Maggie's hands. Connor sucked on a pacifier on Halle's hip while the minister finished up a reading of one of the Psalms.

Over the last few days, Daisy had approached her mother's funeral with an amazing amount of poise and dignity. She'd handled herself far better than Jake had when he'd lost his mother to a heart attack at a similar age.

As the service ended, the minister invited them to approach the casket and say a final farewell. Daisy released Jake and Maggie's hands and picked up a bouquet of daisy flowers bundled at her feet. She took half steps toward the casket, standing on the tips of her toes to lay the flowers on top. She let her fingers trail down the side of the casket.

As she pressed her eyes closed, the tears snaked their way down her face. "Goodbye, Momma."

She turned and darted back to Jake and Maggie, eyes locked on the ground as they rested their arms across her shoulders.

Jake watched her, wondering when the grief would come home to roost and how Daisy would handle it. The girl had been through a terrible trauma, and she'd fielded enough bad life cards to furnish a full deck. As the people from the local AA chapter filed away, Daisy lifted her chin and a scowl appeared.

"What's wrong?" Jake asked.

Daisy ticked her chin up. "That bitch is here to take me away, and I don't want to leave."

Jake spotted Mrs. Robinson, the social worker coming their way with a manila folder in hand and a somber expression on her lined face.

"Language, Daisy," Jake said. "Calling her that isn't going to help anything. Remember what we talked about. Poise and grace."

Daisy's eyes narrowed as Mrs. Robinson paused in front of them. Mrs. Robinson bent over a few degrees closer to Daisy.

"Hello, Daisy," she said. "I'm so sorry to hear about your mother."

"Thank you," Daisy managed to choke out. She squeezed Jake's hand with surprising strength.

"We've been talking," Mrs. Robinson said. "We think it would be best if—"

Daisy's eyes flew wide, and she turned to Jake, tears running down her face as she gripped his hand with both of hers. "Don't make me go, Jake. Please don't make me go back to that place. If you let me stay, I promise I'll—"

Jake wiped her tears away with his thumbs. "Shhh. Hey, it's going to be okay."

"But I'll die if I have to go back to the group home. I just can't..."

Daisy buried her face in Jake's coat and sobbed.

Jake wrapped his arms around her for a moment, gently pushed her back, and looked her in the eye. "Hey, it's going to be alright. Do you trust me?"

Daisy nodded.

Jake turned to the social worker. "Did it come through?"

The social worker handed Jake the manila folder. He stood and opened it, reading what was inside. He handed it to Maggie.

"What is it?" Daisy asked.

Jake smiled. "Guardianship papers."

Daisy's eyes made the rounds of the faces standing above her. "What the hell...sorry, I mean *heck* is that?"

Jake squatted in front of her and took her hands. "Daisy, how would you like to stay with me and Maggie and Connor for a while?"

Her jaw hung open and her eyes darted between Jake and Maggie. "But I thought it was going to take such a long—"

"Special circumstances," Mrs. Robinson said. "There're still some hoops to jump through, but you can stay with Jake and Maggie. If you want to."

The corner of Daisy's mouth curled. "For how long?"

Maggie knelt beside her. "For as long as you'll have us."

Daisy threw her arms around Jake and Maggie. Halle and Connor joined in. After a moment, she pulled back, fresh but happy tears on her face. "I can't believe it."

Connor cooed and reached out, tugging on her hair.

"Believe it," Jake said. "We'll figure the rest out as we go. But for now, you're a part of the family."

Mrs. Robinson said she'd be in touch and headed toward her car.

Bear and Audrey gathered around, Bear leaning heavily on a cane and Audrey supporting him. Bear offered Daisy his hand.

She shook it, the smile dropping a hair. "Are you mad at me?"

"What for?" Bear asked.

"I said some pretty bad things about you."

Bear shrugged. "I probably deserved some of them. Tell you what, I'll let you buy me lunch and we'll call it even."

Daisy grinned. "Deal. I still have the ten bucks I tried to use to hire Jake."

"I'll meet you all at the Rusty Skillet. Ten bucks buys a lot of bacon."

Bear and Audrey shuffled toward Bear's truck as Jake's newly formed tribe gathered around the casket one last time.

Daisy kissed her fingertips and touched them to the wood. "Bye-bye, Momma."

She grasped Jake and Maggie's hands, and they headed toward their car as the sun broke through the overhead clouds.

A LOOK AT: THE CARTEL QUEEN
A SCOTT STILETTO THRILLER BY BRIAN DRAKE

Scott Stiletto returns in this explosive ninth adventure of his best-selling series! You've never read action like this before!

Defecting drug cartel leaders? It's not an assignment Stiletto wants, but it's one he was built for. Carlos and Jackeline Guardado, leaders of a cartel sharing their name, have been funneling information to the US for a decade, damaging cartels world-wide, leading to billions of dollars in losses and the assassinations of high-profile drug thugs. Now they're cashing in on a promise—the promise of a new life and new identities in the US.

But they have to escape alive first.

Stiletto travels to Colombia to coordinate the defection, and right away finds himself hip deep in hostility. Somebody's figured out what Carlos and Jackeline have done, and now they're marked for death. With their teenage daughter in tow, Stiletto risks everything to get them to freedom, or die trying.

AVAILABLE NOW

ABOUT THE AUTHOR

James L Weaver is the Kansas City author of the Jake Caldwell series. He makes his home in Olathe, Kansas with his wife and two children. His previous publishing credits include a six-part story called "The Nuts" and his 5-star rated debut novel Jack & Diane, which is available on Amazon.com and has been optioned.

His limited free time is spent writing into the wee hours of the morning, working out, golfing, running, and binge-watching Netflix, Amazon Prime or Hulu - he's not picky.